AF279302

"Look," said Naomi, "your sister-in-law
is going back to her people and her gods.
Go back with her."
But Ruth replied, "Don't urge me to
leave you or to turn back from you.
Where you go I will go, and where you
stay I will stay. Your people will be my
people and your God my God. Where
you die I will die, and there I will be
buried. May the LORD deal with me,
be it ever so severely, if even death
separates you and me."

—Ruth 1:15–17 (NIV)

Extraordinary Women OF THE BIBLE

HIGHLY FAVORED: MARY'S STORY

SINS AS SCARLET: RAHAB'S STORY

A HARVEST OF GRACE: RUTH AND NAOMI'S STORY

Extraordinary Women OF THE BIBLE

A HARVEST OF GRACE

RUTH AND NAOMI'S STORY

Jenelle Hovde

A HARVEST OF GRACE

RUTH AND NAOMI'S STORY

DEDICATION

To Judy, my wonderful mother-in-law. I am so grateful for your steadfast faith and beautiful heart. Thank you for all your encouragement and love.

ACKNOWLEDGMENTS

When I was approached to write Ruth's story, I could hardly contain my excitement at being a part of the Extraordinary Women of the Bible series. What an honor! I'd like to thank some other extraordinary people who have made this novel possible. My thanks to Tamela Hancock Murray, agent extraordinaire, who mentors and encourages. I'm so grateful for your wisdom. I'd also like to thank the wonderful editors of Guideposts: Jane Haertel, Sabrina Diaz, Caroline Cilento, Ellen Tarver, and others, who shape each novel with finesse and grace. It's a joy to write for you.

To my critique partners: Maddie Morrow, Joanna Politano Davidson, Shannon McNear, Jason, and Gabriella. You each bring thoughtful advice and marvelous encouragement. To my sweet prayer partners, Jeannette Beck, and the Oasis Church—thank you! None of this would be possible without you.

To my husband, who inspires every hero I write, and to my wonderful daughters, who bless me just like Ruth, thank you for your support and cheerful attitudes when Covid hit and surgery followed, and, well, everything felt a little haphazard during a season of writing two novels at the same time. I am extremely grateful to you. I love you.

To my mother-in-law, Judy, who kept my first story and sent a wonderful note of encouragement. You've blessed me in so many ways. I love you.

To my archaeologist friend, M, in Israel, your doctoral research and your invaluable resources came at the perfect time. Thank you for sharing your expertise. I hope I can visit with you in person and on-site one day.

Finally, my thanks to Jesus, who brings more blessings and gifts than I can even imagine. I don't deserve them, but He is rich in mercy and grace. Thank You for being our Redeemer.

Cast of
CHARACTERS

BIBLICAL CHARACTERS

Abraham • Patriarch of the Israelites

Boaz • esteemed leader in Bethlehem, tribe of Judah

Chilion • deceased son of Naomi and husband of Orpah

Elimelech • deceased husband to Naomi

Mahlon • deceased son of Naomi and husband of Ruth

Moses • Patriarch of the Israelites

Naomi • mother-in-law to Ruth and Orpah

Orpah • daughter-in-law to Naomi

Ruth • daughter-in-law to Naomi

LIST OF HISTORICAL NAMES

Chemosh • primary Moabite god

Yarikh • god of the moon

Yahweh • God of the Israelites

LIST OF NONBIBLICAL CHARACTERS

Abigail • fellow gleaner

Aharon • Joab's son

Aviah • friend of Naomi's, resident of Bethlehem

Eshmun • Ruth's older brother

Gilead • Sarah's betrothed

Harim • crippled gleaner

Joab • foreman of Boaz's estate

Levi • kinsman redeemer next in line

Lotan • caravan leader

Machla • half sister to Naomi

Radah • nephew to Naomi, son of Machla

Sarah • field worker for Boaz

Takesh • physician in Moab

Yassib • Ruth's father

Zakai • husband to Machla

Glossary of TERMS

abba • father

Bethlehem • House of Bread, a village

dush • to tread grain during threshing, to crush underfoot

Ein Gedi • an oasis above the Dead Sea

ephah • a grain measurement containing ten omers, 29 pounds

goel • next of kin protector or avenger

hesed • extravagant grace, loving-kindness

imma • mother

kethōneth • inner woolen garment worn next to the skin

Kir-hareseth • Moabite city

mezuzah • Scripture from the book of Deuteronomy written on parchment, placed outside the home

miṭpaḥ • a headscarf

pithoi • large clay storage jar

sadin • long linen garment

senet • a board game from ancient Egypt

simlāh • heavy outer garment or shawl

Yam HaMelaḥ • the Dead Sea

CHAPTER ONE

The massive city gate of Kir-hareseth loomed in the gathering twilight, the sharpened palisades on either side of the walls like a row of jagged teeth, while a faint sickle—the moon—offered only a dim light to illuminate the empty streets. Ruth arched her neck to gaze at the sky, her heart pounding with an erratic rhythm. The Moabite king had ordered the gate closed today, preventing anyone from entering or leaving while a fever swept through the poorest quarters. Above her, the pale moon sliced through the black heavens as wisps of silver clouds fled. It was not a god, as Ruth had been taught as a child. It was Yarikh, whose dew watered blossoms in the desert and who courted his goddess at night. This evening, something felt evil about the celestial body clinging to the dark expanse overhead.

She lowered her head and breathed a prayer to Yahweh, just as her mother-in-law, Naomi, had taught her. *Please deliver Mahlon from the fire eating him from within.* A strangled sound broke free of her as she rushed into another darkened alley, a shortcut leading toward the physician's house. She clamped her teeth tightly together, shaking her head to clear the image of her beloved husband lying helpless on a mat. Mahlon dying? It didn't seem possible.

What if she didn't find Takesh in time? Other healers had refused to come to her house, regardless of the coin offered. What if her husband passed…

No. She mustn't think such morbid thoughts. He would live and tease her as he always had.

"We need to hurry." Orpah's pained voice cut into Ruth's turbulent thoughts. Her sister-in-law panted as she jogged to keep up with Ruth's resumed pace. "We can't be the only ones in need of Takesh's services."

Orpah, two years younger than Ruth, appeared haggard, with dark circles curving beneath her eyes. Her loose tunic, missing a belt, bore evidence of a hard day of work grinding grain, the flour still clinging to the folds, while Ruth tended to her ill husband and brother-in-law. When Mahlon's eyes rolled back in his head, leaving only the white, Naomi had begged both women to find help. Not that she needed to ask Ruth. Ruth had already flung a light blue *miṭpaḥ*, a shawl, over her shoulders, desperation clawing within her to save her unconscious husband. Two women in the city at night provided scant protection, but it was better than going alone.

She glanced down at her worn tunic, just as rumpled and stained as Orpah's. Did she bring sickness with her? She had no desire to hurt anyone, but neither could she let her husband suffer. Dust stirred beneath her leather sandals as she broke into a fresh run while ignoring the throb in her chest.

Don't leave me, Mahlon.

Ten years ago, he had found her hiding behind a perfume market stall, trembling, while another man, one who had assumed she would be his, stalked the rows of shops to find her and drag her home. A teasing glint appeared in Mahlon's eyes when he discovered her crouched to the ground, just as a vial of ointment tipped and fell from the table. His hand shot out and caught the alabaster flask, saving her the exorbitant cost of ruined perfume but not the mortification staining her cheeks.

"Is there a special perfume hidden beneath the table?" he asked with an amiable smile. A hot wind teased the unruly brown curls about his lean face. His brown eyes were warm and kind—a rarity, and far more precious to her than the most expensive nard of myrrh or frankincense.

Her chest fluttering, she ignored his good-natured teasing. "Is he gone? The thickset man who rushed past this table a moment ago?"

All at once, Mahlon sobered. He glanced over his shoulder before turning to her. "I see a fat man at the edge of the market. He turned left in the direction of the temples."

At the mention of Chemosh's temple, she shuddered to the point of her teeth chattering—even when Mahlon reached out a calloused palm for her to take. She felt his fingers wrap around her wrist, pulling her to her feet, just as the old seller spied her with a scowl plastered on his wrinkled face.

Four months later, following a horrible beating from her *abba*, Mahlon insisted on marrying her. To prove his affection, he placed a flask of bittersweet persimmon in her hand as a rare wedding gift. When she protested the cost of the perfume, he merely grinned. Persimmon was the scent of kings and queens, he told her. And he wanted to always remember the day he found her. With an abba who didn't care whether she lived or died, she had moved from a horrible home to one of peace and surprising joy.

Now peace was no more. She was about to lose the man she had grown to respect and love.

Ruth sucked in a pained breath, her lungs aching from running. She studied the exit of the narrow alley, trying to remember the crooked path to Takesh's mud-brick home. After several turns left, then right, she finally spied the large two-story house towering above the other buildings and darted forward. The sound of sandals slapping against the road indicated Orpah struggling to keep pace.

When Ruth reached the house, the walled gate remained locked. She raised her fist and banged on the weathered wood, the sound echoing in the night. A second time, she struck the door until it swung open, revealing an old female servant, her stringy gray hair mussed. Defiant eyes held Ruth's gaze.

"Why do you bother master Takesh's household at this late hour?"

Ruth swallowed, her mouth dry. "My husband and brother-in-law are dying with fever. Please, we need Takesh's help. Can he come with us?"

The old woman glowered, her lined face crumpling further like a shriveled date. "He is treating a nobleman's pregnant wife in the western district, and who can tell how long the delivery will take? Go home."

Orpah's cry of anguish matched the one reverberating in Ruth.

She sagged at the thought that there was no way to save Mahlon. Bracing herself against the wall, she tried again to invoke the servant's pity. "Is there no one who can help us? No other servant of Takesh who might bring herbs? We've tried every physician in the area, and we can't find a single healer."

Grimacing, the woman shuffled backward, raising her arm to shut the door. "Try a little wine mixed with water and pray to Chemosh. I understand the king will offer a sacrifice tomorrow for those who are ill within the city. The gods should be pleased with such a public display of devotion."

Chemosh, the destroyer, the subduer of men, demanded only death, and already the city had lost enough people to the illness. Ruth jerked upright at the news. A sharp rebuttal burst from her lips. "No!"

For years, her parents had forced her to endure the ceremonies. She had been divided on whether to plug her ears with her fingers to shut out the wailing flutes and thumping drums, or to cover her eyes from what would come next.

Mahlon didn't worship Chemosh. With good humor, he tolerated his *imma's* evening stories about Yahweh's faithfulness. He was quick to agree with Naomi's teachings, but he never had the time or the interest to discuss anything deeper. However, Ruth drank in every single word of Naomi's, with a heart hungry for the Creator who offered deliverance. Stories of Abraham and the ram caught in the thicket. Moses escaping Egypt with the Israelites, guided at night by a pillar of fire.

They calmed her troubled soul and brought a hope she had never known.

Yahweh wouldn't abandon her family now, would He?

At Ruth's outburst, the old woman slammed the door, leaving her alone in the alley with Orpah.

"It is too late," the young woman sobbed, wringing her hands in distress. "What can we do?"

"Pray to Yahweh for mercy," Ruth murmured as she clasped her sister-in-law's chilled hand and tugged her away from the barred door.

Surely He would deliver mightily, just as He had in Naomi's stories. Surely He would hear their cry.

As Ruth pushed open the door to her home, a guttural sound greeted her. She rushed into the cramped space, skidding to a halt when she spied Naomi crouched beside one pallet, pressing a knotted fist against her mouth.

"Imma—" Orpah cried as she held back, holding a sleeve against her nose. The stench of sickness and sweat clung to the humid air, revolting after the breeze rustling through the street.

Staring at her husband, Ruth dropped to her knees beside Naomi.

No, not Mahlon.

Grief rose within her like a mighty wave, strong enough to send her rolling into its murky depths. With trembling fingers, she reached out to touch him, his beloved face finally at peace.

Indeed, it seemed as if he only slept and both of them would soon awaken from this nightmare. Surely she must be dreaming. Yet, in the corner of the room, a faint cough rattled from Chilion's chest, indicating the nightmare was real enough.

"Mahlon died shortly after you left," Naomi whispered. She didn't take her eyes off her son, instead pulling the coarse blanket over him as if he was a child about to be tucked in before bedtime.

Ruth's throat and jaw tightened painfully. Why hadn't Yahweh at least allowed her to say goodbye to her husband?

When she spoke, she scarcely recognized herself. "I'm so sorry, Imma. The physician had left long before we reached his house. We rushed home as fast as we could."

If only we had left sooner.

But the fever had moved so quickly and attacked so many. And as Israelites in a Moabite city, Mahlon and Chilion were forced to wait until last for a healer.

Naomi snatched Ruth's hand, squeezing her fingers tightly, her expression bleak.

"We must tend to Chilion and do what we can," Naomi's voice thinned, resigned as if she feared the worst.

Ruth swept her husband's hair away from his forehead, now cool to the touch. She drew a deep, shuddering breath as she studied his features. Was it only a fortnight ago that she had trimmed these shaggy locks, giggling while he snatched her hand to press a heated kiss against her palm? How could a fever snuff out a vibrant life so quickly? How could she live without him?

He never once made her feel inferior for being barren, even if she secretly grieved for a babe. Neither she nor Orpah had borne children. Now, her loss felt doubly painful. She had no bundle to hold close, no small, dimpled face to remind her of him.

Dazed, she tore herself from her husband's side to help Naomi bathe Chilion's forehead, while Orpah shrank against the wall, weeping quietly. Ruth's hands shook as she poured tepid water onto a frayed linen cloth to wash Chilion's limbs. Her mother-in-law had long ago taught her to use water from a pitcher, clean and flowing, instead of letting it swelter in a basin for days. Naomi believed the practice brought health, as proclaimed by the priests of Yahweh. Tonight, the practice proved a futile exercise.

A flickering oil lamp cast a gruesome glow over the claustrophobic room. Chilion felt like fire, burning hotter and hotter despite the water droplets running down his flushed skin. His chest barely fluttered with life, each puff of air from his nostrils less and less.

An image of the bronzed Chemosh, with his rigid arms outstretched for sacrifice, flashed in Ruth's mind, while a great fire in the god's gutted belly roared and crackled, consuming everything given to it.

Please save Chilion for Naomi's sake. We cannot bear to lose anyone else this evening. It's too much loss for anyone to take.

Unlike Ruth's silent, frantic prayers as she wrung out the rag and washed him again, Naomi beseeched out loud, begging for the life of her remaining child. But as rosy dawn flooded through the open door, the battle was lost. Ruth bowed her head while Naomi keened with grief a second time, flinging herself across Chilion's chest. When Ruth tried to pull her mother-in-law away, Naomi resisted, clinging to her son's lifeless body.

Why hadn't the all-powerful Yahweh answered their prayers?

CHAPTER TWO

Ruth rolled over on her pallet, her fingers brushing against the rough, woolen folds of the blanket, searching for the comforting warmth of her husband. Then sharp awareness sank in, tearing her from a dreamless sleep.

He was gone. Agony pierced her afresh, and her eyes burned with unshed tears.

She staggered from her mat as a faint dawn signaled a new day. On the rooftop, she inhaled deeply, the stench of burned debris drifting on the morning breeze. In the city, smoke from several fires stretched wraithlike fingers to the sky. Shivering, she wrapped her arms around her middle again to calm herself. Work had always helped her mute the fear and grief inside, especially when she was a young girl, forced to hide from her abba's rages.

After pulling on a fresh tunic and headscarf, she grabbed a large clay jar, debating whether to wake her sister-in-law or mother-in-law. Yet one glance at their sleeping forms made her resolve to let them rest. The day would be long and trying enough. As she hurried into the street, toward the city well, she discovered several other men and women had also perished in the night. Forced to deal with the dead, the king and city officials allowed the gates to open by early morning.

By the time she arrived at home with a jar sloshing with water, a molten sun had crept over the jagged landscape, the sky deepening to a brilliant crimson. Both Naomi and Orpah lay huddled on their mats. Despite feeling more exhausted than she could remember, Ruth secured arrangements with a neighbor, who had also suffered loss, to bury their loved ones outside the city gates. Carts drawn by donkeys carried shrouded forms from the ramshackle section of the city where homes merged into one long row of tottering apartments, the streets crowded and filthy.

When the driver of the cart arrived at Ruth's courtyard, she roused her mother-in-law. "Imma, it's time to say goodbye."

She looped an arm around Naomi, pulling the older woman to her feet. Chin quivering, Naomi watched the two men place each of her sons on a rough-hewn floor of the cart. "I never thought I would live to see this day."

Ruth kept her arm around Naomi's shoulders. No imma should have to bury her children. Together, they stared at the cart rumbling down the street, taking every hope and dream with it.

The shock of losing half of her family brought only numbness—at least until Ruth burned the fouled pallets and anything that might carry the taint of fever in the courtyard. More fires dotted the city, as similar households struggled to find a sense of normalcy. Yet the spare tunic of Mahlon's consigned to the flames felt unbearably painful and permanent.

"Must you destroy their clothes?" Naomi demanded, her voice ragged.

"Imma, please. We can't leave anything that might carry sickness." Ruth could no longer stand watching the fire where her husband's striped tunic curled into itself.

Mahlon, my beloved. For a moment, she struggled to get enough air into her lungs as dizziness swept through her.

With a sharp cry, Naomi pivoted away from the smoldering embers and drifting ash. "I will have nothing to remember them by."

Biting the inside of her cheek to keep from crying out as well, Ruth wiped the used clay pots with vinegar, while her mother-in-law and sister-in-law spent the morning hidden on the rooftop. She glanced at the flat line of the roof, wishing she could show them some measure of comfort. Naomi was the last person she wanted to injure. Didn't her mother-in-law realize how much the burned tunics hurt Ruth as well?

She refocused her attention to the courtyard and the pot clutched in her unsteady hands. No, she couldn't rest—not when her chest ached so much. Work remained. Instead, she masked her grief with action, moving about the narrow rooms of the house, finding one thing after another to accomplish. There was grain to be ground into flour, a floor to be swept, and a meal to prepare by evening.

While her hands were busy with mundane tasks, inwardly she cried out to Yahweh, searching for answers. He gave no response that she could tell.

By midday, just as Takesh's servant woman had promised, the king ordered the Chemosh priests to invoke the gods to safeguard the inhabitants of the city. The drums rattled the pointed wooden palisades lining the walls, and from the safety of Naomi's home, Ruth's gut clenched as she prepared a simple meal of chickpeas and flatbreads over the firepit in the courtyard. Despite her skill at cooking, she scorched everything.

As the drums echoed over and over, she eyed the courtyard wall blocking the street from view. The sun shone hot and bright in a cloudless sky. With such pleasant weather, the central temple, with its wealth of colonnades supporting a massive courtyard and inner labyrinth of rooms, was certain to be packed with followers. If she needed to leave the house, she would avoid that section of the city where the priests and priestesses cavorted with their devout, if wild, followers.

Retreating into the shadowed house would at least bring a measure of safety.

She climbed to the rooftop and woke Naomi and Oprah from their pallets. "Please, the hour grows late. At least have a cup of honeyed water."

Naomi sat up from the mat, swaying. Without a word, she reached for Ruth's hand and stood. Keeping an arm around Naomi's waist, Ruth guided her mother-in-law to the table while a drowsy Oprah followed, her eyes swollen from weeping.

"You must eat. You need to keep up your strength."

"I cannot." Naomi sounded feeble. "How can I when I hear that awful racket outside our house?"

Orpah, however, nibbled a piece of soft bread, her head bowed. "What will we do now?"

When Naomi didn't answer, Ruth spoke. "It's possible we could find work in the fields. Or we might find something within the city."

"Doing what?" Orpah's usually mellow voice dripped with scorn. She too glanced out the open door, when a piercing shrill echoed across the city.

Ruth got up from the stone bench and shut the door, casting the room in darkness but for a few oil lamps lit, offering a weak light. Even if the sounds still leaked through the gaps between the wood panels, she felt safer with the door shut.

Orpah's question bothered her just as much as the Chemosh temple revelry.

Mahlon and Chilion had labored for several landowners, harvesting grain during the barley season. Though neither one was wealthy, they had carved out a pleasant existence, pooling resources to maintain the modest house with a small courtyard. Two separate alcoves had provided Ruth and Orpah and their husbands with privacy. Ruth didn't object to the cramped quarters. She had never felt more free or safe than in Naomi's humble home.

"Mahlon had wondered about apprenticing for pottery," Ruth answered after a beat. She fingered her bread, a smaller piece than Naomi's or Orpah's, and discovered her appetite had fled. Her suggestion felt foolish as soon as she uttered it. No man would hire a widow as an apprentice. Her brother had taken over the family pottery business, and although she knew enough of the trade to assist Mahlon, they had both agreed to stay far away from her abba.

Orpah's vehement shake of her head showed a similar agreement. No woman could truly apprentice.

Naomi sighed as she nudged aside her wooden bowl. "I'm uncertain it is wise to remain in Kir-hareseth any longer." She eyed the closed door, where sound seeped through, and grimaced. "I lost Elimelech shortly after we moved from Bethlehem. He swore we would find a better life in Moab. During the early years we lived in this community, I agreed with him. We had avoided the famine, which killed so many of our countrymen. But now, I can't bear the idea of living in the same house where my husband and sons died. I see no future here in Moab."

She tucked a strand of long brown hair—so similar to Mahlon's, though weathered with plenty of silver—behind her ear, and gazed steadily at Oprah and Ruth. "I've wanted to go home for a long time. To Bethlehem. Before Chilion died, he told me he had heard rumors that the famine had ended in the Israelite land. Of course, he had no desire to leave. This was home to him, full of excitement and opportunity, and I hadn't the heart to argue. But now..."

Ruth waited, hardly daring to breathe as she stared at her mother-in-law. Surely Naomi saw her and Orpah as family, didn't she? Surely she wouldn't abandon them so easily?

Orpah didn't hide her confusion as she pushed away from the table. "What are you saying?"

Naomi closed her eyes momentarily. "If we sell our house and most of our items, you both will return to your abbas with something of value. You can marry again. I want to see your dowries renewed. You are both lovely women with plenty of years ahead of you. Why stay with me? I can't provide for you in the years to come. Find new husbands, carry babes in your bellies, and be blessed by Yahweh."

Ruth swallowed hard. She couldn't live with her abba. He was a cruel man. Greedy and careless. Ready to solve any issue with his scarred fists. When Mahlon had offered for her hand and asked for barely a coin of dowry, Yassib counted himself fortunate to have gotten rid of one extra mouth to feed. Of course, the man who had stalked Ruth in the marketplace, an older merchant, soon tired of pursuing her and found a younger, more compliant girl.

Desperate to escape her household, she accepted Mahlon's urgent offer to escape with him. And though she feared the worst from an unknown mother-in-law, Naomi proved to be the loving imma Ruth had never known. With a rag soaked in vinegar and a pot of oily salve, Naomi had gently tended to Ruth's bruises on her back and cheekbone.

"Shh. You are home now. Safe." Naomi had promised when Ruth's teeth chattered loudly. "You never have to see your abba again, if you don't want to."

How could she possibly abandon her mother-in-law after such kindness?

"If you give us most of the money, you won't survive. I can't bear the thought of you with nothing," Ruth replied quickly before her sister-in-law could respond.

"I agree," Orpah added, though after a moment of hesitation. "We will take care of each other."

Naomi's mouth tilted to the side as she reached for Ruth's hand, then Orpah's. "You bless me with such kind words. But to stay with me will ensure poverty. Without Mahlon's plans for a pottery business, and Chilion working in the fields, we will be destitute within a few months."

Orpah's dark eyebrows rose high as she glanced at Ruth. A polished amber bead necklace hung about her neck—a gift from Chilion in better days. She fingered the round gemstones, her bottom lip quivering. With her raven hair tumbled about her face, her cheeks flushed from tears, Orpah's beauty remained undimmed. Without delay, she would attract another suitor.

"It's true," Ruth said. Only a few clay jars lined the courtyard walls, each stuffed with wheat and oil. She estimated the three of them had enough for a journey but not much longer. Her stomach growled loudly in the silence. "I'm happy to sell what we can, including this house. We won't allow anyone to go hungry."

"No! We can't sell our home," Orpah breathed, but Ruth noticed her young sister-in-law didn't protest as loudly as before.

"We must," Naomi said firmly as she rose from the table. Without another word, she left Ruth and Orpah. Ruth covered her face with her hands and tried to think. Surely Naomi wouldn't readily give up this life they had built together as a family? Who would take care of her mother-in-law? Most widows were forced to marry quickly or face ignoble work to survive.

"She is grieving, Ruth," Orpah said, reaching for the last of the bread. "How can we reason with her when she's gone through so much? She will reconsider in days to come." Despite its slight burns, she tore off a piece. "We are the only family she has."

Ruth sighed as she picked up Naomi's bowl, still filled with scorched chickpeas. She planned to cover it with a scrap of linen and save it for later. Or, better yet, cook something fresh a second time, though they could ill afford the waste. She would do anything to ease the burden plaguing her family. But this tragedy was far beyond even what she could fix.

CHAPTER THREE

Naomi slipped into the courtyard as if she were but a shadow. She hadn't the strength to reassure Orpah or Ruth that everything would turn out well in the end. Bless Ruth, whose large green eyes had widened with Naomi's ruthless assessment. She couldn't ask her daughters to leave their land, their culture. It was all they had known. Kir-hareseth's wealth and security were more than enough to entice anyone to stay. They were Moabites. They belonged to this city.

Yet Ruth had indicated a far greater interest in Yahweh than anyone else in the house. Naomi dreaded leaving her daughter-in-law behind. Even her sons had brushed aside her motherly concerns with a teasing kiss, telling her not to worry about the city's influences. But she had worried. For years, especially after Elimelech's death. How could two Israelite men refrain from being eventually soiled by Moabite ways?

A fresh sob threatened to break free. She wanted to do nothing more than to rend her robe and pour ashes onto her head in grief. She had no choice but to submit and follow when her husband left everything behind to seek a better opportunity. He had refused to see his sons wither away in starvation.

Reluctantly, she had agreed with Elimelech's plan—even though Moses had warned against mingling with outsiders.

The cost had been high—too high in hindsight. A memory surfaced of her boys wrapping their arms around her after Elimelech's passing nearly ten years ago. "You are not alone, Imma," Chilion had promised her.

But she had never felt so alone or so afraid as she did right now.

Had Yahweh abandoned her? Surely she was cursed. It would be better to go to Bethlehem and hide away from everyone.

She caught her bottom lip between her teeth before the hateful thought vocalized within her. *I am a burden. I will be unwanted, with no hopes of marriage. It would be better if I died too.*

A soft warning pricked her as the traitorous thought filled her with dread. Who would take in an older widow? She had no sons to take care of her in her old age. She had no grandsons to rock to sleep in her arms. Fear blossomed into panic as her breathing quickened and her heartbeat raced like the drums in the center of the city.

Forgive me, Yahweh. I don't have the strength to even make it to Bethlehem.

But from beyond the courtyard gate, smoke billowed from the temples, dirty with ash and debris—a blight against the bright blue sky. Naomi felt the warning right down to her innermost being. Moses wrote it.

You shall not intermarry with them, giving your daughters to their sons or taking their daughters for your sons, for they would turn away your sons from following me, to serve other gods. Then the anger of the Lord would be kindled against you, and He would destroy you quickly.

Nothing could intermingle, not even the fabric woven by the Israelites. No mixing of linen and wool in the same garment. No worship of other gods. No eating of foul meats, such as the rabbit or the pig, or other crustacean delicacies favored in the Moabite market.

Despite these warnings, she could never see Ruth or Orpah as a mistake, and had instead viewed their entry into her home as an opportunity to share Yahweh's love. Ruth, particularly, needed such love. She always served Mahlon as if she didn't quite deserve any affection at all. Naomi had immediately felt a powerful pull to her older daughter-in-law, a protective tenderness to show Ruth a better way.

She would truly lose her closest family if she left this city. But what would she lose if she continued to stay?

Her resolve strengthened as she stared in the direction of the city square, where the two-story temple with its seven inner chambers reflected the brilliance of the sun. The music lessened in the distance, less harsh and frantic, and far more celebratory, as if bleeding a cathartic release of tension from the prior drums. Before long, the drunken worshipers of Chemosh would pour into the streets, hollering and cavorting past her little mud-brick haven.

She didn't belong here. She had family in Bethlehem, including a younger half sister. She and Machla, however, had never been close, even if they shared the same abba. Naomi would be truly destitute to rely on a sullen younger sister, who had married one of Bethlehem's most prominent men. Years prior, Zakai had reluctantly promised to tend to the land during Elimelech's absence. She hadn't heard a word from either Zakai or Machla. Nor could she shake an undercurrent of dread. Machla had always resented Naomi. It wasn't Naomi's fault her abba cared for her imma more than Machla's imma.

Perhaps she might beg work from her family and find a new beginning. Even though she hated to lose Ruth and Orpah, she had no choice but to escape Moab and the memories of her loved ones. Regardless of her decision, her heart tore afresh. Her daughters-in-law were family, even if not flesh and blood.

But only a selfish woman would beg them to tie their lives to her sinking stone.

***

Two days later, Ruth knew her mother-in-law had decided to leave the city. She couldn't hide a flush of dismay when Naomi riffled through the small chest hidden beneath the table, where a meager stash of coins lay tucked inside. Her mother-in-law's jaw firmed into a bullish line. Never a good sign. After counting the coins, Naomi rose to her feet.

"Have we enough money to last a month?" Ruth dared to ask, although she dreaded the answer.

"Not quite." Naomi folded her arms across her chest, as if reluctant to share more. After a pause, she added, "I'll speak with our neighbor tonight and ask if he will purchase our home. A fortnight ago, I overheard him stating that he wanted more space for his second wife and children. Perhaps he will offer a fair price."

Orpah shot Ruth a warning look as she mended a basket while sitting cross-legged on a mat.

"Of course," Ruth murmured, surprised. So much change in such a brief span of time. It was enough to make her head spin. But she also knew once Naomi's mind was made up, there would be no retreat.

Naomi took the jug from the table and poured a small amount of water into a clean basin. She washed her face, removing any evidence of recent tear stains. Straightening her headscarf, she inhaled deeply. "I will ask him now before courage flees me."

The door slammed shut, leaving Ruth to feel as though her world might collapse at any moment. Orpah pressed her lips into a bloodless line as she tucked the strands of loose reeds into a familiar pattern.

Ruth offered conversation to break the heavy silence. "We'll need more baskets if we are to leave as soon as Naomi insists."

Her sister-in-law stilled over the half-finished lid. "You really want to go to Bethlehem with her?"

"I..."

Orpah narrowed her eyes as her nimble fingers resumed threading more slender reeds into the loops. "You realize what the Israelites think of us Moabites? They think we are unclean swine. They hate us."

A chill swept through Ruth at Orpah's declaration. Following Naomi seemed even more risk-filled, especially since the Israelites considered Moab as enemy territory.

However, when Naomi reentered the courtyard, her face was crestfallen. She brushed past Ruth with nary a word. Her footsteps echoed hollow as she climbed to the flat roof, where an awning attached to poles provided scant respite against the scorching sun.

Ruth flinched as she tended to the cooking fire in the courtyard. Clearly, Naomi's plan had not gone as expected.

The next morning, Ruth forced herself to walk faster, past the cluttered marketplace where voices shouted at her to buy a vial of perfume, a luxurious woven tunic, or raisin pastries. She ignored the cacophony on either side of her, quickening her stride when she reached the dreaded temple of Chemosh, the fish god. The squat pillars as thick as three men standing side by side, stained halfway with bloodred paint, and the bronzed bowls of sickly sweet incense at the front of the entrance made her stomach roil.

She knew what waited inside the main hall. A metal and clay creature, part man, mostly sea serpent, trapped in a writhing form with bulging eyes, gaping mouth, and razor-sharp scales, each grotesque feature carved by her abba.

With a moan, she forced the image aside and focused on the road ahead. If not for Naomi, she would never have chosen to visit this section of Kir-hareseth. Eshmun's pottery business flourished near the center of the city, close to the temple. Ruth spied the familiar collection of wares, the cheapest pots lining the front of her brother's business. The most expensive pieces remained inside the shop, safe from pilfering fingers. His chief specialty, however, included exquisite idols with painted faces so real, one might assume the figurines could awaken any moment. The eerie artistry had earned the praise of the priests and nobility alike, earning her family a coveted spot within the city as the premier artisans.

She halted in front of the shop, struggling to control her rapid breathing.

Six years her senior, Eshmun stood to inherit everything her abba had created. When Mahlon had thought to apprentice for a pottery business, they both agreed to avoid her family and possibly join with another artisan whose wares were just as lovely.

Now, she would enter the fox's den and beg for help.

A tingle ran down her spine as she entered the vast workshop. Sturdy shelves contained a variety of hand-painted wares of every size. Urns and bowls bore scenes of the gods and goddesses, frolicking or fighting with each other. Another section of the wall contained cups, goblets, and shapely goddesses with voluptuous figures.

Toward the back of the shop, Eshmun had left his potter's wheel, his thick fingers dried with a gray mud and his apron splotched with paint and clay dust. Startled, he gaped at Ruth, still standing at the shop's front.

At once, she thought of her abba. Her brother was handsome and big-boned, with long black hair, now thinning at the top. Unlike the men in the family, Ruth took after her deceased imma's tiny stature. As it was, she barely reached her brother's chin, forcing her to look up at him.

"Ruth? Is that you?" Eshmun asked as he peered intently at her.

She strove to sound natural, and failed. "It's me. I've come with a business proposition for you."

He studied her from head to toe. "You look well."

Except she didn't feel well. Her grief, far too raw this morning, choked her blunt answer. "My husband passed away, and my brother-in-law. My mother-in-law wishes to leave for Bethlehem and needs someone to purchase her house."

He folded his arms across his burly chest, a bushy eyebrow cocked. No sympathy for her loss. No expression of grief. "You want me to buy that hut in the seediest part of Kir-hareseth? For what purpose? Why would I want property more in need of a teardown?"

"Lease it, or do as you wish with it. My husband"—her tongue tripped over her next words—"took good care of his property."

Eshmun rubbed his bearded chin, his silence more distressing the longer it continued. Since the neighbor had rejected Naomi's offer, Ruth hoped she could do better for her mother-in-law. At least, she hoped she hadn't made a mistake coming to her family's shop. Naomi had agreed with the idea, eager to sell immediately.

"And what are your plans if I purchase the house?" he finally asked, unfolding his massive arms.

"I'll leave with Naomi for Bethlehem."

He frowned, the lines bunching in his forehead. "I could arrange a marriage for you. A profitable one, with a man who can provide far better for you than Mahlon."

Her heart slammed in her rib cage at the idea of marrying an idol worshiper. Her brother likely wouldn't understand why she was so drawn to her husband and his family. Nor would Eshmun understand her desire to avoid a household devoted to Chemosh. "I was happy with Mahlon. He treated me very well."

Eshmun blew out an exasperated breath, placing his hands on his hips. "You were poor with that spindly Israelite. A house in the southern section is barely worth the cost of the wood."

Her hopes plummeted as he continued to stare at her. He wouldn't help. Perhaps he was too much like her abba, only concerned with personal gain. As if reading her thoughts, Eshmun added in a disarming voice, "Abba is ill. Bedridden with fever, and you don't have to see him again, if you wish. I will find you a match with someone far more suitable for a daughter of Moab. I swear on my life, I won't send you to a man like Abba. There is a merchant who purchases pottery from me. He needs a wife to raise his young boys. No doubt you'll have strapping sons of your own before long."

A shocking promise, and one that would ease her situation greatly. But what of Naomi? No future husband would allow a former mother-in-law to move into his home. Not a single person would take care of her if Ruth didn't step in to fill the role.

Regardless, her brother was grossly mistaken. She was not a daughter of Moab. She had long ceased to identify with her people and their gods. "Thank you, but I have made my decision. I will leave with Naomi in a fortnight."

Eshmun grunted. An unnerving light entered his beady eyes—a cunning look, when a man realizes the gain to be had. When he finally quoted her an offer, her heart sank further. It was indeed low. Too paltry an amount for Naomi to last the year.

"That sum won't be enough for us to survive," Ruth protested.

He shrugged as if wearied with the conversation. "Take it or leave it, sister. It's the best I can do. I have four sons to raise. I can't jeopardize their future inheritance by coddling foolish whims. You'll die on the road to Bethlehem along with that Israelite. Why should I encourage your demise?"

A sliver of fear crept into Ruth. Could he be right? Leaving the city would likely prove dangerous for two women without protection. Regardless, she felt manipulated as he continued to stare at her. Perhaps her brother was more like her abba than she realized. She gritted her teeth, furious that Naomi would be essentially cheated out of her meager store of money. "We will accept your offer."

Naomi was determined to make the long journey to Bethlehem before the harvest season, and truthfully, they had no choice. Naomi had encouraged her to take whatever was negotiated, especially since an Israelite widow in Moabite territory had precious little bargaining power.

He called over his shoulder as he left to provide her with the coins, "If you stay, you'll be a wealthy woman. I'll make certain of it."

But she had decided her future course when she accepted the small sack weighted with shekels. She couldn't let Naomi—broken and grieving Naomi—travel alone through the wilderness with an unknown caravan. Nor did Ruth want to lose the only other person who had shown her compassion. Not even the promise of wealth or children could tempt her away from where she was needed most.

CHAPTER FOUR

The sound of weeping followed Naomi as she marched outside the massive city gates of Kir-hareseth. With a ragged sigh, she stopped in the middle of the dirt road and faced her two daughters-in-law. Ruth, though pale, appeared resolute despite gripping a satchel loaded with three tunics, a woolen blanket, a bronze pan to cook with, and an assortment of dried herbs, flour, and several flatbreads carefully wrapped in clean linen. Mahlon's leather sling lay tucked in her daughter-in-law's waistband—the only memento Ruth had kept. Lastly, a bulging, oiled waterskin draped across her diminutive form.

Orpah, with her eyes and nose reddened, sniffled loudly before dabbing at her tears with the edge of her crimson veil. She wore the amber beads draped about her neck, reluctant to part with them in the end, and Naomi had no wish to deprive her younger daughter-in-law of one last remembrance. Orpah's bundle remained the smallest, comprising clothes and a tightly rolled blanket and an additional waterskin recently filled from the city well.

Naomi refused to take one more step until she addressed both women. "Orpah, please, you needn't come with me. Why leave Kir-hareseth, when it has always been your home? Your imma waits for you."

Orpah hiccupped as she offered a tiny shake of her head. "No, no, we belong with you."

To Naomi's left, a noisy caravan, complete with braying, spitting camels and arguing caravan guards with daggers dangling from their hips, demanded an immediate answer. Alarm flared within her, particularly when the leader of the caravan, Lotan, sauntered up to Naomi. His one filmy eye, which didn't quite track with the opposite eye, and a missing earlobe gave him a menacing appearance. She flattened her expression to hide her distaste.

Not caring how he came across, he openly leered at Orpah, whose beauty had caught Chilion's attention. Then Lotan flickered his smug gaze to Ruth, his grin revealing a missing front tooth. "We leave now, old woman. My men won't wait for your daughter's tears to subside. I'll need to sell passages on boats if she keeps bawling."

She squared her shoulders, refusing to appear weak. "Just a moment. We will join you shortly." Her curt voice, sharp enough to make most men shrink, only made the caravan leader widen his grin. Her gut roiled when he moved only a few feet away, as if determined to listen to every word of her conversation.

She grasped both Ruth's and Orpah's shoulders and pulled them close despite the supplies bumping into each other. "Listen to me. Go back, each of you to your imma's home. May Yahweh show you loving devotion as you have shown to your dead and to me. May Yahweh enable each of you to find rest in the home of your new husband."

She placed her hands first on Orpah's wet cheeks and pulled her in to plant a kiss on the young woman's forehead. Then Ruth, who stiffened when Naomi kissed her on the temple. When Naomi released Ruth, the young woman's eyes shimmered.

Ruth's gaze pleaded. "Surely we will accompany you to your people."

Naomi shook her head. "Return home, my daughters. Why would you go with me? Are there sons in my womb to become your husbands? Go home." She pushed them away, gently, hoping to make her point clear. "Go on, for I am too old to have another husband. Even if I thought there was hope for me to have a husband tonight and to bear sons, would you wait for them to grow up? Would you refrain from having husbands? No, my daughters, it grieves me very much for your sakes that the hand of Yahweh has gone out against me."

It hurt to admit that Yahweh had turned His back on her, but what else could she think? She felt cursed beyond measure, and she would condemn her loved ones to share in her misery if they left with her.

The sound of sobbing intensified. Despite her resolve to be strong, Naomi broke down and cried with her daughters. They belonged to her. Truly, even though she had never carried them or raised them, she loved both women as her own. How could she see harm come to either of them, especially when the caravan leader couldn't take his molten gaze off Orpah?

Orpah nodded, despite the tears streaming down her cheeks. She flung her arms around Naomi and kissed her soundly on the cheek. "I will never forget you, Imma. Never."

Ruth stepped in to hug Naomi, and for a moment, Naomi felt a keen sorrow pierce her. They would listen to her, as they usually had. Such dutiful daughters, who had given her so much. When she patted Ruth on the back and tried to step away, Ruth wouldn't release her grip.

The younger woman rasped, "Please, Imma. Don't send me away. I need you."

Orpah clasped Ruth's shoulder before snatching her bedroll and bag. She unslung her waterskin and handed it to Naomi. "Goodbye, Ruth. I couldn't have asked for a better sister. If you won't stay with your brother, at least come to my home."

But Ruth shook her head, her lips pressed together as if she couldn't speak. She covered Orpah's hand with hers until at last, Orpah pulled away with a sad smile, waving when it was clear no one else would follow. She swiftly melted into the bustle of the men and women leading donkeys and carts loaded with produce as farmers and merchants clamored to enter the city.

"Look," said Naomi as she pointed to the open city gate, "your sister-in-law has gone back to her people and her gods. Follow her back home. Please, Ruth. For my sake. I can't take care of you."

Ruth disentangled herself from Naomi. Her jaw jutted outward in a rare show of defiance, and her eyes glowed with a fire. "Do not urge me to leave you or turn from following you. For wherever you go, I will go, and wherever you live, I will live. Your people will be my people, and your God will be my God. Where you die, I will die, and there I will be buried. May Yahweh punish me, and ever so severely, if anything but death separates you and me."

Naomi opened her mouth and shut it. How could she argue with such an impassioned speech?

She heard Lotan shout to the men, signaling that the caravan would leave at any moment. "I won't stop you from coming, but I am afraid for you. Don't ruin your life, Ruth."

Her tone was brusque enough to make Ruth duck her head while securing the supplies, but Naomi felt only fear and frustration bubble up within her, along with a sharp stab of guilt, because deep down inside, she couldn't quite deny that it would be good to have someone she trusted beside her in the days to come.

Glancing over her shoulder, Naomi took one last look at the city perched high above the rest of the land, supported by powdery cliffs. Regret stalked her, refusing to let go. What if she had pressured her husband or her sons to leave the city? Would they still be alive? She had been content to follow their lead, and now she had nothing.

Balancing on an ornery donkey while the blistering sun beat down on her head and shoulders brought a quiver to her chest. She wasn't sure how much more travel she could take. Yet the intense discomfort did one thing. It distracted from the pain of her loss, forcing her to pay attention to the rutted path strewn with rocks and steer her donkey to stable ground.

Naomi smarted everywhere, including joints and muscles she didn't realize existed. When Lotan yelled out the command to camp for the night, she almost flashed a relieved smile at him, catching herself at the last moment.

Not once did Ruth complain as she rode behind Naomi. Surely Ruth needed as much rest as everyone else did. The evening sunset proved brilliant and surreal, a painting of vivid purple and pink, while the sun, a ball of fire, melted into the horizon. Dust stirred along the pathway, swirling in small eddies. Holding the edge of her veil over her nose, Naomi longed to take a breath of fresh air. She was tired of coughing. Tired of aching in every muscle.

"Look at the sunset," Ruth said with a hint of awe as she pointed to the sprawling vista.

The horizon, now a dusky amethyst, offered a breathtaking view of craggy hills and hollows, perfect hiding places for foxes or desert horned vipers. But Naomi could hardly enjoy the sunset, even if it was a luxury after living in a crowded city.

She gestured to Ruth once they dismounted with dough-like limbs, beaten from the swaying of the donkeys. "Stay close to me. I don't trust Lotan one bit."

Before they had left the city, Naomi had divided the coins into two leather pouches. She placed one pouch in her blanket, secured away so no one could see it. The other pouch lay hidden in Ruth's blanket.

Lotan had demanded a ridiculous price up front for the caravan, and Naomi knew he had cheated her out of an exorbitant amount. But to travel alone, where robbers or venomous snakes lurked in the forbidding landscape, would be foolish.

Ruth nodded, silent as she darted a quick look in the direction of the caravan leader. In the dying light, his bald head gleamed with sweat. A sword constantly dangled by his side as he barked orders to his subordinates, forcing men and a haggard female slave to rush to do his bidding.

Did he sleep with that formidable sword? Naomi had no defense other than her son's sling. Mahlon had tried to teach her how to use it, but the only one with the patience to listen had been Ruth. Naomi knew her daughter-in-law had packed a few smooth oval stones, slipping them into the wide sash tied at her waist. A shepherd's sling against a slew of battle-hardened swords brought no reassurance, though.

Ruth's next question cut into Naomi's observations. "Where should we sleep, Imma?"

Naomi glanced about the campsite, searching for a decent place to rest. "I don't know yet. Beside the fire would prove safer from animals, but it's not the wild beasts I fear. Let's see where the men throw their pallets and choose the opposite spots."

Ruth carried her supplies and the rolled blanket with Naomi as they searched for a level place free of snakes or scorpions. The men of the caravan nabbed the area closest to the crackling fire, spreading out their mats and blankets in a circle. Farther away, Naomi set her supplies to the left and sank down on the wool blanket spread on the ground.

Silently, Ruth supplied the waterskin. The water tasted stale and warm, mingled with a hint of cured leather. Regardless, it quenched Naomi's thirst as she shared the skin with her daughter-in-law.

When Ruth offered a larger portion of bread, now crumbly and tasteless from the journey, Naomi held up a hand. "You must eat the same as me. I don't need any special favors on our journey."

Ruth's eyes darkened, but again, she said nothing as she slowly chewed the bread they had baked before dawn. Naomi mentally chided herself for her churlish command. Surely Ruth would see she cared. She bit into the bread, her mouth as dry as sawdust.

They discreetly watched Lotan, who brought out a waterskin of his own. Naomi highly doubted it contained water. A few of the men ogled Ruth, now that Orpah was no longer traveling in the company. Another young couple traveled with Naomi and Ruth. The man and his wife intended to travel past Bethlehem to Hebron, their unwillingness to share much understandable. They too kept to the edge of the encampment, nervously listening to the caravan leader's boisterous laugh as he lounged by the fire. Lotan's sharp features, illuminated by the dancing flames, matched that of the Chemosh idols sold at the market—exaggerated nose and thick lips pulled back in a snarl. When he yanked on the arm of the female slave, Naomi ducked her head, wishing more than ever for her bold sons to be by her side. They never would have tolerated seeing a woman treated so disgracefully.

Ruth's next question brought a welcome distraction. "How much longer must we travel?"

"We have eight to twelve days on the road if we move swiftly. Lotan mentioned we would stop at inns and settlements, if possible. We'll go around the southern portion of the Yam HaMelaḥ, the sea of salt, past the Moab plains and past the city Jericho, and a mighty river. Then you will see Bethlehem. It's full of hills and caves, with the rocks bleached by the sun. Hot and windy. Yet in the plains, the grain grows this high." Naomi gestured with her hand. "When you stand in a field, it is like a sheet of the purest hammered gold, rippling in the breeze. Stunning in every direction, as far as you can see. Even the name, Bethlehem, means House of Bread."

"Sounds beautiful indeed—a promised land, as you once described to me," Ruth stated quietly. She leaned an elbow against the blanket, no longer studying Lotan and his men carousing by the fire. Instead, Ruth glanced at the deepening sky and the scattered stars glowing brightly. Her face softened as she studied the sparkling constellations springing to life, one by one, as the darkness stretched outward like a heavy veil.

Naomi recognized a few of the patterns. A hunter notching his arrow. The ram bellowing while stomping its hoof into the heavens. The virgin clasping her wheat, signaling the coming season of harvest.

Ruth's innocent question startled Naomi from observing the sky. "It's astounding to think our Creator made the heavenly tent stretching above us. If Yahweh watched over Abraham and Moses during their travels, do you think He watches over us? At this very moment?"

Naomi bit her tongue until it throbbed. She knew the correct answer to give, yet grief stole the words from her mouth. Did Yahweh see her or Ruth, truly? If so, why had He allowed so much loss, condemning both of them to a life of miserable want?

She dropped her gaze from the glittering display high above and pressed a hand against her abdomen, where hunger threatened. Though she wouldn't utter the traitorous words aloud, her soul railed in protest.

I don't see You, Yahweh. Where are You when we need You?

She rolled over on her blanket while pulling a worn cloak over her shoulders, her tender ribs, arms, and legs failing to find a patch of comfort on the hard, rock-strewn ground. "Good night, Ruth."

CHAPTER FIVE

Five days of travel. Ruth's skin burned despite the scarf wrapped around her head. She was certain she shared the same aroma as the dusty donkey who had been her constant companion. Naomi too had a red nose and cheeks. The water-skins looped around their torsos no longer burst to the brim, trickling water over the side when opened. Ruth hoped Lotan would stop soon and allow an urgent refill at the next well.

Tongue cleaving to the roof of her mouth, Ruth watched the horizon shimmer and dance, as if a great lake waited over the hill.

Lotan told them it was only a mirage. The closer she rode, the farther the lake shifted away, always in sight but never in reach. They rode during the cooler part of the morning, rising before the sun crested over the horizon. Lotan kept the camels moving at a decent pace, yet whenever they stopped at a walled settlement or a well from a nearby farm, he often offered to water her donkey.

She didn't care for the attention, nor the way he tried to brush against her body. Naomi noticed as well.

"Be firm with him," Naomi advised with that sharp voice of hers. "Like a lion in the desert, without fear or shame."

Easy enough advice, yet for Ruth, extremely difficult. How could she not shudder or stare at her dust-coated sandals whenever the caravan leader drifted her way, reeking of garlic and sour wine? Instead, Ruth forced herself to raise her chin and meet his continual leer with a withering glare.

Mahlon had been so gentle and protective of her after her abba's last violent outburst. But truthfully, she couldn't afford to remain timid when Naomi needed her. Yet the memory of her fierce abba still brought a whisper of insecurity, of unworthiness. Shame too, for letting others treat her so poorly for so long. Did that mean there was something truly wrong with her?

Twilight bathed the craggy landscape in hues of purple when Lotan demanded the caravan halt. At the edge of the Judean desert, sparkling like a jewel in the harsh arid dust, lay Ein Gedi. Ruth tugged at her filthy scarf to better see the lush vegetation, promising shade and respite. Previously, Naomi told her of the four rivers flowing year-round to provide fresh water. Beyond the oasis, the sea of salt waited, harsh and forbidding with patches of crystalized white beaches devoid of life.

No one complained about the stop. Bethlehem would soon appear on the horizon if they left early enough in the morning.

Naomi said nothing as she brushed the sand from her robes. Ruth thought her mother-in-law appeared exhausted. Fresh lines crept beneath her eyes and near her mouth, as if she had aged ten years overnight. Surely they weren't the only ones to desire a comfortable mat and a thick blanket. The young couple who had traveled with the caravan could go no farther, not with the wife keeling over on her donkey, her face a sickly hue.

After speaking with the caravan guards, Lotan sauntered toward Ruth. His hand rested at the leather-wrapped hilt of his sword, ever menacing.

She dismounted from the donkey, even if in a clumsy, haphazard manner with the hem of her tunic unfortunately riding up to her lower calves, before he reached her side. She gathered the reins and jerked the obstinate beast closer to the freshwater pool, but the donkey dug its hooves into the sand and brayed in protest.

The caravan leader reached out a long arm as if to snag the leather straps from her hands. "The other woman needs your help. Gather your mother-in-law and see if you can be useful." He nodded at the male traveler who stumbled as he carried his wife in his arms to find shade beneath a tree. "Says she's with child. I can't afford to wait while they deliver a babe."

This time, Ruth didn't fight Lotan as he snatched the reins, his thick fingers grazing hers. She hurried to the traveler. Behind her, she heard Lotan order Naomi to do the same.

"Is she in any pain?" Ruth asked the man as he laid his wife carefully on the ground. The sight of a man caring for his wife renewed the ache in Ruth's chest. Had she really lost Mahlon only a short while ago? It felt forever, and yet as if it was only yesterday. The ache intensified until she could scarcely breathe again. She felt as barren as the sea of salt, where nothing lived.

The woman hissed through clenched teeth as she clutched her belly, the swell formerly hidden beneath the loose robes.

The youthful husband, with a soft beard and crooked teeth, pointed to his wife. "We won't be able to travel any farther to Bethlehem, and the caravan leader refuses to wait for us. I've heard there might be a midwife in Ein Gedi. Will you stay with her until I find someone capable?"

"I will watch over your wife," she assured him as she knelt beside the pregnant woman, who lay flat on the ground.

The young mother's hair, damp with sweat, curled around her neck. She bit her lower lip as she moaned. "It's too soon to deliver the baby, far too soon."

Naomi sank down beside the young woman, whose name they discovered was Rebecca. Her husband, Reuben, left with a caravan guard and two donkeys to search the nearby village for a midwife.

"Breathe deeply and try to relax. Some women have discomforting pains, and riding a donkey this long—" Naomi's voice dropped as if she didn't want to finish her thought out loud, while she brushed Rebecca's hair from her face. The husband might soon rue his decision to have his pregnant wife travel such a distance, and in her condition. "If you gather the blankets, Ruth, I could make her more comfortable."

Ruth found her items and the blankets near the pool of water fed by a narrow waterfall. Her donkeys lingered by a muddy bank pitted with hoofprints, drinking their fill with the other caravan animals. Lotan was nowhere in sight.

The top blanket, however, appeared folded oddly, unlike her careful packing. Alarmed by the change, she instinctively reached inside Naomi's blanket, her fingers grasping for the satchel of coins cleverly hidden inside the scratchy folds. Shock rippled through her when she touched only the rough wool.

***

"What have you done with our money!" Naomi seethed as she stared at Lotan.

With a smirk, he planted his hands on his hips and tipped forward. "I've done nothing with your coins, old woman."

"You took our donkeys and ordered us to help that poor mother, allowing you enough time to pilfer my money!" She resisted the urge to jab at his chest with her finger.

Lotan's smirk deepened as he studied her. "You have no proof. Maybe the coins scattered across the terrain, thanks to your sloppy packing. I'll let your insult pass and consider it ravings of a heat-addled traveler."

Naomi growled low in her throat.

At least Ruth had found the other portion of the coins secured within the additional blanket. She hid them in the one tunic Naomi had insisted on bringing, a colorful wedding gown with rich embroidery in saffron and crimson. A pair of silver earrings, beaten as fine as papyrus, brought a wealth of memories. Naomi wouldn't—couldn't—give up that costly outfit, a reminder of better days when she was young and full of hope and about to marry Elimelech.

Lotan rocked forward on his heels, clearly pleased with her reaction. "If you have no money, how will you pay the rest of the fare when I reach Bethlehem?"

She gasped, her ire fading into horror. "What do you mean? I paid you in full before we left Kir-hareseth."

"You will owe me additional funds, and I'll find payment one way or another." His mouth twisted into a feral grin.

Nausea pooled in her belly as she watched him stride away. No one would help her. The man and his wife had already abandoned the caravan, finding refuge in Ein-Gedi. Naomi hoped the new mother wouldn't miscarry her first child.

An image of her sweet sons flashed before her. Mahlon tripping and scraping his knee and her arms wrapping around him to pick him up and kiss away the tears. Chilion snuggling in her arms, his baby cheeks flushed from eating.

So much loss. So much suffering welling inside her until she felt like a desert stream about to overflow and erode the land. Now she had Lotan's threat to contend with in. How much more torment could she endure?

Pressing a fist against her mouth, Naomi bent at the waist, suddenly woozy and wanting to retch. She dare not travel with this man, not with his malevolent intent shining so clearly in his one bright eye. She hadn't enough money to survive in Ein-Gedi. She needed to get to Bethlehem and find Elimelech's old home. At least she and Ruth could garden there, and maybe use the last of the coins to buy a goat. To stay in this oasis would bring her and Ruth to ruin.

And to stay in the company of Lotan, two widows with no protector…

Bile gurgled in the back of her throat.

"Imma, imma—" Ruth's voice came from behind Naomi. Naomi felt gentle hands pull her shaking form close. "What is wrong?"

Fresh anger coursed through Naomi as she straightened to her full height. "The caravan leader stole our money. He insists I owe him for the rest of the journey. He will take everything we have. I don't trust him not to steal the coins in your blanket, if given the chance."

Ruth led Naomi to a nearby fig tree. They both eased to the ground, overcome. Ruth hugged her knees close to her chest. Finally, she rested her head against her knees, while Naomi struggled to control her racing pulse.

She couldn't even utter what her heart feared most.

Yahweh had truly abandoned her and Ruth.

CHAPTER SIX

Stars brought only a sprinkle of light to the gathering gloom. The waxing moon limned the bubbling, freshwater spring near the campsite, and the caravan animals, mostly quiet, munched on cud. Naomi had moved their blankets to the far edge of the camp, staying close to the gnarled fig tree with its outstretched branches raised high over their heads. The leaves rustled like sheets of papyrus, and a donkey brayed its discontent. Somewhere in the foliage, an animal darted across dried leaves and branches in the hurry to either hunt or escape.

At sunset, the men had appeared more boisterous than usual, including Lotan, who nursed his wineskin through the evening. Naomi had witnessed evil in the Moabite city, including the flat stare of eyes more dead than alive. When the men had exited the temples of Chemosh, glutted with their so-called worship, she had bolted her door as a precaution. She was mightily sick of Lotan watching her and Ruth with the same predatory curl to his lips.

As soon as the fire died to spitting embers and sifting ash and the men were mostly asleep with the occasional snore, Naomi shook Ruth awake. Her daughter-in-law sat up, silent, her long hair tumbling about her shoulders.

Naomi's whisper seemed unnaturally loud. "We must go now. If we do not leave while the men are asleep, I don't think we will make it to Bethlehem. Lotan will force us into slavery."

Ruth paused, her pupils so huge that her eyes were nearly black as she studied Naomi. Then she swiftly folded her blanket and collected her assortment of items, including her sling. When everyone else had been preoccupied during the evening meal, she had hidden the remaining coins, precious few, along with the magnificent wedding tunic, tucked into a dusty cloak. Lotan hadn't examined everything.

While Ruth hid the coins, Naomi had at least refilled the waterskins. Enough bread and dates remained to make it by foot to Bethlehem. If they walked through the night, they would reach their destination by morning.

With quiet footsteps, they crept from the lush oasis amid the rattling snores of the men. Before Naomi, a path of sand and dust waited, now shifting silver in the moonlight.

"Shall we pray, Imma, for Yahweh to guide our path?" Ruth asked in a low voice.

"If you must," Naomi replied, but her heart felt as though it would rend in two.

She adjusted the leather strap of her waterskin to a more comfortable position on her shoulder and hefted her meager belongings in her arms before stepping into the unknown. If it wasn't for her daughter-in-law by her side, Naomi might have collapsed up by the side of the road and begged for death, but she couldn't stop—not when Ruth needed her.

Once the campsite could be viewed no longer, Ruth prayed out loud, her voice hoarse.

Naomi flinched as she struggled to put one sandal in front of the other, the journey by foot already wearing on her. All around her, danger lurked. Bandits or wild animals, snakes, or perhaps the caravan leader, should he arise and notice his two travelers missing.

She couldn't worry about such fearsome thoughts. Indeed, she felt too paralyzed at the moment to think about more than surviving this walk.

There was only Bethlehem. But the irony of fleeing her birthplace for security and a far better life and now returning with only the things she could carry on her back and in her arms was far too bitter to contemplate.

By the time the sun crested over the hillside, a thrill of wonder darted through Ruth despite her bone-deep weariness. A vast plain of fields stretched before her, the shining wheat and barley rippling in the breeze, undulating like the waves of the salt sea. She rubbed her dry eyes, but the mirage didn't disappear. She had never seen such a bountiful harvest when Mahlon and Chilion worked on Moabite land. Along the hills, terraced strips of land cut into the slope like a staircase for a giant. Farmers wasted nothing in Bethlehem. They transformed every bit of decent soil into crops.

Naomi came to a halt, wheezing from the long journey on foot.

"How different this looks," she gestured with a slight tremor. "When we left, we saw nothing but cracked earth and blowing dust."

Ruth remembered Naomi's tales told across a supper table with Chilion and Mahlon and Orpah listening raptly. Yahweh's judgment had fallen on Bethlehem. The more the Israelites turned to false gods, the less He could remain with them. He was, after all, a holy God, without sin.

She shivered as she studied the vast land before her. Would the residents welcome her? Or would they deem her as corrupt as the city she left?

"Come," Naomi rasped as she took the lead. She pointed to the town surrounded by rolling hills. "Hopefully, we'll find the well less crowded this early in the morning."

As they limped down the hill, Ruth couldn't help but wonder if her mother-in-law wished to hide away before anyone recognized her.

***

The Bethlehem stone well, as in Moab, was a gathering place for women in the dawn's cool or the evening. Women of all ages brought their jugs to plumb the depths of fresh water. An awning, supported by thick posts of wood, offered a decent shade. A long trough leading from the well allowed women to share the precious resource.

Ruth heard Naomi's sharp intake of breath when she spied a group of women in colorful robes next to the stone rim.

Their lighthearted chatter and giggles traveled easily through the hush of the morning.

Naomi stumbled midstep and righted herself as she clutched Ruth's arm. "We need water. I don't know what condition the cistern might be in at the old house."

Ruth nodded. She briefly clasped Naomi's shoulder and was rewarded with a wobbly smile.

Surely returning home without kin while covered with swollen mosquito bites and smelling like donkeys would cause any woman to quake. Her heart lurched for Naomi's anxiety at facing a community she had known in a previous life.

The Bethlehem women stopped talking when they saw Ruth and Naomi approach. The oldest woman, her auburn locks caught beneath a saffron veil and silver bracelets tinkling at her wrists, cried out when she spied Naomi. "N-Naomi, is that you?"

Both women stared at each other for a long moment. Ruth's mother-in-law sighed as she unhooked her waterskin and approached the ledge. "Yes, Aviah, it is Naomi, but you should call me Mara, for the Almighty has dealt bitterly with me. I went away full, and Yahweh has brought me back empty. Why call me Naomi, when the Lord has testified against me and brought calamity upon me? We have come home to Bethlehem now that my husband and sons have passed away."

Stunned silence swept through the women as they cradled their jars. The shock was so great, Ruth might have been standing in a hall of carved wooden statues.

She had never heard such acerbity in Naomi. Unfortunately, the name *Mara* felt wholly inappropriate. It meant "acrid" or "bitter," unlike *Naomi*, which meant "pleasant." Had her mother-in-law lost all hope in Yahweh after such crushing losses? The woman standing beside her felt more a stranger than kin. In Moab, Naomi had been the epitome of kindness and trust in her God, a friend and mentor, convincing Ruth to believe. This new demeanor was disturbing to say the least.

Aviah blinked rapidly at the harsh answer before turning her attention to Ruth. "What a tragic loss. I am so sorry to hear of it. And who is this with you?"

Naomi placed a hand on Ruth's back, nudging her forward. "This is my beautiful daughter-in-law, Ruth."

She tried to hide her cringe but failed as the women whispered to each other. Aviah's groomed eyebrows arched high as she studied Ruth. "Your sons married Moabite women? Isn't the union to foreigners forbidden by Moses?"

Ruth felt Naomi's fingers grip her shoulder, as if to prevent her from running away. Summoning fortitude, Ruth forced herself to meet the other women's gazes as Naomi spoke. "Yahweh blessed me with the sweetest of daughters. One rejoined her family, but Ruth has faithfully remained by my side, showing me every kindness even though she could have married again in Kir-hareseth. She is truly a gift from Yahweh."

"How commendable," Aviah murmured as she clutched her water jar closer, regardless of the water dripping down her tunic. She didn't sound entirely convinced. "You both have had quite a journey, I'm sure."

The rest of the women retreated as Naomi approached the well. Studying their sandals, or her faded gown, they continued to avoid Ruth's direct gaze. Offering a bright smile to the women next to her, she attempted to appear at ease even as her anxiety increased. She refused to cower and bring further embarrassment to Naomi.

"Where will you stay?" Aviah asked, her gaze narrowing. "Your brother-in-law, Zakai, has absorbed Elimelech's lands. Hasn't your sister, Machla, sent word to you?"

"My husband never sold his land. My family offered only to tend it in our absence," Naomi confessed with a frown. Her knuckles whitened as she clenched the strap of the waterskin. "But I will speak with Zakai as soon as possible."

"Hmm," Aviah hummed as she shot a look at another woman, one full of hidden meaning. The older woman's face smoothed, the lack of expression almost as disturbing as the prior raised eyebrows. "Welcome to Bethlehem."

And just like that, the conversation ended, and the women turned their backs on Ruth and her mother-in-law, focusing on other gossip in the village. No one took Naomi seriously enough to call her Mara. No one gave Ruth a second glance.

The dismissal pinched. What she could say or do to break through the coldness? Even her mother-in-law appeared subdued as she quietly drew a bucket of water and used the trough to refill her wineskin. She said her farewells before whispering to Ruth it was time to leave. Moisture prickled the back of Ruth's eyelids, for she sensed the women had found her somehow wanting, and likely because of her heritage. But far worse, none of the women had offered to help Naomi. How much more did her mother-in-law suffer from such rudeness?

Indeed, the village women had already gathered together, their heads nearly touching as furious whispers raced back and forth in the cool morning air.

No doubt she and Naomi were the source of such gossip.

Naomi didn't break her brisk stride. "Pay them no heed, Ruth. They will get used to you. A small village is far different from a great city. You can't hide here in anonymity, my sweet girl. You've got to keep your chin up and show them who you really are. In time, they will see you as I do. People fear what they do not know."

Her mother-in-law linked her arm through Ruth's, demonstrating her approval should anyone continue to watch. And it warmed Ruth's heart despite her discouragement with the encounter at the well. This was the Naomi she remembered and loved.

"I fear they may not look past the fact that I am a Moabitess."

Naomi shook her head with impatience. "You are an Israelite now. Don't let anyone else tell you differently. I suspect their discomfort has as much to do with my misfortunes. When I left Bethlehem, my husband had more wealth than most, and Yahweh had blessed me with two sons. Now I have nothing, and it reminds them of how loss can strike any of us, at any time."

Naomi's confession burrowed into Ruth, bringing fresh grief. She had dealt with her sorrow by staying busy during the journey, but when faced with rejection by the women, somehow everything she had endured stung all the more this morning.

When she raised her head, a man watched her from outside the Bethlehem gate. A crooked nose, as if broken once, and dark eyes immediately drew her. He was very tall—more so than her brother, if such a feat was possible, with strong shoulders built from hard labor. Yet the tunic he wore was of the finest linen, soft spun, and cinched to a narrow waist with an embroidered belt woven in a vibrant malachite hue. His beard and black hair reminded of her strangely of Mahlon, yet this was no youth with untamed curls, not with those streaks of white at his temples. His sober assessment of her was the opposite of the caravan leader's lecherous stare.

She didn't like big men—they resembled her abba with his sinewy hands capable of crushing anything.

This stranger was undoubtably rich and used to power, judging from his clothing and confident stance as he waited in the middle of the gate, next to the stone benches lining the city wall where leaders waited to discuss matters in a public forum. And here she appeared like a frail little bird caught in a rainstorm, bedraggled and weary, without a place to rest. No wonder she made such a poor impression on the Bethlehem women at the well.

The man's gaze lingered on her—almost as if he recognized her or, more likely, Naomi. Other men gathered about him, everyone speaking at once. He tore his attention away from her, refocusing on the person closest to him. In Kir-hareseth, the elders often resolved important business matters at the city gates, and Bethlehem, though vastly smaller, appeared much the same.

Was this man a judge or a city leader? He remained calm even when the other man waved his arms, stabbing at the air, his voice shrill.

"We'll need to push through the people to get to the market, and from there, we'll find Machla's home and see if she'll take us in for the time being." Naomi sounded resigned, and maybe a tad fearful. She tripped on a small rock, reaching a hand to grasp at Ruth's cloak to right herself.

Worried for her mother-in-law, Ruth lent an arm for Naomi to take. Snatches of arguments tugged at Ruth's interest, but amid the morning crush of people trying to enter through the open gates, she didn't dare stop.

"He stole my sheep!" someone shouted above the noise. "I recognized my brand on the hindquarters!"

"You lie, you worthless cur!" another retorted, sounding equally livid.

She kept moving, pausing only to make sure Naomi kept pace without getting winded. Edging past heated conversations and clusters of men, some old, some young, Ruth kept her gaze lowered as she weaved through the crowd of merchants, farmers, and people curious to be entertained by the drama unfolding outside the walls of Bethlehem.

When she approached the crowded gate, she suddenly found herself in front of the giant she had noticed earlier. He listened intently to an argument between two rugged men with untamed beards and shepherd staffs, while others pressed in, blocking the entrance.

Standing on her tiptoes, she searched for a way to enter Bethlehem, one that would not cause a commotion or involve her stepping on feet. The tall man glanced down at her and Naomi. He immediately moved aside to let her pass, his gaze snagging on hers for just a moment. He opened his mouth as if to speak to her, but someone else demanded his immediate attention.

One of the hairy shepherds accusing the other of theft bellowed his outrage to the tall stranger. "The law demands retribution! An eye for an eye, I say!"

Then, without warning, the hairy man charged the other shepherd, his fist swinging wide. The shepherds grappled with each other, grunting as each one sought to break free and land another jab. So intent on fighting, they nearly bumped into Ruth and Naomi. With a cry, Naomi dropped her rolled blanket. Ruth edged in front of her pale mother-in-law as a shield while Naomi scrambled to retrieve her scattered supplies. The shepherds were both red-faced and spitting insults, their punches flying fast.

Ruth flinched as though one of those fists was aimed at her jaw. Sickening memories of her abba rushed to the forefront and suddenly, she couldn't move as the brawling men thrashed near her. Worse, the crowd hemmed her in, allowing no room for escape.

To her astonishment, the tall man dashed into the fight, blocking her and Naomi from a flying elbow or sandaled foot. Ruth snatched Naomi's cold hand and yanked her mother-in-law away from the melee, but she couldn't quite tear her gaze from the large man who acted as a leader in the city and now as a buffer for her and Naomi. His face hidden from view, he reached out and grabbed a fistful of the closest shepherd's tunic, jerking him backward just before the fighting men collided with each other a second time.

"We don't settle arguments this way! Stop with this foolishness before you hurt an innocent bystander." His voice boomed over the gathering crowd, eager for a skirmish. "Take your complaints to the elders. They are waiting for you at the gate."

With a shudder at the visceral hatred from the shepherds and pity for the stranger forced to deal with them like an abba with misbehaving children, she hurried past the gated arch with Naomi in tow. Other than Mahlon, she had never had a man move aside for her, or protect her, for that matter. Certainly, no Moabite citizen ever showed such courtesy. She glanced over her shoulder. But the giant, grasping the two ornery shepherds by the arms, had disappeared into the gathering throng of harvesters and merchants clamoring to see the result of the latest dispute to be decided by officials before heading to the fields.

"Did you see that man?" Ruth asked Naomi as they finally broke free of the crowd and passed through the gate.

Her mother-in-law groaned under her breath as she examined her dirty blanket. "What man? Too many men surrounded and jostled us on all sides."

"The one who moved aside for us and later chastised those quarreling shepherds? He looked as though he recognized you."

Naomi shook her head, her weary gaze seemingly captured by the marketplace of Bethlehem, where farmers brought carts loaded with colorful wares—pottery, melons, stacked tapestries, and far more than a person could take in with one glance. "I've been gone so long, Ruth. Will everyone recognize me? People change, and I've changed too. If he's truly a friend or an acquaintance, hopefully we'll meet later. For now, I must get to Machla and secure a place for us." Naomi continued to stare at the market stalls, her expression dreamlike, as if caught in a wealth of memories.

Ruth let her mother-in-law stop and drink in the familiar sights and sounds. Despite her best effort, a shiver trailed down her spine.

They had made it, despite a hair-raising journey.

But the town had not extended the welcome Ruth had hoped for. Was Bethlehem all that much different than Kir-hareseth? She fervently hoped so. But no matter what trials came next, Naomi was home, and Ruth dearly hoped, in time, it would feel like home to her too.

CHAPTER SEVEN

R uth followed Naomi to an estate outside the noisy bustle of the village. It clung to the hillside with a blue scrolling trim painted along the upper walls. More olive trees than she could count broke the monotonous color of the hills swathed with brown grass. Large cedar doors opened into a magnificent courtyard, complete with a central pool of rainwater. Ruth longed to take off her sandals and dip her feet in the refreshing depths. She hadn't had time to wash at the last oasis, nor had she had felt safe enough to do so, even with her mother-in-law present.

Tempted to splash her face, a sigh of longing escaped her. At the last moment, she snatched her hand back from the water. She would be considered unclean, fouling another's ritual cleansing pool.

"I see things have been very profitable in Bethlehem during my absence," Naomi said as she set her bundle onto the stone pavement. Ruth did the same. She ran her hands down her tunic, as if somehow she could will the wrinkles away. Carefully, she tucked the loose strands of hair beneath her headscarf and did her very best to appear the demure Israelite maiden.

The door to the house opened, and a young woman, perhaps no older than fourteen years of age, approached them,

Her clothing was spotless and her hair neatly braided, but no smile of welcome graced her round face. Instead, she wrinkled her pert nose as she looked at Ruth, then at Naomi.

"My mistress has a headache and cannot see any guests."

Naomi waved a hand, dismissing the refusal with a false smile. "Tell Machla her sister, Naomi, wishes to pay her respects."

"I will pass her the message, but I wouldn't expect a visit today." The girl flounced away before slipping into the hall. By now, the morning sun had risen high in the sky. Ruth squinted against the brightness. She longed more than anything to sink to the ground and take a nap. She had walked throughout the night, intent on escaping Lotan. All she wanted was a place to lie down in peace.

After an interminably long wait, the door to the house creaked open a second time. The young girl entered the courtyard, her face set like granite. "My mistress says Naomi may come, but alone."

Naomi startled beside Ruth, her frustration clear. "Ruth is my daughter-in-law. Is there no hospitality to be extended to her?"

The girl had the decency to blush. Regardless, she pointed to a bench pushed at the edge of the wall. "She may wait there until my mistress is finished with you."

That last comment didn't bode well. Naomi snorted her disgust. She folded her arms across her chest, as if she were about to protest, but Ruth had no desire to have a repeat of the situation at the well.

"I'll wait on the bench. Truly, I'm exhausted."

Naomi frowned, but since they had no choice, she followed the girl into the home.

Ruth sighed and sank onto the bench, already pleasantly warm from the sun. She rested her back against the plastered wall. A breeze passed over the pool, bringing a hint of freshness from the valley. Somewhere a bird called overhead, the sound sweet and trilling. Her muscles ached and her stomach rumbled. Yet, in the beauty of the courtyard, she closed her eyes. Just for a moment, of course.

At some point, she realized someone was close to her. Very close. Alarmed, she opened one eye and jerked upright, only to see a man, a youth, really, stare at her with sly amusement. He also wore an expensive tunic, a *sadin*, long to the ground as befitting a wealthy man. Deep blue tassels hung from the *simlāh*, a light covering draped over the tunic. Pimples dotted his skin, and a beard, or at least a few sparse hairs, straggled from his pointed chin.

"The servant quarters are to the left, but we don't allow sleeping during the day. Especially in the family living quarters."

Her mouth dried at the insult. "I am not a servant. I'm with my mother-in-law, Naomi, sister to the lady of the house."

Instead of being embarrassed, he appeared even haughtier with a nose lifted high. "If you are searching for a handout, you won't find it here. My abba doesn't tolerate laziness. No woman sleeping during the morning is worth any salt."

Ire heated her cheeks as she struggled to come up with a coherent reply that would preserve her dignity and not embarrass Naomi.

He glanced at her through hooded eyes while adding, "No matter how pretty either."

Since Naomi hoped for help from her relatives, Ruth could hardly refute his previous statement. But his second only made matters worse.

She struggled to keep her voice even. "My apologies for resting in your courtyard. We traveled during the night and have only just arrived in Bethlehem."

He sniffed and opened his mouth to say something when the massive door to the house flung open with a bang. Naomi marched across the stone pavement, her cheeks as red as Ruth's and her nostrils flaring. The door slammed behind her, the sound echoing across the courtyard.

She didn't even acknowledge the young man beside Ruth. "I've had enough visiting for one day. Shall we leave?"

Eager to escape the obnoxious youth, Ruth jumped from the bench and grabbed her items. For someone with such lordly manners, he certainly didn't seem to be in a hurry to go anywhere and, as he so callously put it—work hard.

They hurried out of the courtyard and down the sloping terrain. Ruth had to lengthen her stride to keep up with Naomi's pace. "I can tell by your face the visit went terribly awry. I had a strange encounter in the courtyard, though he appeared too young to be the owner."

Naomi blew out a harsh breath, the sound almost comical if their situation wasn't so desperate. "You met Machla's son, Radah. Pompous child, isn't he? He was just a baby when I left Bethlehem. He unfortunately takes after his imma. I've never been treated so—so shamefully in all my life. Israelites pride themselves on their hospitality, but since I've left, things have indeed changed. Maybe not all for the better."

"Is it because of me?" Ruth asked, dreading the answer.

Naomi shifted her blanket to a more comfortable spot beneath her arm. "Machla did state she won't entertain foreigners. But it's more than that. She's furious we came back to claim Elimelech's old land, and states we have no right. She swears my husband sold it to her husband. Ridiculous claims. Elimelech would have never sold his land, not when he had sons. He left it because he wasn't a patient man and he saw no reason to plant crops in parched soil with no promise of rain. Nor did he want to see his family starve before his eyes, so he bolted, and headed to the closest place providing work."

The sinking feeling in Ruth became a millstone, capable of crushing her. They could not count on Machla for the slightest mercy. Nor the women at the well. Was there anyone in all of Bethlehem who would take pity on two desperate widows? Why had Yahweh brought them to this place?

"What do we do now?" she asked, partly afraid of what Naomi might answer.

Naomi pushed back her scarf, her face ashen, each line in her forehead deepening from worry. "We will go home. Elimelech had a house on the southern edge of the property. Clearly, Machla isn't living there, and if there are no workers who have taken it over, then we have every right to find shelter."

CHAPTER EIGHT

The house, perhaps once a lovely residence, lay like a blight on the land. Despite the burnished fields nearby and the terraced hillside, a few fig trees struggled to survive on the arid property, producing minimal fruit, much of which appeared shriveled. Around the house, fields had turned fallow, with sheep munching on fragrant grass.

Naomi hissed when she saw the flock, and the few shepherds drifting through the sea of white wool. "Not a single crop remains? Zakai must have allowed his animals to completely take over our property."

A troubling thought.

However, Ruth wanted to shout for joy when she saw the house, the cramped courtyard, and the straggling garden tucked beside the western wall. If she had dared, she might have even kissed the ground.

A fresh burst of energy filled her once she approached the sandstone threshold, but the dismay on Naomi's face was enough to make Ruth halt midstep.

"Oh no," Naomi breathed as she slowly turned around in the center of the courtyard. "I'm afraid of what we'll find." Although the modest home, like many in the area, had no windows, a weathered door swung with the breeze, creaking in protest. At least the door, which was attached to a pole inserted into hollowed-out stones above and below, continued to pivot in the sockets.

Ruth glanced at the cracked mud-brick walls built upon a stone base. Expensive homes were comprised of layered rock, but not this building. Naomi stared at the deepened cracks and webbing of delicate lines running every which way through the mud plaster. "I've never plastered a wall."

Ruth brushed her fingertips against the roughened surface. "We'll learn together. How hard can it be?"

Naomi shot Ruth a disbelieving look.

"Don't forget I helped my abba with his pottery. We can fix this property."

No, she would not let Naomi fall into despair. Without hope, they would achieve nothing, and lose whatever they had left.

The small courtyard contained tamped earth, beaten level and smooth from years of use. Lining the walls, a row of *pithoi*, massive jars for storing water, grain, and olive oil, appeared relatively intact. She wandered to the nearest one and sniffed to determine the contents. Gagging, she jerked away from the pot and the rancid stench clinging to it. Had an animal found its way inside the jar? How would she clean such a huge jar that reached nearly to her waist?

The rest of the jars remained empty. No wheat. No water either. But the handles bore Elimelech's name, once scratched into the soft clay.

Placing her hands on her hips, she sighed, just like Naomi. But at least the building housed a room on one side for storage, and on the opposite side, a stall for a cow or a mule. The room at the end was reserved for living and sleeping. Thankfully, Naomi rediscovered the small stone well, which was more of a cistern used to collect rainwater.

When Ruth reached the doorway, her breath caught. There, just as in Moab, Elimelech had inserted a carved-out hollow near the door. The *mezuzah*. Moses's commandment had initially sounded strange when Mahlon tried to explain the symbolism and the meaning behind it.

The words that I shall tell you this day: that you shall love your God, believe only in Him, keep His commandments, and pass all of this on to your children.

Her fingers trailed outside the cleft. To her amazement, the mezuzah, a tapered clay jar with a lid, remained tucked into the narrow space. Inside the jar, the words of the law waited. Mahlon had explained that the container must not be sealed permanently, because twice in seven years, the parchment should be opened and inspected to see if any of the letters had faded or become damaged. Only a priest could rewrite the letters.

It was a comforting sign, one of many during the journey, that Yahweh remained close to her and Naomi, His words breathing life and encouragement when they needed it most.

She bowed her head with a silent plea, her palm splayed flat against the wall. However, once she stepped inside the room, she paused before taking off her sandals as dictated by the law. One glance at the ceiling and she cried aloud. Rotten wood beams sagged, in danger of collapsing at any moment. Pillars, placed at crucial points around the house, supported part of the roof. They appeared solid enough. Yet water stains traced grotesque patterns across the plaster walls. Naomi didn't remove her sandals either. The ceiling was made up of an interlocking series of branches covered with dried mud. Gaps had eroded between the branches, flooding the room with dots of wavering sunlight.

Naomi glanced up at the ceiling. "We'll need to replace the beams at some point. If only someone had sealed the wood with clay, but I suspect Elimelech was the last to weatherproof everything. Otherwise, we wouldn't see such damage." She glanced at Ruth. "Still think we are up for the challenge?"

Ruth caught her bottom lip between her teeth. This was significantly worse than she could have imagined. Her prior bravado easily evaporated beneath the weight of repairs needed.

Dirt and grit crunched beneath her sandals as she moved across the floor. They could use the two stone benches on either side of the wall as seating, or to provide a spot for a bed-roll. A hearth near the center of the home allowed the comfort of a fire, but most of the cooking would take place in the court-yard over a circular pit. One rare luxury remained—a table. She was relieved to see it was mostly sturdy, despite some warping of the wood. A second luxury made her smile—a staircase outside the house led to the upstairs rooms.

At least she wouldn't need to balance on a clumsy ladder to reach her pallet.

An animal hidden by the shadows scurried away when Naomi joined Ruth's side. She prayed the scurrying sound she had just heard wasn't rats. Anything but rats.

She found a broom with missing straw at the end. A chewed-up pallet rested near one wall, and the straw stuffing scattered across the floor promised more rodents. Black droppings the size of seeds were likely the gift of the rat or the mouse.

"Imma—"

"I know. We have our work cut out for us. But I can't move another step. I think we need an hour of rest, or two, then we will clean and repair as much as we can." Naomi dragged a palm over her face as if she couldn't quite believe what she saw.

"Can I do anything to help?" Ruth asked.

Naomi said nothing as she stood in the center of her home that was ruined beyond all imagination.

Her shoulders shook as if she was weeping. Ruth went to her, intending to offer comfort. But Naomi held up a warning hand. "I need a moment to myself. I can't even think clearly right now. If you take the outside stairs, you may find a serviceable chamber overhead to sleep, but avoid the flat roof. It won't support our weight. At least, I hope the other rooms will be usable. Let's rest, and then we can figure out what we need to do."

Ruth stepped backward. Disappointment surged through her yet again to be dismissed, but she grabbed her blanket and meager supplies before heading up the stairs. Naomi needed to grieve in private.

As promised, another room awaited at the top of the stairs. A rush of stale air greeted Ruth as she pushed open the door. She laid her blanket on the floor and found a large rock on the floor, a perfect doorstop, and propped open the door to bring in a fresh breeze.

She removed her sandals and unwound her sweaty headscarf while exhaustion washed in waves over her. Next came the dust-encrusted sash, her fingers stiff as she tugged it free from the knot. The stones clattered to the ground, along with Mahlon's sling, two thin leather straps flanking a round pouch. During the journey, the stones had brought a comforting presence, as if he remained with her.

She fingered the leather, now worn smooth from use. Closing her eyes, she pictured his swarthy face. They had been nearly the same height, and she had felt so safe with him. He had included her in nearly every area of his life, inviting her outside the city to learn how to use the sling.

"Come here," he had told her with a hint of a smile, wrapping one hard arm around her waist. "Anyone can learn to toss a rock. It's all in the snap of a wrist. First, you must spin and release." He raised her right hand, his fingers firm. "Hold both strings, and as you whip the sling in a circle, sight your target, and let your arm extend, releasing the second string at the same moment. You can do this, Ruth. It doesn't matter how tiny you are."

He made it look so easy, striking a clay jar perched on a craggy outcropping. And, of course, when she tucked the rock into the pouch, he had snuck a kiss or two just to throw her off balance.

Helpless to fight the onslaught of bittersweet memories, or her choked sobs, she stretched out her blanket and lay down, cradling the sling next to her chest.

When Ruth sat up, the sun had moved west, signaling late afternoon. She had overslept despite intending only a quick nap. Struggling to rise, every muscle afire, she stumbled to her feet. Naomi hadn't joined her.

Tonight, they would surely fall into a deep sleep again. In fact, she wanted nothing more than to rest an entire week. A thump resounded downstairs, and a squeal pierced the calm. She didn't bother with the headscarf or shawl, running down the steps to see Naomi standing on a chair with the sad excuse of a broom while battling massive cobwebs draped across the ceiling. White filmy web and dust clung to her hair. She swatted at the ceiling like a warrior of old, grumbling at each new web she found.

A thick cobweb strand swung in an arc from the broom, landing on Ruth's hair. She yelped, clawing at her hair for the invisible spider sure to follow from such a massive web. They glanced at each other and broke into shocked giggles, pointing to each other.

"You've got cobwebs in your hair." Ruth gestured to her forehead and side locks. "Right here and here."

Naomi touched her hair, her lips quirking with wry amusement. "It's like a new scarf, far more delicate than anything Machla can spin, I'm sure."

Relief filled Ruth at the sight of her mother-in-law in better spirits. "She is certainly a spider, that one."

Naomi rolled her eyes, the reaction so comical that they both sputtered again, this time from laughter instead of tears.

A faint spark lit within Ruth as she reached out a hand for Naomi to take as the older woman stepped down from the stool. If they could laugh despite everything that had happened, then perhaps Yahweh had not left them yet. Perhaps His presence had been here all along.

A smile lingering on her lips, Ruth left Naomi to the cleaning.

She surveyed the garden, or what remained of it. Weeds sprouted everywhere in profusion, most bursting with seed. A small fence had collapsed with age, but then, they didn't have a goat for a fence to keep out. As she walked through the garden, she spied legumes. She grabbed ahold of a few and yanked them out of the soil. Her stomach protested loudly as she nibbled on the tip of one. The acidic taste felt almost pleasant on her tongue, especially after a week of bland bread. If only she had meat or milk to make a proper stew to fill the hollow of her belly.

Tonight, she needed to count the remaining funds with Naomi and hope they could purchase an animal. A sinking feeling told her there wouldn't be enough for such a necessity. She had nothing of value to barter with. Beneath the weeds, bland mallow leaves grew in clumps. At least they could eat the leaves without getting sick. As she brushed aside the growth, she recognized garlic and cried out.

Life resided in this abandoned garden. Hopefully, the fig trees next to the house would produce fruit within four months following the barley harvest. After gathering what treasure she could, she hurried to the house. She found Naomi wrestling with a large stone, attempting to drag it into the patch of light.

Naomi's skin was flushed from effort, but a spark remained in her eyes. "I thought I remembered leaving a millstone for grinding grain. I also found a loom."

Ruth placed the mallow and legumes on the linen spread over the freshly washed table. With a grinding stone, fresh water, and a garden, hope unfurled in Ruth, like tender shoots emerging from the soil to reach for the sun.

She grabbed the end of the millstone, and together they lifted it, grunting and groaning, their fingers slipping with the strain of the heavy piece, when a long shadow fell across the floor.

Both Ruth and Naomi set the stone on the ground, thankfully, with no crushed fingers.

Naomi straightened, a strange expression crossing her face as Ruth pivoted to see a paunchy man blocking the doorway. He spread his hands out to Naomi, as if greeting an old friend. A black, oiled beard covered a double chin.

His mouth, the lips far too red, creased into a toothy smile. "Ah, Naomi. Look at you. Why, you've not changed these past years."

"Zakai," Naomi greeted curtly as she brushed aside hair falling loose from her braid.

Unease slivered through Ruth, despite the fawning greeting. So, this was Machla's husband. He immediately conjured the image of the rat hiding within the walls, scurrying and chewing at most inopportune times.

He stepped inside the house, his eyes darting around the walls and the ceiling in need of repair. "You've cleaned this old hut, I see." He made no effort to remove his sandals.

"Indeed," Naomi said as she wiped her hands free from dust. "A fitting action for one's home."

"Your home?" He chuckled, his eyes round. "I bought your husband's lands before he fled Bethlehem. I paid more than a fair price to help you move to Moab land, and this property belongs, every stone, every beam, every item, to me!"

"You most certainly did not buy it from Elimelech. You stopped paying us rent four years ago. As things stand between us, you owe me."

"Naomi, Naomi, let's not bicker like sullen children—not when we are family. I'm certain your husband wouldn't have wanted it so." Zakai tugged at his beard, but despite the condescending tone, his eyes narrowed to slits.

"Then pay me, Zakai, and leave me in peace to fix this house—unless you've come to help, as you so kindly noted, being family and all."

"I will allow you to live here for the time being." His hard gaze flickered to Ruth, scouring her from head to toe. "Who is this?"

Judging from his tone, Ruth felt he might already know. She rubbed her arms, chilled at the lack of warmth in his expression.

"Meet Ruth, my daughter-in-law."

His upper lip curled with disdain. "I don't want a woman from Moab living here in my house. Nor does Machla. Why must you bring further reproach to the family? Isn't it enough that God has taken everything away from you because of such stubbornness?"

"Ruth has brought only honor to my family. She believes in Yahweh, not Chemosh. I won't have you say anything further against her." Naomi's former bluster faded. She swayed as if she might collapse at any moment.

Had Naomi even rested? Or had she quietly cleaned the house while Ruth slept? She chided herself for the nap, especially when her mother-in-law blanched to a frightening hue.

"We've asked you to leave," Ruth added as she stood beside Naomi, ready to provide what support she could.

Ignoring the challenge, Zakai's gaze slid to the flat millstone and the rolling top stone responsible for crushing the grain. "I will expect payment when you are able. Don't make me take the millstone, Naomi."

A cry escaped Ruth. Only a cruel lender would demand the millstone as payment, forcing someone to starvation. No doubt Zakai had wrongfully absorbed lands not his own. Instead of tending them as a good steward would, he demanded ownership.

"Get out." Naomi pointed to her door. "You want to shame me when it is you who practices no hospitality and shows no willingness to help a family in need? I won't listen to your threats."

Muttering, he pivoted on his heel and marched out of the house. The courtyard gate banged behind him.

Ruth had never felt so tempted to lock a door. "Has Zakai truly a claim to the land?"

"I don't think so. Oh, I hope not. As long as Elimelech didn't do business at the gate in front of the elders…" Naomi's voice trailed as she sat on the bench. "He didn't always include me in his transactions, but I would think he would have shared something as important as selling our land. Every man must keep his property in his tribe."

"Zakai has the money to pay you, considering what we saw of his olive grove and estate."

"And yet what he owns isn't enough to satisfy him. I saw the hunger in Machla's face when I visited with her. She fully supports his actions. He won't stop until he steals this farm. If he takes my house, we will have nothing left." Naomi ran her hands up and down her arms, as if to soothe herself.

The law ensured that Naomi, or her children, could buy land back at a discounted price or see it restored to the family at the fiftieth Jubilee year. However, such a boon would hardly matter. They had no sons to inherit.

Nor could two women break the fallowed ground and plant crops by themselves.

Naomi shivered uncontrollably, her voice frail. "We will be homeless, living outside the town gate and begging for our next meal. I can't live like that."

Dismayed but uncertain of what to say next, Ruth could only watch as Naomi retreated into herself, her eyes vacant and unseeing. As the sun set, Ruth found an oil lamp set high on a shelf. She had unpacked a flint earlier and struck the metal pieces until a spark resulted. With a prayer, she hoped enough oil remained. Something sloshed inside the rounded clay bowl with a pinched spout. The lamp flickered to life. After placing it on the table, she went to light the newly cleaned hearth.

Ruth made a simple supper from the greens she found in the garden and the last of their supplies, including bread and a hard chunk of goat cheese. Tomorrow she would head to the village and purchase more to help last through the next few weeks. After that? Who knew how they would feed themselves? Perhaps she might find work. Until then, she had a roof over her head and a warm blanket.

Yahweh had even provided the small lamp, an item left behind so many years ago.

Naomi barely picked at her food, the lines deepening in her forehead. "We should conserve the oil in the lamp."

"Yet Yahweh ensured that the oil still burns, after all this time."

Her mother-in-law picked up a piece of limp mallow and dangled it between two fingers. She dropped the bruised leaf into her bowl. "A lamp is hardly miraculous. If Yahweh could bring about a lamp, why not a bigger miracle?"

Shocked, Ruth couldn't find the right answer to Naomi's bitterness.

Naomi cannot see the miracle of a lamp or the mix of green vegetables in her bowl. She cannot see the cistern filled with fresh rainwater, nor the escape from Lotan's plans. Help me, Yahweh. My mother-in-law only sees despair. Ruth bowed her head, her plea silent.

Naomi pushed away her food and left the bench, signaling any further conversation finished. Her slow footsteps trudged up the stairs to the bedroom. Ruth exhaled as she cleaned up after her mother-in-law. Naomi desperately needed rest. Perhaps after a good night's sleep, she would feel differently in the morning. As Ruth dragged the broom across the stone floor, she couldn't help but think about the previous conversation with Zakai. Naomi had avoided stating that she believed in Yahweh, mentioning only Ruth's faith.

She had left Moab because she couldn't imagine living for Yahweh without Naomi's encouragement or guidance. What now, if her mother-in-law no longer believed?

CHAPTER NINE

Two weeks later

The dawn brought a fresh breeze and the sound of birds singing. Ruth rose, intending to light a fire in the courtyard. She glanced at her mother-in-law, sprawled beneath a blanket. How frail Naomi appeared as she slept on the floor. Pausing, Ruth studied the form, relieved when she saw the slow rise and fall of Naomi's chest.

She tiptoed out of the room as quietly as she could, hoping Naomi would at least recover some of her former strength and mood. Without animals to tend to, the morning chores felt far more manageable, yet Ruth wished for more to do. Peace remained impossible, for in those hushed moments, she wrestled with grief. In a sense, her husband was everywhere in his childhood home. How easily she could picture his gleaming smile. Recall the affectionate whispers in her ear.

Work was far preferable than the emptiness in her heart.

An eerie silence filled the house, lonely without the rattle of wagons or the shouts of men, or the howl of a dog echoing from the city, Mahlon's jests, or even Orpah's endless chatter. Instead, Ruth washed her face and combed her hair to the sound of wind brushing against the walls of the house. Today, she would walk to Bethlehem and purchase supplies—a quick trip, at least.

She unfolded the spare tunics, which lay on the table. Naomi's wedding garment, a deep blue with intricate scarlet embroidery at the neck and sleeves, gleamed in the morning sunlight. Perhaps she should sell the tunic and the silver earrings.

It might buy enough food to last a few additional weeks. She needed a more permanent solution, and she wouldn't sell it without permission.

Footsteps padded toward Ruth. "Perhaps you will wear the tunic again, one day soon."

Ruth raised her head, meeting Naomi's bloodshot eyes.

The older woman pointed to the gown, unfolded on the table. "I wore it in this house. A day of blessing—" she sounded choked.

Ruth let her fingers skim across the embroidered trim and delicate weave of the fabric. It caught against her roughened fingertips. A sigh escaped her. She was a Moabitess, a widow of no means, and barren—why would Naomi assume any Bethlehem man would seek her? "I fear it will bring more value if sold at the market. If the women at the well wish to have nothing to do with me, and Zakai insists I'm trouble, then it won't matter how I dress."

She was also short, unlike Naomi's willowy frame. Nor was Ruth curved in the right places like Orpah. Glancing down at her belted tunic served as a reminder that she wasn't as plump as she once was. This morning, she had tied the belt extra tight to cinch in the voluminous material.

She had already lost weight. And stood to lose far more.

Naomi sank onto the nearest bench. Her hair remained uncombed, the locks snarled with dust and grease. She glanced out the open door and said nothing more, even when Ruth offered the last barley cake.

"I'm going to buy supplies, Imma. And maybe find work."

Naomi gave the barest of nods, her gaze still captured on the rolling landscape covered with barley fields. "So much wealth lies outside our house, yet we suffer from so much want."

"What would you recommend I do? Are there any families who might hire me?"

"I don't know, child."

Again, the abject weariness—as if Naomi had given up on life altogether, without a care for the future.

Ruth swallowed hard against her own mourning. She would find a way to help Naomi, no matter what dismissal came from the villagers or her mother-in-law.

The midmorning sun felt warm against Ruth's back. She walked toward the walls of Bethlehem and the gate. On her walk, she felt slightly better, putting distance between her and the once-abandoned house and the oppressive silence.

Shielding her eyes against the bright light, she spied several workers in the fields. Men and women and children. Men grasping moon-shaped sickles swung out in large arcs, felling the golden stalks, while at a greater distance behind, women of all ages gathered the cut wheat from the ground. The sound of laughter trilled in the air despite the hard physical labor.

She stopped on the road to watch the light flash against the blades as the men moved swiftly. Alternating crops of barley, like patches on a garment, suggested an unusually profitable harvest. Her perusal of the fields halted when she heard the heavy thud of hooves coming to the left. Startled, she stepped back. Behind her, a horse and rider galloped along the road edging a field, the man leaning over his mount's neck, urging it to go faster. Dirt churned beneath the beast's hooves.

The horse was magnificent. A reddish coat brushed to a sheen, as if carved from polished malachite. The man, one with the beast, shouted his glee as he raced along the edge of the field. Despite her fatigue, she chuckled at the sight of someone so thoroughly enjoying himself, not caring how dignified or undignified he appeared to the rest of the world. Mahlon would have done something similar. He had always brought a smile to her face with his antics.

A few workers lifted their hands in welcome at his approach. If he was lord of this plot of land, he at least appeared well loved. He waved and dismounted with an effortless grace, leading his horse to a servant or slave waiting nearby.

He looked so familiar.

Was it the same stranger she had nearly bumped into at the edge of the Bethlehem gate? The man who had separated quarreling shepherds? He was her neighbor?

Self-conscious at spying, she resumed her walk to the village.

Once past the gate, she headed toward the bustling market area. Though she resembled most of the other women in appearance, she felt different, wearing a tunic with a frayed hem and a faded shawl about her shoulders.

She drifted past wagons loaded with goods. Draped fabrics in vibrant crimson and the deepest indigo, and surprisingly, a few jars of perfume glinting beneath the sun. The sight made her yearn for her husband and she swiftly averted her gaze from that table. Her perfume from Mahlon had long since been used up, and thoroughly enjoyed.

Other tables contained baskets of flatbreads, lightly browned, aromatic spices such as cumin and coriander and even expensive saffron. How wonderful if she could afford just one spice to add to the next meal.

Everywhere she searched for work, she found a similar answer. A resounding no.

Not even the potter, whose lumpy wares were far beneath her abba's craftsmanship, had any interest in her help. She refrained from giving him advice, pointing out the uneven shapes due to too much water in the clay mix. A smidgen of fine sand would stabilize his clay, but his foul answer was enough to curb her tongue when he realized she wouldn't buy anything. One of many rebuffs this day.

By noon, she was hot and dusty and tired. And maybe a touch irritable. Having brought her waterskin, she headed to the well, hoping to find it mostly quiet during the heat of the day. When she approached it, another woman drew water from the depths. Ruth recognized her as Aviah. Today, the older the woman wore a brilliant scarf of green wrapped around her head. She drew the bucket up again, carefully filling a clay jar resting on the stone ledge, while another waited on the ground.

Ruth waited patiently for her turn.

Aviah raised her head to see who stood next to her. The older woman's expression cooled. "Ah, Naomi's daughter-in-law. How is Naomi these days?"

It was better to be honest. "It's been a shock."

A weighted silence, and then Aviah blinked rapidly, her hardened gaze flickering. "I would assume so. And for you too. Few women would follow their mother-in-law into a foreign land."

Was there a compliment hidden in Aviah's acrid tone?

"I would never abandon her," Ruth admitted.

Aviah placed the full jug on the ground and picked up the second empty jug. She appeared thoughtful as she poured. When finished, she prepared to lower the bucket into the well, her hand gripping the rope. Her expression grew distant. "I knew Naomi when we were girls. You might even say we were close friends, long, long ago. We used to draw water together in the early morning. I was here, standing in this very spot, when her future husband, Elimelech, followed her. How we giggled after he gave her a handful of wildflowers he had picked just for her. We asked him how she could balance her jug and flowers at the same time? He ended up carrying her jug all the way home."

Ruth couldn't help but smile at the story—a new one for her and yet somehow familiar, so similar to what Mahlon might have done. "I never knew Elimelech. He passed shortly after arriving in Kir-hareseth."

Aviah frowned as she gripped the rope. "Did he? Somehow, I always pictured Naomi living a life of ease and luxury over there in Moab."

Nothing could have been further from the truth. She sensed a frigid undercurrent beneath Aviah's words, one hinting at judgment and condemnation. Aviah released the rope, the bucket dropping with a slosh.

Unwilling to let the conversation end on such a note, Ruth took a risk. "May I help you with your water?"

Aviah's eyes widened. "You are offering to help me?"

"I have a strong arm, if you need."

Tilting her head, Aviah offered a lopsided smile. "Then you may indeed."

Ruth took the nearest full jar, hoisting it to a comfortable position in her arms, while watching Aviah readjust her headscarf. Would Naomi's former friend show compassion and give advice?

The older woman added as an afterthought, "My daughter and her infant twins are ill. Normally, I wouldn't come to the well at noon, but we've had to clean every surface with vinegar. I'm drawing for them, besides my household."

"Please let me know if there is anything more I can do for you," Ruth said as they walked toward the marketplace.

Aviah shot her a curious glance. "You are very thoughtful. I must confess you are not what I expected from a Moabite."

Ruth let the comment roll off her shoulders. Keeping her expression neutral only piqued Aviah's curiosity further as they passed beneath the gate.

"And you lost your husband. How? Illness?"

Ruth nodded, her chest tightening as she struggled to keep pace with Aviah's long-legged stride.

Aviah clucked her tongue. "Both Mahlon and Chilion were so sickly when I saw them last. So not even Moab territory could strengthen them. What a terrible burden for an imma to bear. But you, you seem to be holding up well enough."

Ruth sucked in a pained breath at the observation. Was that how she appeared? Unfeeling? She had always kept a tight rein on her emotions, but it didn't mean she felt nothing. At night, when her mother-in-law slept, she descended to the bedraggled garden and wept in private.

A shudder rippled through Ruth, one that made Aviah take notice. "You're right. It's too much for a woman to handle on her own. Naomi's grief is still so raw, as is mine. I know some company would do her good."

Aviah glanced at her, her expression unreadable. By now, they had reached the colored awnings over the marketplace wares. A few women shopping beneath the canopies stirred at Ruth's arrival, their curious gazes sliding from Aviah to Ruth.

"I know a shortcut. Follow me," Aviah ordered as she made a sharp left turn into a different street, avoiding the overt stares and whispers.

Aviah's pace slowed once the marketplace remained no longer in view. Instead of speaking of Naomi's suffering, the other woman changed the subject. "I understand you and Naomi have reclaimed Elimelech's home."

Hungry for conversation, Ruth readily answered, "It needs some work, yes, but we have a garden and a few fig trees. It was once a pleasant home and could be again with some hard work."

"Watch Zakai. He is a sly one. If he can, he'll charge you for the dust you tread."

Ruth gripped the heavy water jar, disturbed by the allegation. One, no doubt, easily proven true. How soon would Zakai carry out his threat to take Naomi's millstone? "Perhaps you might offer some advice. I need to work. Can you recommend anything?"

Dare she hope Aviah might offer something in her household? The street they traversed appeared wealthier than the other streets, with well-appointed homes hiding behind large courtyards and rustling palms.

The older woman was silent for a moment. "You could glean in the fields. Our law provides for the widow and orphan and the poor. According to Yahweh, no one can reap to the border of the land, nor can the workers pick any leftover grain once reaped. Forgotten sheaves must remain as they were. You might find enough barley and grain to last for a season or two."

Had she heard Aviah correctly? "Glean in fields?"

"It's respectable work for a widow or orphan," Aviah added dryly, studying Ruth as if searching for any sign of weakness.

Heat bloomed up Ruth's neck and cheeks. Her ears rang, drowning out the rest of Aviah's condescending speech.

Instead, she felt shame. What Aviah suggested truly would be reserved for only the most desperate. Yet wasn't she desperate? She had no choice. Nor did Naomi.

"But you'll need to find a landowner who won't harass you," Aviah said matter-of-factly, cutting into Ruth's turbulent thoughts. "One who keeps his hands to himself."

"Is there anyone you can recommend?" Ruth croaked.

Aviah merely shrugged as she pointed to her gated entrance.

"I would avoid Zakai and his friend Levi, if possible. They leave only the barest of edges in their fields. Hardly anything to glean at all."

Aviah opened the door and motioned for Ruth's jar. With a muttered thanks, the older woman slipped inside and firmly shut the door, the echo thudding with a hollow sound. Ruth stood alone in the street, mortified by Aviah's abruptness and her humiliating suggestion.

Her cheeks burned hotter. What to make of that encounter? Had Aviah used her to carry the heavy jar? The conversation felt more like the prying of a gossip than a friend.

Ruth retraced her steps to the marketplace. It wasn't until she ducked past booths with silver necklaces, baskets of an assortment of breads, and jars of oils, that realized she had forgotten to fill her waterskin. She gulped when she walked past the baskets of almonds, pistachios, and walnuts. Nor did she dare stare too long at the ripe cucumbers and melons. All items she couldn't afford. Her heart sank as she rummaged through her meager supply to pay for the additional supplies. She didn't have enough money for a goat or a chicken.

Too tired and weary to do anything else, she departed for home. Again, to her left, she spied the same workers in the fields. The women gathered grain, their faces flushed from the labor. The men, several feet ahead, continued to the cut the harvest, the scythes and sickles moving almost as one, while a foreman led the procession deeper into the fields.

She didn't see the tall man in the field, or the magnificent reddish horse. Somewhat disappointed, she followed the path leading to her decrepit house. Inside, she deposited her items on the table. Naomi was nowhere to be found. Not in the straggling garden, nor near the withered fig trees. Ruth headed up the stairs, her footsteps echoing.

Inside the upper room, Naomi's even breaths barely stirred the stale, hot air. After opening the door to allow a fresh breeze, Ruth knelt down and touched her mother-in-law's forehead. Cool to the touch, at least.

Naomi's eyes fluttered open. She stared at Ruth, unseeing at first.

Ruth brushed the tangle of knotted hair away from Naomi's forehead. "Forgive me. I didn't mean to waken you."

"I haven't slept long," Naomi said in a flat tone.

"Have you eaten?" How could she possibly tempt Naomi with limp mallow roots? A bath and a fresh tunic were needed. A comb too.

"There is nothing to eat."

"I came from the market with a few supplies. Why don't you come with me and we can chat together over the fire, just like we used to?"

Naomi shut her eyes tightly. "I don't want to remember Kir-hareseth."

Ruth chewed on the inside of her cheek to prevent herself from saying anything she might regret. She grieved just as much as Naomi, albeit differently. Was it wrong for her to feel impatient with her mother-in-law's giving up on life?

"Come with me, Imma. I have much to tell you. I—I've found the possibility of work."

Interest flickered in Naomi's eyes. She sat up front on the mat, her hair cascading down her shoulders in snarled curls. "What do you mean?"

"I met Aviah at the well. I helped her carry her jugs of water home." She avoided mentioning Aviah's family being ill. "When I asked what might be available in Bethlehem for a woman such as I, she mentioned gleaning in the fields." Ruth kept her voice deliberately light and cheerful.

Naomi snorted as she folded her arms tightly across her chest, rocking back and forth.

"Imma—"

A defeated sigh escaped Naomi. "Only the poorest of the poor glean."

"We certainly fit the description. No one would hire me, and I don't know what else to suggest."

Naomi lay down again on the thin mat, her features tight and drawn.

"Imma, what do you think of the idea?"

Naomi's answer was faint. "Go, my daughter. Do what you deem best."

CHAPTER TEN

Ruth lit the fire and left a covered plate of cheese and bread for Naomi. She hoped the visitor scratching in the night wouldn't get to it first. Exhaustion pressed on her as she found the most worn of her garments—not a hard choice—and threw it over her shoulders. Carefully, she braided her hair without the help of a bronzed mirror. She wrapped a scarf over her head, pinning back any rebellious curls. Tying the shapeless tunic the color of mud with a woven belt, she hated to think about the sight she must present. A tiny brown bird with wings practically clipped. But she wasn't dressing for the wealthy citizens of Kir-hareseth. Nor for her beloved Mahlon.

As she slid her sandals onto her feet, she trudged upstairs to check on Naomi, who again lay on the pallet, this time with her back to Ruth. Naomi didn't respond to Ruth's farewell.

Yahweh, she doesn't even want me to help her.

What more could Ruth do? She could hardly dress Naomi, nor push bland chickpeas into her mouth. Her presence apparently brought no real comfort. In the night, a host of thoughts plagued her, robbing her of sleep. What if Naomi resented her? Wasn't Ruth a constant reminder of all that her mother-in-law had lost? She much preferred strong-willed Naomi, tough Naomi, willing to stare down a ruthless caravan leader or a pack of women gossiping at the well.

This new, silent Naomi, devoid of faith or future, frightened Ruth to her very core. But she couldn't collapse with her mother-in-law on a moldy pallet and wait helplessly for the inevitable to happen.

The more Ruth worked, the less she dwelled on all she had lost. It brought a relief, at least until evening when everything slowed enough for her to think and remember. And then, if she was fortunate enough to be so exhausted, she would fall into a dreamless slumber and rise with the next dawn and do it all over again.

If only Naomi had shared where Ruth might glean safely. However, Naomi remained mute, barely speaking even when spoken to.

Ruth grabbed her filled waterskin and headed for the fields. As she walked, she studied the fields, already swarming with harvesters. She knew nothing of the men of Bethlehem. Zakai and Lotan had instilled only fear within her. If she went to the wrong landowner, she would be helpless to resist unwanted attention from either the owner or the male workers.

Her prayer was simple. *Yahweh, please show me where to go.*

Again, the field with the tall man filled her memory. Aviah's warning clung to Ruth as she shut the door behind her and turned south, toward the field with the cheerful workers. She hoped she wouldn't find a repeat of Lotan.

Ruth waited at the edge of the field, her pulse pounding with an erratic beat. She inhaled the spicy scent of earth and grain, both mingled together, dusty and sweet. Men wearing short tunics wrapped about bronzed legs walked past, their curious gazes on her as she struggled to keep her face serene. Did she need to ask the tall man for permission? She didn't see him this morning, or his horse. Perhaps she needed to find the supervisor and ask him? What exactly was the polite thing to do? Her belly fluttered as she worried about what to do next.

With so many harvesters gathered in the morning, she wasn't certain who the foreman was, until at last she guessed she found the right person. A short, wiry leader shouted commands to the waiting men surrounding him. He gestured his thin arms, pointing to different sections of the fields. Like a general about to lead his army into battle, he organized the workers into groups. Sunlight glinted off the horn slung from his neck. He was about to raise that instrument to his lips when she hurried in his direction, edging through a row of harvesters.

She offered a slight bow as she rushed to explain in one breath. "My lord, may I glean at your field? I am Naomi's daughter-in-law, Ruth."

"Elimelech's Naomi from Moab? *You* are with Naomi?" The man asked as his black eyebrows arched high. A large wart trembled at his chin as his mouth rounded with shock. "Glean as you must, but you'll need to stay with the women and avoid the sickles or the scythes. The harvesters won't look out for you, and I'd hate to see you sliced like a ripe melon. Go back to the end of the field and stay put. Don't ever barge to the front again." He jerked his thumb over his shoulder, indicating the end of the field.

"Thank you, my lord." She bowed a second time, relieved the foreman proved willing, even if crusty. Embarrassed at her blunder to interrupt the harvest, she didn't miss the curious stares, this time coming from the workers surrounding her on all sides.

Somewhere, she heard a snicker and a man sneer beneath his breath. "Is she truly a Moabitess? Do you think she might dance for us?"

"I intend to ask her this evening. Have you ever seen such green eyes?" Another man laughed from behind her.

She hurried to the women clustered together at the end of the field, with baskets or satchels in hand, and tried to ignore the sick feeling bubbling up inside her. Maybe there was no place safe for her.

Someone blew a horn, the sound piercing across the fields, and she found a place beside another young woman with hair the color of honey. The rest of the women were Naomi's age or older. A few children also hovered nearby with their immas, with features pinched and gaunt.

"You're new, aren't you?" the young woman said as she eyed Ruth's attire. An amused twinkle appeared in her eyes. "Bethlehem is a small village, and everyone knows everyone else's business."

"I've never gleaned before," Ruth admitted sheepishly before sharing her name.

The woman offered a half smile as she pointed to Ruth's hands. "I'm Abigail. You'll need salve by the end of the night for those soft lily fingers. Plenty to drink too. It gets hot out there beneath the sun, and a few can faint if they are not careful. But Lord Boaz is far more generous than most. He offers bread soaked in vinegar and roasted wheat at lunch—which is more than I can say for the other landowners."

Boaz. Now she knew the landowner's name.

"You mustn't go ahead too far—as you've just heard from the foreman. His name is Joab. He's reasonably kind, but he won't let you interfere with the harvest again. The men will grab the grain with one hand and slice with the sickle. Stay away from that blade. Boaz insists on only the sharpest of flint or bronze. The men carry as much as they can until their arms are full. They will let the cut grain fall to the ground. Then the female servants bind it into sheaves. Finally, the bundles are carried to storage to await the threshing floor. So you see, we are the very last in the field, gathering what leftovers we can find."

Would she be able to glean enough wheat for Naomi? Especially with a crowd of other gleaners intent on feeding families?

Abigail chuckled as she glanced at Ruth. "Don't look so worried. The men drop plenty." She planted a hand on her slender hip. "I know for a fact several of them leave grain just for me. I'll take the center of the field and you take the left. You'll be fine if you follow my lead."

The horn blew again, the echo stirring men and women to action. Ruth searched for Boaz, but to her disappointment, he hadn't arrived this morning. Like a commander leading an army into battle, the foreman raised his hand high over his head, signaling everyone to advance. The men followed with their scythes or handheld sickles, marching together as one. The sheer breadth of the harvest operation and the practiced movements of the workers ensured a surprising speed.

As Abigail noted, Ruth's skin soon felt scratched and poked by straws. Fingers, palms, wrists, and even her toes peeking beneath her sandals. She opened her satchel wide and tried to follow the other gleaners's actions, snatching fallen heads of barley among the stubble. A white-haired man with a limp remained behind her. His leg dragged as he struggled to keep up with the women and children. To her chagrin, he missed retrieving much of the barley. The fields were already plucked clean by the time he reached them. Sidestepping to the left, she motioned for him to join her.

"There's room enough for both of us," she said as she pointed to an unclaimed cluster of barley.

He hurried, his gait wobbly and the limp more pronounced, but the wide smile he gave her brought a lightness to her step.

"My thanks," he said, his chest heaving with effort. "I'm not as young as I once was, and under this heat, it's enough to slow a man down."

She wanted to inquire his name, but he resumed plucking with knobby hands tanned a deep hue—a testament to the hours spent outside, beneath nature's canopy. Inhaling sharply, she turned her attention to the ground. The scent of earth and barley on her heated skin filled her nostrils. Not an unpleasant smell, considering the overripe stench of the city she had left.

If she focused on the minor triumphs, perhaps she wouldn't feel the sharp prick of shame. No, she would choose to see only the blessing before her.

There would be provisions to last through the season. She had a bright blue sky overhead, with the occasional hawk zooming with wings outstretched. She might even make a new friend by the end of the day. Abigail, however, reserved most of her attention for the men, waving to a choice few with coy laughter.

Despite the flirtations, Abigail moved faster than most of the women, snatching the fallen barley with nimble fingers. She tossed a glance over her shoulder at Ruth but never stopped.

Before long, Ruth's back ached from the constant bending and straightening. She lost herself in the work's rhythm, taking whatever she could find. Abigail was right. Ruth would have plenty by the end of the day, even if it was hard work. Her bag filled step by step, and without realizing it, she hummed a song beneath her breath.

So intent on her work was she that she nearly missed the thunder of hooves pounding the earth. When she straightened, she looked directly at the man on the reddish horse. It was *him*. The man she had observed at the city gate breaking up a tussle between shepherds. He watched her from the edge of the field, a frown lining his forehead. She froze, caught with the gleanings trapped beneath her arm. As he dismounted in a fluid motion, he never took his gaze from her, pausing only to hand the reins to a servant waiting close by. He spoke with the youth, his words too muted to discern, and then he glanced again at her.

While she slowly shoved her grain into her satchel, he stalked toward Joab.

Oh no.

Had she misjudged his character and made a mistake in coming to this field? Was it possible the owner, Boaz, didn't want her with the others? Worse, would he hurt her if he knew she was a Moabite? If he could easily quell two men, she didn't want to imagine what he could do to her.

The familiar heat from shame and self-doubt bloomed across her chest and neck, nearly exploding at her temples. At least she had some grain to bring home to Naomi. Enough to last several days, if they were careful. Unless he took it from her.

To her surprise, he held up his hand as if in benediction as he passed the workers.

"The Lord be with you," his voice echoed across the field. The workers readily parted for the owner of the field, some bowing or shouting a jovial greeting. "The Lord bless you!"

Abigail also watched the master as she slid the stalks into her basket. Her scarf had slipped back, revealing a tawny wealth of hair she didn't bother to hide.

Not knowing what else to do, Ruth continued to glean. She bit back a murmur when a stalk scratched against the back of her hand. A faint red line welled. Wringing her hand, she willed away the sting.

The sun blazed white hot, and the weather no longer felt as delightful as it had earlier in the morning. Out of the corner of her eye, she saw Boaz approach Joab, their heads nearly touching as they discussed something. The foreman nodded as

Boaz clapped him on the back. To Ruth's surprise, Joab blew on the horn. He gathered the men toward him. A few of the male workers glanced at her then listened to Joab.

The foreman's harsh voice reached her ears. "Leave her be, or else…"

What would she give to listen to that particularly menacing conversation? What woman did Joab reference? The field was filled with women and girls.

With a soft grunt, she bent again at the waist and snatched the closest strands of barley. Sweat trickled down her shoulder blades. She felt hot and sticky. Dirt embedded deep in her cracked fingernails. Dully, she realized she hadn't had a drink from the tepid waterskin by her side. Her vision blurred and her ears rang loudly.

She closed her eyes and rubbed them with her thumb and forefinger. When she opened them again, she saw Joab hurrying over to her. His eyes narrowed.

"Ruth, that is your name? Master Boaz wishes to speak with you immediately."

Before she could answer Joab, the owner himself came to her, his long legs rapidly eating the distance between them. His fine tunic, a deep indigo, stood out among a field of gold and brown. Did she see a bit of silver glinting from his collar?

Joab respectfully stepped away, his attention directed to a few female servants bringing baskets. But Ruth could not tear her attention from the master of the field. He came to a halt in front of her. She barely reached his massive shoulder. Raising her head, she saw the same crooked nose and chiseled mouth. Hair tousled by the wind and nearly black. However, his eyes were brown, a rich brown like the cinnamon sold in the market. She shivered despite the heat. Boaz's eyes were far too similar to Mahlon's. All at once, she was keenly aware of her filthy tunic and short stature. Surely her cheeks were smudged from dirt, the way his gaze lingered on her face.

An unreadable expression flickered in his eyes.

Her pulse thrummed. Her initial fear had been correct. He would now ask her to leave the field and never bother his workers again. Perhaps the law of the Israelites made no provision for an old enemy.

"My daughter—" His voice suited his height. A deep rumble, low in pitch.

She startled. Did she hear him correctly? Had he referred to her as a…?

"My daughter, listen to me. Don't go to any other field. Please. I want you to stay here and work with the women in this field." He swung out his arm, showing the land belonging to him. "Watch the field where the men are harvesting, and follow along after the women. I have told the men not to lay a hand on you. And whenever you are thirsty, go and get a drink from the water jars the men have filled."

Shock numbed her fingers, and the satchel nearly slipped from her grasp. He reached out, almost catching the satchel, had she not tightened her grip.

Of all the likely reactions playing in her mind, never would she have dreamed of such kindness or respect.

Knees weak, she knelt and bowed, her forehead hovering above the powdery dirt and remnants of straw. Tears filled her eyes and her voice trembled. "My lord, why have I found such favor in your eyes that you notice me—a foreigner?"

His sandaled feet shifted, as if he might be uncomfortable with her lying nearly prostrate before him. Something lightly touched her shoulder, and she saw a sun-browned hand extended to her. After a moment of hesitation, she took it. He easily pulled her to her feet, his hand warm and strong. He let go immediately once she stood.

He peered intently at her. "I've been told all about what you have done for your mother-in-law since the death of your husband—how you left your abba and imma and your homeland and came to live with a people you did not know."

"It is an honor to love and serve Naomi," she answered readily.

He smiled with something akin to awe as he raised a hand as if to touch her. To her surprise, he kept his hand outstretched. "May the Lord repay you for what you have done. May you be richly rewarded by the Lord, the God of Israel, under whose wings you take refuge."

Dumbfounded, she could only gape at him. He had *blessed* her, invoking Yahweh in a way similar to Naomi's prayers and encouragement. Not only had he praised Ruth, he did it in such a bold manner that those closest to Boaz surely would have heard every single word. A public blessing intended to show his approval of her.

"I—I thank you for your generosity," she whispered. "May I continue to find favor in your eyes, my lord. You have put me at ease by speaking kindly to your servant—though I do not have the standing of one of your workers."

He smiled, his eyes crinkling at the corners. "It is my pleasure to welcome you to Bethlehem and to this field. I thought I saw you at the gate a few weeks ago. Naomi too. I would have greeted her, but I was a bit preoccupied."

She remembered the shepherd intent on vengeance. "Did that theft ever get resolved?"

"Yes, it did," Boaz answered slowly, offering no more information. "A terrible reception for both of you, no doubt."

The memories of the caravan trip and the women at the well weren't exactly thoughts she cared to dwell on. Suddenly she swayed, the heat overwhelming. He stepped closer to her, a frown marring his brow a second time. By now, they had gathered the attention of the workers. Many in the field stopped to stare at her and Boaz.

She licked her lips, wishing she could creep away and find privacy from all the prying stares.

"Have you had anything to drink or eat? My foreman tells me you've been working hard since the early morning."

She shook her head.

He pointed to a group of women bringing baskets laden with food. "Come," he ordered. His tone, though winsome, allowed no disagreement. "I will show you where you can rest."

CHAPTER ELEVEN

Despite having to use precious water from her waterskin, Ruth washed her face and hands, while ignoring the red, stinging cuts on her palms and fingers. She refused to eat with unclean hands, and now that she knew where the water jugs were stored, she could drink anytime she chose. As she flung the water droplets from her hands, she realized her actions were studied by all, including Abigail, who cast a shuttered look in Ruth's direction. The young woman made no further effort to chat with Ruth as she waited with the other servants sitting in a large circle.

Not all the gleaners ate alongside Boaz's men. Several of them reclined in separate circles, and a few, including the man with a limp with his injured leg outstretched, rested alone. Someone brought him a round loaf of bread. She discovered his name was Harim, and he remembered Naomi from the early days.

After Boaz prayed a blessing over the food, women passed bread and bowls of pungent vinegar. The men sat in their area, already shoving food into their mouths, their hands dipping into the wooden bowls laden with roasted grains. For the most part, they kept their gazes trained on the food, and the laughter and crude comments had all but disappeared when she walked past them. Her cheeks warmed at the idea that Boaz was watching out for her.

She was about to approach the women, who sat side by side around the circle, none of them making room for her, when Boaz called her name.

He pointed to a rug on the ground, where she might join him.

Her breath caught. Surely he had only the best intentions, didn't he? Perhaps this invitation was nothing more than a simple courtesy, especially when the women had done exactly the opposite, whispering behind their hands, glancing over their shoulders. Not one of them scooted over to offer her a place to sit among them. When Joab hunkered down onto the large rug, she breathed a sigh of relief and joined Boaz, tucking her legs beneath her.

A servant brought bowls of roasted grain, a delicacy, and another brought a platter of bread and glistening dates. Boaz ordered the last servant to serve Ruth. To her surprise, the plate offered her contained a larger portion than Joab's.

"Eat, please," Boaz said as he nudged a bowl toward her, loaded with dried figs. "The bread is especially good with vinegar, and the figs are perfection."

Despite her best effort, her mouth watered. As delicately as she could, she scooped a handful of roasted grain and nearly groaned aloud when the nutty flavor hit her tongue.

Both Joab and Boaz averted their eyes as she ate. It took everything in her to exercise control and chew slowly when her growling stomach cried for more. When Boaz and Joab spoke about a southern field, she took the bread from her plate and eased it carefully into her satchel for Naomi.

Boaz seemed not to notice—or so she thought until he asked his servant for more bread and promptly handed her a second serving.

"We work hard in the fields, and it can stir quite an appetite," he said. The barest hint of a smile touched the corner of his lips. But mostly, she felt the kindness of the gesture, and his attempt to preserve her dignity.

She nodded, and as she reached for more bread, the sleeve of her tunic fell backward, revealing the sad state of her hands.

Boaz winced when he saw her scratched fingers. "Have you any hyssop?"

"I have olive oil, my lord. It will work well enough."

He didn't argue with her. Regardless, she found herself moved by his concern.

He left the food on his plate untouched, still watching her. "I haven't asked how Naomi fares. Is she…well?"

Ruth hesitated, a dripping piece of vinegar-soaked bread in her hand. What could she say without giving away too much information? "Naomi deeply grieves over the death of her husband and sons."

To her surprise, Boaz released a sigh as he rubbed the back of his neck. "I am truly sorry for her loss. I remember Elimelech. He was older than I by several years, but he was the first to teach me how to use a sling. Give my condolences to your mother-in-law. If she needs anything, let me know. I will help any way I can."

Joab shot his master an enigmatic look as he bit into a chunk of mutton.

A wave of longing suffused her. She had enjoyed watching Mahlon show off his incredible skill with the sling, no doubt passed on from Elimelech. With a wink and a grin, her husband would swing it around so fast she could feel the air rush and hear the sling whine. At just the right moment, he would maneuver the sling to let the rock fly. And fly it did.

"Thank you, my lord. I am certain Naomi would also wish to thank you for such wonderful generosity." Her words must have carried louder than she intended.

Whispers and murmurs floated on the breeze from the other workers, especially the women sitting closest to Boaz. Despite her best effort, Ruth felt keenly aware of him as he reclined with elegant manners. Had he a wife, or a son or a daughter, perhaps?

Boaz glanced at the women, his neck reddening. Had he also heard their idle chatter? She fervently hoped not. When he turned to Ruth, his voice was kindness itself. "It is truly my pleasure. I am grateful Naomi has such a loyal family to count on during such a trial. Grief should not be borne alone."

The admission hinted at personal pain, and she wondered about his story that he would understand so much about loss. Before she could probe for more, another servant approached, a young man this time. The youth whispered a message to Boaz, who pushed up from the rug. "Forgive me, but I have several sheep who ran away and refuse to come home."

Sheep, grain, and barley. Just how much did Boaz own?

As if reading her thoughts, Joab nodded toward Boaz's retreating back. "He hardly sleeps. He rises before the dawn and is the last to bed. My master is one of the largest landowners, his holdings far exceeding most men, including Zakai, who spies from across the road, coveting everything he sees."

She decided it would be best to ignore the calloused remark about Zakai, even if she agreed with it. "Your lord is blessed, and his family as well."

Joab shook his head, his lips pursed as if tasting something unpleasant. "No family. Lord Boaz's wife died four years ago, along with their only child, a son not quite fifteen years of age. They drowned in a flash flood. He will never forgive himself for not rescuing them."

She had heard of similar floods, carving out fresh ravines, digging deep into the soft earth with a torrent of muddy water, snatching stray animals or people in the way. Such dangerous rivers came out of nowhere, unrelenting and devastating.

Oh, Boaz.

Of course he would understand Naomi's grief so well, and hers too.

"I'm truly sorry to hear of his loss," she said, her words so inadequate and helpless in the face of such devastation. She had never lost a child. No one could understand such raw grief until tasting it first. No wonder Boaz showed such compassion to her and Naomi.

Joab nodded as he snatched another piece of bread, rolling it in his hand. He rose to his feet. "Take as much food as you wish for your mother-in-law. I suspect Boaz asked you to sit here for this reason. Even though he feeds everyone well, you won't find much left over with the other workers."

Tears filled her eyes as she sat alone. But the wetness beneath her lashes was not made entirely of sorrow, even though her heart stirred with compassion for Naomi, and now, Boaz. Overwhelmed, she breathed a prayer of thanksgiving for Yahweh's immense love.

He watched over her. And He would continue to provide.

***

She didn't see Boaz again until late afternoon. He avoided her as he strode through the fields. Not once did he look her way, which was perhaps for the best. After the noon meal, she worried about how others might perceive the extra attention, even if she was grateful for it.

Beside Ruth, Abigail gleaned swiftly, moving closer and closer to Ruth's area. Once or twice, Abigail reached to snatch the remaining barley before Ruth could. She let the slight pass, especially when her satchel hung with a pleasing weight, bumping against her leg with a solid thump. She had harvested a great deal today, and she could hardly wait to rush home and show Naomi the contents of the satchel. Surely such a blessing would bring a new smile to her mother-in-law's face.

Several feet ahead of the gleaners, Boaz found Joab halting the harvest. Snatches of their conversation drifted her way in the sultry breeze.

"Let her gather among the sheaves and don't reprimand her. Even pull out some stalks for her from the bundles and leave them for her to pick up, and don't rebuke her."

Did Boaz intend to leave additional food in her path?

A soft gasp came from Ruth's left. Abigail's mouth rounded with shock. "My, my. What exactly did you say to him over lunch to warrant such treatment?"

"Nothing." Ruth frowned as she reached for another stalk loaded with plump kernels. "Lord Boaz knew my father-in-law and wanted to inquire about my mother-in-law's health. Nothing more."

The mere thought raked her composure. Only a foolish woman would assume more from his attentions. She was no fool. She was a barren, older Moabite widow without a dowry.

Abigail chuckled, but there was no mirth in it. "Truly, he hasn't shown any woman attention in years, and believe me, plenty of women have tried to catch him."

Had Abigail tried and failed?

"He is generous to many. He even made certain the man who sat alone with a crippled leg received food," Ruth agreed, keeping her tone indifferent.

Abigail picked up her basket, already overflowing with harvest. "Yes, you are right. He's the most generous man in all of Bethlehem." She winked at Ruth as a sly grin curved her lips. "And also the richest. Not to mention, he could practically hoist a ram over his head with those arms and—"

Ruth coughed to cover her embarrassment. The last thing she needed was to indulge in such idle chatter, sure to cast an unfavorable light on the women unwise enough to engage in it. Thankfully, Boaz remained blissfully unaware as he strode through the shorn sections of the field, pausing here and there to speak with workers. She dearly hoped anyone nearby missed Abigail's overt fawning.

Abigail laughed as she readjusted her headscarf. "I didn't realize Moabite women could blush so red."

Ruth drew her satchel near as a protective barrier. Inwardly, she flinched at the assumption Abigail so easily blurted out loud. "Moabite women are not that different from Israelite women."

Abigail tilted her head as she watched Ruth. "I've heard about your gods and your poles in high places. Are the rumors true about what happens in the hills? Do Moabite women wear veils to cover their faces?"

The question brought an unnerving sensation, and suddenly Ruth was awash with childhood memories, far too frightening and full of sorrow to share openly with a stranger. "I don't wish to discuss such things. Chemosh and his consorts are not my gods. I serve Yahweh, as I hope you do."

Naomi had told her years ago it was an abomination to speak of things done in private, or worse, during the idol worship, and Ruth wholeheartedly agreed. She hated her country's vile history of ancient Lot and his daughters cohabiting. Despised the story with all her being, and yet it was a part of her. How could she help where she was born? Or to whom? She could only choose those who entered her life, and she had gladly bound herself to Naomi and Mahlon. Because of her beloved adopted family, she had found Yahweh.

Nor did she care for Abigail's assumption about head coverings. Only prostitutes wore full veils. Not all Moabite women were so loose.

She decided to be bold and offer a similar verbal challenge to Abigail. "I understand Israel turned from Yahweh to worship false gods, even to the point of erecting similar poles. I hope they never embrace idols of gold or wood ever again. The price is far too high, wouldn't you agree?"

Abigail retrieved her basket, her good humor rapidly evaporating. "You're a strange one, I'll give you that. Imagine a Moabite offering a morality lesson to an Israelite." The young woman leaned in, just within Ruth's hearing. "But I do like you, Ruth the Moabitess. I'll see you tomorrow, yes?"

Ruth smiled just as her gaze collided with Boaz's. In the gathering evening, as the fields lost the golden luster and faded to purple twilight, it was too dark to decipher his expression.

CHAPTER TWELVE

Naomi struggled to rise from her pallet. She knew deep down inside that she needed to move beyond the thick gloom and stale air of the bedchamber. The shadows had hemmed her in—at first a safe cocoon promising comfort, but later, as the day wore, an oppressive prison cell trapping her.

She knew grief hurt. She hadn't been prepared for how much it hurt physically.

Her arms and legs. Her chest and stomach. Her head. Her heart. Everything throbbed, just like the drums she had escaped from in Kir-hareseth.

She had fled Moab and the memories of her children suffering. Yet, in this very room, more memories lingered. She had delivered her firstborn son, Mahlon, on a similar straw-filled pallet placed next to the wall. How Elimelech celebrated, singing and dancing in the courtyard, his hollering loud enough to draw the chastisement of her imma!

Despite herself, Naomi tittered, remembering how irate her imma had been, demanding Elimelech cease braying like a donkey and let his young wife sleep. Her laughter sounded so strange in the hush as the wind moaned against the walls of the house, sweeping through the courtyard and through the open slats in the roof.

Oh, these memories had the power to bring her to her knees. She didn't want to remember. Or feel, ever again.

Why did You let me live to see such days, Yahweh? Will You deliver me and Ruth, or have I misplaced my trust in You?

She sat up from the mat and brought her knees close to her chest.

"Yahweh, I don't have the faith to believe in You right now. I'm like an empty vessel, drained to the bitter dregs. I don't know what to do anymore. I want to believe. Help me in my unbelief."

She hadn't prayed, not since the night her sons passed. The words felt stiff and strange, her lips barely moving and her voice a thick rasp.

Moments passed, or was it hours? Since Zakai's threats, she had no sense of time, especially after so much sleep. If he cast her from her home, her last place of refuge, she didn't know what she would do. Terror pooled within her, and the mat seemed the only safe place left for her. She was so tired, despite resting. She was so tired of fighting and trying to be strong.

Rise.

She heard no voice, but the thought would not let her go. It rippled deep inside her, like a pebble cast into her cistern, refusing to let her consider the darkness a place of comfort. She obeyed, her legs weak and quivering. As she pushed open the door, which opened to the flat roof, she saw several shapes in the distance. The sun had moved to the west, casting a mellow glow over the fields. On the dusty road, a few workers in the fields walked home to Bethlehem. However, one person walked toward Naomi's home.

Ruth. She strode as swiftly as she could with those short legs, the bulging satchel at her side.

Though Naomi longed to dart across the flat roof and lean over the side to better view the road and Ruth, she dared not test the integrity of the beams with her weight. She edged to the most secure section of the roof closest to the ledge and watched. It creaked ominously, forcing her to retreat. Straining to see her daughter-in-law, she had to grasp the mud-brick ledge to keep from tumbling over the side.

At the right moment, Ruth saw her. She nearly jumped up and down on the road, pointing to her bag, her excitement contagious.

With a cry, Naomi backed away from the ledge and rushed down the steps and into the courtyard. She flung open the weathered door at the gate and waited for Ruth, who, bless her, had broken into a jog while holding her satchel. When her daughter-in-law reached the courtyard, her cheeks were flushed from work and sun. Triumph shone in her eyes.

"Imma, look at what I harvested today!" She unslung the satchel and handed it to Naomi.

Naomi could only stare at the wealth of barley filling the bag, as she struggled to comprehend such a bounty.

"I'll need your flail to beat out the grains. I'm certain I'll find an *ephah* of barley," Ruth continued, out of breath, "but first, I have so much to tell you."

"Come and sit by the fire," Naomi said as she carried the bag. How tired Ruth must be, working so hard in the field.

Guilt for resting stole some of the excitement. Why hadn't she thought to start a fire?

"Forgive me. I have no food for you this evening, and you must be famished."

Ruth laughed, a delighted, bubbling sound. "I ate more than I could stomach. Roasted grains and breads dipped in vinegar. Delicious dates. I wanted to bring you slices of melon, but I feared they wouldn't last in the heat, squished to a pulp inside my bag. But I've brought plenty of extra for you to eat tonight."

Naomi could only stare at her daughter-in-law. "Who would feed a widow so well? Where did you glean? Blessed be the man who took notice of you!"

"His name is Boaz. I saw him at the village gate when we first arrived at Bethlehem, and I asked if you noticed him. You hadn't. But he moved aside for us, Imma, without a word of complaint. And he removed those awful shepherds from our path. Imagine such courtesy from the strutting city leaders in Kir-hareseth? Later, I saw him racing across his fields with that magnificent horse. The gleaners tell me Boaz is the largest landowner in the area, even over Zakai. You can hardly compare the two men, even if they are of the same age. Boaz treats his workers like family. He instructed the men not to harass me, and he ordered the harvesters to leave extra gleanings in my path."

Naomi's heart raced. She knew Boaz! He had been a close friend and relative of her husband. "He did?"

"Yes, he even invited me to eat lunch with him and the foreman."

"Oh?" A wealth of meaning lay behind that syllable. Naomi couldn't help but notice her daughter-in-law's animated hand gestures as she discussed Boaz.

"I don't have to fear him. He saw that the others excluded me and wanted to ensure I had enough to eat. He asked about you too."

Intrigued, Naomi sank onto the stone next to the circular fire-pit. She found the flint rocks and struck until a spark flashed. As the spark lit a small curl of kindling resting on top of the feathery ash, another thought rose to the surface, one she hardly dared vocalize but decided she must. "I remember Boaz, as a young man, of course. He is Elimelech's first cousin. They used to race their horses in the valley together. No one could ride quite like Boaz."

A soft smile lit Ruth's face. "I saw him race."

Naomi arched an eyebrow at the wistful expression, but it didn't displease her. Not at all. She doubted Ruth even realized it herself. "Is he married?"

Ruth shook her head with a sad murmur in the back of her throat. "No, Imma. His wife and son died in a rare flood. He has not remarried."

Naomi fumbled for the firewood kept in a basket. She ached afresh at the idea of sharing so much loss with another. She had especially liked Boaz. "Bless him. I don't understand why some of the gentlest people go through so much loss and pain. It hardly seems fair."

Ruth placed a hand on Naomi's shoulder. "He expressed his grief for you too. He said if there is anything you might need, he would help."

This changed everything. Naomi strove to sound calm as she found the right-sized twigs to toss onto the fire. "The Lord bless him! He has not stopped showing his kindness to the living and the dead." She added as an afterthought, "You understand he is our close relative, one of our kinsman-redeemers, don't you?"

In fact, Naomi could barely contain herself the more the idea kindled with her, an insistent flame consuming everything else. Could this be the answer to their trouble? Dare she hope Ruth might see the same?

Ruth's brows dipped down, her expression confused. "I don't understand what that term means."

Naomi hid her smile. "He is a *goel,* one who helps family when they are in terrible circumstances. A goel is a protector and a deliverer. When someone is enslaved, the goel can purchase the person back, restoring full rights and freedom. He redeems property and even…"

Ruth leaned forward, her eyes wide. "Yes?"

"Widows."

If possible, Ruth's green eyes shimmered like the stars at night. She blinked and shook her head, as if chasing the notion away.

"It's true. The kinsman-redeemer offers marriage. If a son is born, he will keep the name of the lost brother or relative, ensuring the line continues."

All at once, the light in Ruth's gaze died. "I wondered why I saw Mahlon's resemblance in Boaz. Now it makes sense how they share the same eye color. They even share the love of a sling."

Naomi held her breath, not daring to speak further. She had been so lost in her own grief that she had somehow forgotten how much Ruth cared for Mahlon. And though the knowledge of such devotion warmed an imma right down to her bones, she also realized Ruth couldn't afford to be alone forever.

Ruth rubbed her eyes, likely wearied from such a long, hard day of labor. "I also understand why he showed me so much favor, especially if we are related. He even said to me, 'Stay with my workers until they finish harvesting all my grain.'"

Naomi nodded. "It makes sense to go with his girls, because in someone else's field, you might be harmed."

After Lotan, Ruth needed no further warning to be careful.

Naomi darted a glance at her daughter-in-law. Did Ruth understand what a tremendous opportunity it was to work near Boaz? He would see her nearly every day. How could he not be charmed by her?

Instead of excitement, Ruth clasped her hands tightly together, her head bowed. "How very generous Boaz is. I couldn't ask for anything more when he has already given so much."

"You are not unworthy, Ruth." Naomi's words might as well have fallen on deaf ears.

Ruth shut her eyes tightly, her voice strained. "I have no dowry. I am barren, and I'm hardly a young maiden."

Nonsense. Utter nonsense. Ruth was still young, and lovely too, if only she could see her own worth. But Naomi was used to her daughter-in-law's self-deprecating ways. She knew who to blame for such self-loathing. Her hands curled into fists when she remembered how abused Ruth was when she came into her home.

"And I'm a Moabitess." Ruth's last protest was so soft, Naomi could barely hear it.

Naomi curbed her next words. She would need to tread carefully or she would frighten Ruth away from a beautiful possibility, one Ruth didn't believe she deserved.

Is this Your answer, Yahweh? Dare I hope again?

She wanted to hope. She was afraid to hope.

So Naomi chose the safest answer she could think of. "I'm in awe that Yahweh brought you to Boaz's field. Surely His hand must be in this. You asked about miracles? The barley you brought is truly a gift."

Ruth reached with one arm and pulled Naomi close. "You said we needed a bigger sign, and Yahweh provided one. I'll glean enough to last the winter months."

Naomi returned the hug. She didn't want to tell Ruth the gleaning wouldn't likely be enough to survive for an entire year, but it was a promising start. She could only hope and pray that Boaz would realize what a treasure Ruth was before the harvest season ended.

Ruth wrinkled her nose. With an impish grin, she pulled away from Naomi. "I'll also haul water for both of us tonight. I think we both need it."

A rusty chuckle escaped Naomi, the third time she had laughed since arriving in Bethlehem. She clasped Ruth's shoulder and squeezed gently. "I'll help you. We can heat the water and take turns bathing this evening. Tomorrow, I might even find some flowers to distill with oil and mix some pleasing scents for you. The garden outside has some blue lupine blossoms. They won't last more than a few days."

As soon as the words escaped her, something settled within her as soft as a whisper but full of solid truth. How good it felt to take care of someone else.

CHAPTER THIRTEEN

Ruth slung her satchel and waterskin over her shoulder and waved goodbye to Naomi in the courtyard. The previous week, they had decided Naomi would do what she could around the house and tend the garden while Ruth collected the barley and wheat. Naomi's fearful silence appeared to be at an end. For now. Her mother-in-law hadn't completely recovered. What was lost could never be reclaimed. Instead, they both focused on living one day at a time.

A song of thanksgiving filled her heart as she walked the now familiar path. Thanks to Abigail's willingness to share information—or perhaps *gossip* was the better word for it—Ruth had a better sense of who owned what sections and which roads to avoid. It pleased her to no end to realize the land leading up to the border of Elimelech's farm belonged to Boaz. To her right, Boaz's lands spread out, including an ancient olive grove with silver-hued trees gnarled in fantastic shapes. Though she hadn't seen it, Boaz's new vineyard remained the talk of Bethlehem.

As she eyed the crops to the left, she could hardly suppress a twinge of unease. Zakai's holdings dotted the landscape, as if in defiant rivalry to Boaz's increasing lands. Most of the workers clamored for work with Boaz, although a few tried to harvest Zakai's fields.

Aviah had spoken the truth about Zakai's harvest methods. His fields appeared stripped clean of barley, with hardly any crop remaining at the edge of the fields. Nor did he allow the harvesters to move as quickly, insisting they claim every single kernel. Only the most desperate worked for him, unlike Boaz, who kept the same loyal workers year after year.

Somehow Boaz's harvest, despite the overabundance of generosity, burst with seed, a rolling sea of barley and wheat. Not true for Zakai. Abigail had shared that the farmers were required by the law to let the land rest in order to restore the soil. Zakai's crop grew sparse in the shallow points, and the grains appeared shrunken.

While studying Zakia's holdings, Ruth hurried along the path, not bothering to glance at her feet. A sudden wrench of her ankle, and she tumbled forward as her sandal loosened. Lowering her satchel, she paused long enough to slip her foot back into the sandal and secure the leather ties around her ankle.

When she glanced down the road she had just traveled, the fine hair on the back of her neck stood on end.

Someone stood on the crest of the hill, watching her.

Perhaps it was foolish to worry. Many farmers and shepherds used this road to reach Bethlehem. The fierce pounding in her chest would likely amount to nothing. As she joined the gathering crowd of men and women, she saw the lean figure hang back far from Boaz's property. The stranger's features were obscured because of the distance he maintained, yet he had tracked her all the same, keeping an even pace.

Who followed her? She decided it was a man. By the time she took a steadying breath, he had disappeared when she looked again. Pulse speeding, she hurried to join the cluster of men and women at the edge of the field. No sign of Abigail, or Boaz either.

Harim waved to her, the limp in his crippled leg more pronounced than the day before. She joined him, pleased with the welcome. Unlike the other women, who held back, avoiding her at every turn, he offered much-needed conversation.

She also realized he liked to glean next to her since she shared so readily. "My mother-in-law tells me she remembers you," she said to him.

He shifted his weight to his good leg, his craggy features lighting up with a ready smile. "That news is a balm to my heart. Tell Naomi I remember her as if it was yesterday. No one could haggle prices quite like she could. But I liked to give her the special price, as I called it."

Had he experienced a change in fortune similar to Ruth's, losing nearly everything at once? "Were you a merchant, then?"

He guffawed at her assumption. "Not anything nearly that elite. But I thank you for assuming so of me. No, I worked for an olive grove farmer, just north of Bethlehem."

She didn't dare pry, nor did she have to, as Harim continued his tale. "I harvested the olives and manned the olive press, and then I brought the wares into the village and sold them. I broke my leg while fixing my master's barns and soon discovered I was no longer of any use. Lord Boaz graciously allowed me to glean on his property and recently offered that I might sell his wine and oil following the barley harvest. Tell Naomi to come to Harim in a few months. I'll take good care of her as I once did."

She couldn't help but smile at his enthusiasm and the twinkle in his eye when he mentioned Naomi's name. "I'm sure sitting under a tent in the marketplace would be vastly preferable to working the fields."

He sobered. "Yes. You're right. But I would far rather glean in Boaz's field than be a foreman hired to someone cruel or greedy. The other landowner swore I stole his wine, and hence, he had no obligation to help me."

How strange to think that callousness and neglect resided in Israel just as much as Moab. She slowed her walk to accompany Harim. "Who was your former master?"

With a scowl, he answered, "A man I hope you never chance to meet. He is friends with Zakai, which says plenty. His name is Levi. You won't find a more stingy man obsessed with counting his hoard of shekels. He lives only for the coins he collects."

She mentally stored the name for future reference. Hadn't Aviah also mentioned a Levi to be avoided? No one needed to ask Ruth twice to stay away from Zakai, considering the last encounter with him.

The work soon began with the blast of the horn, and she fell into the now familiar rhythm. Within moments, her muscles complained, particularly in her abdomen and arms, and other muscles she hadn't even considered. Never had she bent at the waist so often. By the first hour, she was tempted to wrap linen scraps around her hands as she snatched the barley from the ground.

A woman ran onto the field, her chest heaving with effort as she edged sideways between a pair of gleaners. Ruth recognized Abigail. The young woman kept her head down, her long hair falling against one side of her cheek. When she rose at the same moment as Ruth, the curtain of hair swayed to reveal a purple bruise on the cheekbone and a swollen eye.

A cry escaped Ruth before she could help herself. Abigail refused to look her way, so Ruth reluctantly focused on the scattered barley. Unfortunately, she knew only too well how such occurrences happened. Abigail had insinuated she was unmarried. Did she live with an abba or older brother who used his fists to control and intimidate?

By noon, the workers paused for lunch. Boaz had yet to visit the fields and eat with his harvesters. Ruth squeezed in among the other young women and found more than enough to eat, although, as Joab promised, the workers devoured the round loaves of bread and bowls of vinegar, stuffing themselves on the roasted grains and leaving only crumbs behind. She secured several pieces of bread and tucked them carefully into her satchel to take home to Naomi.

Abigail sat at the opposite end of the circle. To Ruth's chagrin, no one seemed to notice or care about the younger woman's injured face. The woman closest to Ruth, Sarah, readily shared additional bread with Ruth, the gesture a bright moment during a dull day.

Gossip about life in Bethlehem, including Boaz, was passed back and forth like a bowl of dates.

"You should see the feasting after the barley festival." Sarah grinned as she pointed to the mound of roasted grain in a bowl. "There is so much meat. It's enough to last for a week."

"I'd like some of that roasted lamb. I don't think it's fair Joab relegates us to the back to gather a few kernels when Boaz is so rich," someone mumbled from Ruth's right.

Murmurs swept through the group, rumblings of discontent rippling outward. At noon, the water was too stale to drink. The sun was too hot, and the gleanings were not enough. The day was too long, and the gleaners were too many to count.

If only she could sprout wings and fly away as she listened to the women pour out their frustrations. Hadn't they walked past Zakai's stripped fields morning and night? Were they *blind*?

Another young woman with loose curls elbowed Sarah in the ribs, changing the direction of the conversation. "It's pointless to wear your nicest tunic in front of the lord. He won't notice you in that shade of green."

A third woman, her hair gray as Naomi's, chuckled. "Sarah knows better than most. She has tried for the past two harvests to catch his eye."

Sarah didn't appear the least offended by the comment. She merely laughed with the workers. "I've settled my sights on one harvester. Gilead." She waved to a young man with a thick beard and hair with streaks bleached in the sun. He raised his hand, surrounded by a group of men who whistled their approval. "My betrothed has worked for Boaz just as long as I have. Gilead wants to build a house for me. So why shouldn't I please him with a green tunic? He says it complements the shade of my hair and my eyes." She fluttered her eyelashes with a false simper.

The murmurs of congratulations rippled through the women, including some good-natured teasing about the other men missing out on the prospect of a stunning bride.

"What about you, Abigail? Any progress with finding a husband?"

Abigail sniffed loudly as she tossed her glossy hair behind her back. "I promise I won't settle, if that's what you mean."

Sarah's smile faded as she shifted on the woven mat. "I haven't settled. I've accepted my fate. There's a difference. I refuse to sway my hips to attract the men."

"Joab's son, Aharon, wouldn't object to settling for Abigail," a woman snickered under her breath. Titters rippled through the group, the women smirking.

Abigail narrowed her gaze as she scooped a generous portion of roasted grains, leaving none behind for the other women. "I'm not settling for any average field hand, including Aharon."

Her arrogance, in the face of her impoverished circumstances, clearly grated on the other workers. Someone clucked her disgust. Though Ruth hadn't formally met Aharon, she wondered if he might be the young man standing next to Gilead. A slender, black-haired youth with a sullen turn to his mouth, staring at the women whenever he had a free moment. Usually, he carried a bow and quiver full of arrows strapped to his back. Boaz kept some of the workers armed in case of thieves.

"And what of you, Ruth?" an older woman, another widow with a young son and a pleasant, round face asked. Her name was Chayna. "Does Naomi have plans of marriage for you? You're young enough."

The question hung in the air. All the women became silent as they watched Ruth.

The memory of Naomi's enthusiasm when learning about Boaz made Ruth's stomach churn—as if she had eaten unripe fruit. She didn't have time to worry about matchmaking, not when poverty and starvation loomed in the horizon. Considering the age of the young women around her, she was older too. Nearly twenty-five years of age. If Chayna hadn't found a respectable Israelite by now, why would Ruth expect more for herself?

"As Sarah said, I am content with what Yahweh has brought me. He has proven faithful in all areas, including the gleaning. I am grateful for His continued provision."

Someone snorted at her answer, and at once, Ruth felt herself shrinking inside, but she wouldn't back down from her statement. She glanced down at her hands, dismayed to see her fingers tremble. Didn't the women realize the gift they were given? Or did their hearts hunger for more and more, never finding true satisfaction?

"A Moabite has no business marrying an Israelite or receiving charity."

When Ruth immediately raised her head at the vicious slur, none of the other women would meet her gaze. Abigail continued to chew slowly, her eyes remote.

Sarah cleared her throat after the awkward silence, and then Ruth realized why the women were silent. Boaz walked past them, a muscle in his square jaw flexing. Inwardly, she groaned. Why must he appear at the most inopportune times? Had he heard the women's presumptuous comments? He didn't deserve such rudeness.

The horn blared again, rousing the men and women from the ground.

Ruth rose with the other women, keenly aware that Boaz kept his distance. Not that she could blame him. Some women were exhausting with their henpecking type of gossip, their endless complaints, and their constant need for attention.

She found herself beside Abigail once again.

The young woman smirked as she patted her bag. "I intend to glean beside you, since the owner has left you the best." A light challenge lay behind Abigail's teasing.

Ruth nodded. "I think there will be enough for both of us."

Abigail's smile faltered as she clutched her bag. "You are entirely too good, Ruth. You can't trust everyone, you realize."

She ignored the odd comment, choosing instead to focus on Abigail's injury. Had anyone shown compassion to Abigail? "I couldn't help but worry over your eye when you entered the fields."

Abigail moved swiftly, picking barley left and right, her hand darting like an asp striking. She kept her bruised side averted. "You needn't fuss. I can take care of myself. It was naught but an accident at home." Her jaw clenched, belying the truth of that statement.

"I do worry. I've seen such accidents before. If there is a way I can help you, let me know."

"And what, exactly, would you do for me?" Abigail laughed under her breath, though Ruth thought she heard the undertone of barely restrained tears.

Would Naomi be open to sharing with someone else in trouble? Perhaps Ruth had been too swift to offer help, but neither could she stand by and do nothing.

"What do you need?"

"A miracle." Abigail smiled darkly. "But those don't exist for women like me, and I've learned to carve my path."

"What of the Israelites and the miracle of the manna in the wilderness? What if Yahweh gives us exactly what we need for the day? Nothing greater, nothing less, but completely enough so we depend on Him?"

Abigail made a sound in the back of her throat, a sign that Ruth's comment might have hit the mark. But instead of sharing more, Abigail tilted her head, her gaze thoughtful. "I couldn't help but hear the women talk of marriage and you. Are you truly not interested in any man?"

Ruth shook her head, tamping down on her frustration to discuss her marital state yet again. "My only concern is to gather enough barley for winter. Yahweh will see to the rest."

Yet the more she worked, the more exhaustion she felt pressing down onto her aching shoulder blades. Her days had blended into an indistinguishable blur, marked by gleaning most of the day, and then patching the roof and tending the garden at home.

She couldn't remember feeling so tired. Or so discouraged.

When evening came, she said goodbye to Abigail and the other women. Harim broke free from a conversation with Joab, hobbling as fast as he could to reach her side. "Please greet your mother-in-law for me. It's been too long since I've seen her."

She placed a hand on his arm. "I would be happy to pass your greeting. It will lift her spirits."

Naomi so desperately needed encouragement. As did Abigail, despite her flippant manner. As Ruth trudged home, her movements slowed. The bag slung over her shoulder felt comfortable, full of barley yet again. Stifling a yawn, she saw her home and yearned for a cool bath.

But as she approached the courtyard, a familiar shape emerged a second time, far down the road, watching her from afar.

Waiting.

CHAPTER FOURTEEN

Naomi greeted her daughter-in-law with a hug, eager to fill the house with conversation after a lonely day with nothing but the sound of bleating sheep for company. Ruth remained silent, drawing back from the embrace, bluish shadows ringed beneath her eyes. She deposited her satchel of barley onto the ground this evening as if it were a burden and not a new triumph.

After grabbing the heavy satchel, Naomi drew Ruth to the center of the courtyard. "Come and eat."

Roasted grains filled bowls next to a welcoming fire crackling in the courtyard. After pulling off her filthy headscarf and washing her hands, Ruth sank down onto the mat positioned next to the fire. She rubbed her bloodshot eyes and yawned, perhaps too tired to catch her mouth opening in such a cavernous manner.

Naomi poured a cup of honeyed water for her daughter-in-law. "You are exhausted, Ruth. This gleaning is too much for you."

Ruth rubbed her arms, where the muscles were sure to throb from so much physical labor. "I'll be fine, Imma. We need the barley. Unless I sell myself as a servant or slave to help bring income, I don't know what else to do."

"We will do no such thing!" Perhaps pride—and fear—made Naomi bite out the last remark, but Ruth merely smiled as she tucked her legs beneath her. The last thing Naomi wanted was for her daughter-in-law to be held captive to a dangerous master.

"Then glean, I must."

"At least you will be safe in Boaz's fields. I take great comfort in that thought of him watching over you."

Ruth stiffened. "I saw someone on the road today. I think it was a man. He followed me all the way to Boaz's field. I never saw his face. Tonight, when I left Boaz's field, he was there. Watching me from afar."

Unable to believe her ears, Naomi handed her daughter-in-law a bowl of chickpeas mixed with fresh garlic. She was heartily sick of the same meal, but Ruth thanked her all the same. "Are you sure?"

"I'm sure. He didn't want to be recognized."

A chill swept through Naomi as she glanced at the weather-beaten courtyard door, so easily breached. She had no animal to warn of an approaching stranger. She had no weapon beyond Ruth's sling and one rusted knife incapable of slicing fruit, much less damaging anything.

"Hopefully it is nothing. Plenty of men and women walk that road to Bethlehem."

They ate together in companionable silence while the fire popped and hissed.

"Did you speak with Boaz today?" Naomi dared to ask as she brought a scoop of grain to her mouth.

Ruth kept her gaze downcast as she picked at the contents in her bowl. "No. I saw him walk past the workers. He's a very busy man and doesn't have time to chat with the gleaners."

Naomi frowned. It didn't exactly bode well for her plans if Boaz didn't speak with Ruth for two days straight.

"I'm thinking we need to repair the roof before the seasonal rains come. I don't dare let more water damage into the house, or we'll be forced out due to mold."

"Can we trade barley for supplies to fix the roof?"

Naomi hated to part with a single kernel. How had it come to this, deciding between encroaching mold or a hungry stomach? If she didn't take care of the ceiling, a priest would soon declare her home unclean and uninhabitable.

She leaned forward, opening her mouth to share her plan. Why not ask Boaz for help, since he so readily agreed? Yet Ruth's deep sigh prevented her from speaking about Boaz just yet.

"You are troubled today, and it's more than just strangers on the road."

Ruth poked at her chickpeas. "Several of the workers don't want me in the fields, although Harim has been friendly enough. He was most insistent passing a greeting to you."

Naomi pictured a much younger man, one who sold her oil with a flirtatious wink and steeply discounted prices. She brushed aside the image, focusing on Ruth. "The other women are not friendly?"

"Two women speak with me. But I'm uncertain I'll ever find my place in this village, not as a Moabitess."

Naomi felt the old familiar rush of anger mingled with protectiveness course through her veins. "You must raise your chin—"

"And stare down the lion. I know, Imma. Mind you, it's not one lion but a pride. A very hungry pride, watching me for any mistake, no matter how small. I don't want my actions to reflect poorly on you either."

Naomi inwardly flinched. Ruth was ever bound by the need to be perfect and constantly please the fickle whims of others. Her meek spirit had originally drawn Mahlon, and Naomi too, but as time passed, Naomi couldn't help but worry about her hurting daughter-in-law. When would Ruth realize that her worth didn't rely on the opinions of others, especially strangers?

She answered firmly. "Don't waste your time or energy worrying about them. Village women often have nothing better to do than gossip. They are indeed a pride, looking for a new gazelle to hunt. Lucky for you, your feet are swift and sure. You can't continue to stew over every silly comment that comes your way."

Satisfied with her succinct answer, Naomi reached for Ruth's bowl and heaped a second portion of chickpeas. She would gladly forgo extra food to help Ruth, but to her shock, Ruth got up from the mat and hurried into the house without another word.

Ruth was asleep by the time Naomi crept up the stairs with a clay lamp in hand. The flame flickered, casting her shadow across the wall. She settled onto her mat, carefully cradling the light. She blew out the flame, rewarded with a thin stream of smoke visible in the waning moonlight.

A soft snore rattled from Ruth as she lay on her back beneath a threadbare blanket.

Sitting by the fire alone, Naomi had puzzled over Ruth's abrupt departure. Surely her daughter-in-law had no reason to be offended, did she? Naomi had uttered good advice—solid and weathered from years of experience. Yet neither could she deny an underlying sense of worry. Had she pushed Ruth too far?

Conviction soured her well-intentioned words.

Yahweh, help me encourage Ruth—not stifle her sweet spirit. She dearly missed the blunt communication she had enjoyed with her sons. They had been so easy to read, so quick to push back when necessary. Sometimes, she forgot Ruth's wounded past.

Naomi wiggled her toes beneath her blanket, her movement arrested when she heard a rustle downstairs. She sat up, flinging the blanket aside, her breathing noisy. Had she imagined the sound? Living alone was more than enough to do strange things to a person, and she hadn't had company other than Ruth.

A twig cracked beneath something heavy. It was not the resident mouse, which liked to visit during the night. Naomi would far prefer it to whatever waited downstairs. Was the stranger Ruth had described outside the courtyard or inside?

Her heart pounding in her throat, she crept to the stairs. In her haste, she accidentally kicked the lamp. It rolled away from her, out the door, and promptly shattered on the first step leading to the courtyard. A few shards tinkled to the ground.

Silence greeted her as she waited.

Lion. She was a lion, forced to take her own advice, which had felt so brave and fierce only hours prior. "Who is there! Show yourself!"

Behind Naomi, she heard Ruth slip from beneath her blanket and pad toward her on bare feet.

"Imma?"

"Stay back," Naomi whispered. "I heard someone downstairs."

After several moments, with only the sound of their harsh breathing filling the silence, she finally exhaled. "I think he's gone, whoever he was. I'd like to check the courtyard before I sleep." *If I sleep.*

"I'm coming with you." Ruth sounded resolute as she bent to pick up her sling.

The courtyard remained empty. The storage jars, the barley that slowly filled them over the past days, remained untouched. Ruth had ducked into the lower part of the house and found a lamp. After lighting it, Naomi cupped a hand over the feeble flame and gathered her courage to check the garden. She had tended it carefully this past week, watering the plants. Something had unfurled within her as she weeded around mallow and the garlic. Not joy but something restful and almost pleasant.

She raised the lamp higher, the hot oil dribbling over the clay spout, as she surveyed the grounds. A muffled cry escaped her, but it wasn't from the lamp. Someone had blundered through the garden with heavy steps, crushing the fragile leaves. He had escaped into the fields now swathed with shadow.

"You shouldn't walk alone in the morning or evening," Naomi told her daughter-in-law.

Ruth picked up a ruined leaf and twirled it between her fingers. "We have nothing of value to steal. Many know who we are and why we've reclaimed the farm."

"That's what troubles me," Naomi said as she studied the rippling fields before her. On one side, Boaz's holdings lay to the right. Across the road, Zakai's land rolled with swells, like that of an encroaching sea, rising higher and higher.

Someone was intent on frightening her and Ruth away from Elimelech's land. Her land.

Naomi poured a handful of barley onto the milling stone. Its curved surface, similar to a saddle, made the tedious morning chore easier. With the golden kernels puddled in the center, she positioned herself on the mat and slid back and forth with a second stone, flat on the bottom and rounded on the top for gripping. Over and over, the routine action provided scant comfort while troubled thoughts plagued her. To think Zakai threatened to take away her grinding stone…

He had no right to her property, and he knew it.

Dare she speak to Boaz about the matter and seek his advice? Ruth was far too shy to speak up for herself, and Boaz, based on Ruth's latest stories, was far too distant for Naomi's liking.

What if she nudged the two of them together? How could she help them to see each other as something more?

She hated waiting for answers.

Grinding barley occupied most of her morning. Later, in the afternoon, she planned to add oil and leavening to the flour to make bread in time for the evening meal. Flicking away a stray lock tugged free by the breeze, she resumed her work. Today Ruth would be in the fields, her work ethic above most women. A full day waited for both of them, with far too many things to do than worry.

Yet the rhythm of the grinding did nothing to soothe the anxious fluttering in Naomi's belly as she recalled her morning. As soon as the sky blushed pink with the rising dawn, she had inspected the damage in the garden. Somehow, the crushed leaves felt even more alarming—violating, even— when viewed in the light of day. Her daughter-in-law had silently tucked her sling into her sash and poked around the ground, her fingers easily finding another stone.

Were they both overreacting, considering all they had gone through? Was Ruth in danger? Naomi had offered to escort Ruth to the fields, but her daughter-in-law refused. Too much work waited at home, Ruth had claimed.

An unbidden prayer whispered within Naomi, one tainted with ripe anger.

Protect Ruth. I can't lose her too, Yahweh. You've taken so much away from me. Will You take away my closest friend and only daughter?

When the door to the gate creaked open, she jumped. Aviah stood at the gate, her gaze glancing from Naomi to the run-down courtyard with the cracked walls, and back to Naomi.

To Naomi's surprise, her old friend had brought a satchel, holding it out as if bringing a peace offering. Aviah's sharp gaze softened when she studied Naomi. "To see you in this courtyard again, it brings back so many good memories."

Her statement reminded Naomi of the past, when she had joyfully entertained women around the hearth. Elimelech had been prosperous, and she had been quick to share her blessings.

How different the two of them appeared after all these years. Naomi's hair was threaded with far too much gray, while Aviah maintained some of her youthful glow, with her shiny locks carefully braided and her tunic a vibrant blue. Silver bracelets tinkled at her ankles and wrists, and the wind rustled her outer robe, a *kethōneth*, revealing a fine linen sadin beneath the outer cover.

Naomi rested on her haunches, her back aching from hunching over the millstone. She gestured toward the courtyard hearth and the woven mats of frond leaf surrounding the cold ashes. "It's good to see you too."

How long had it been since her old friend had come for a visit? She had wondered if she would ever see Aviah again.

Aviah sank down onto the nearest mat, folding her legs beneath her. She handed the satchel to Naomi, the weight surprising. "I thought I would bring a welcome gift in honor of your arrival."

More than a fortnight had passed since Naomi's return, yet none of her friends had bothered to visit. A sting of bitterness stole from the gift, piercing her with fresh doubt.

She wiped her hands free of flour, her gaze on the bag and not Aviah. Inside the leather satchel lay an assortment of wrapped herbs, including milled turmeric and garlic, roasted grain, and bread from the day before. But it was the number of dried figs and dates and the two pots of honey that made her gasp with delight.

"You still harvest from the bees?"

Aviah smirked, her face almost impish with pride. "I do. I like to think I have the finest honey, other than Boaz."

"I've heard about his blessings," Naomi admitted carefully. "My daughter-in-law has you to thank for word of the gleaning, I understand. Boaz has been very generous, leaving extra barley in the fields for us."

Though it hurt to admit she needed the charity, she couldn't help but take pride because Boaz had blessed Ruth and extended so much favor. Had Aviah and the other women heard that bit of gossip? Perhaps they wouldn't be so quick to judge Ruth if they knew of Boaz's approval.

"I am truly sorry, Naomi. I've been a terrible friend." Aviah dropped her gaze to her lap. She toyed with a silver bracelet on her wrist. "When you left Bethlehem, I resented you at first. Part of me wanted to escape the famine. But my husband adamantly refused to entertain the idea of abandoning his father's land. We lost so much those first years when Yahweh shut the heavens, bringing drought. When I thought of you, I imagined how wonderful your life must be. And yet how wrong I was. You suffered, more than most."

Naomi pressed a hand against the throb in her chest. Aviah's raw honesty touched her deeply. "My sons were so sickly when they were born. Unfortunately, I couldn't produce enough milk to feed them. By the time the famine came, and they were young boys, Elimelech feared he would lose them both. He refused to stay and do nothing. But I never wanted to leave Bethlehem or my family and friends. It is just as much my home as yours."

If she hadn't lost her sons and husband, she likely would live in Kir-hareseth, right at this moment, not needing to reclaim her land.

Aviah sighed. "I don't always understand Yahweh's ways or why He allows such suffering."

Naomi busied herself with Aviah's satchel, removing the dates to share with her friend. She had always loved Yahweh and tried to serve Him faithfully, no matter where she lived. She realized she ought to say something in response to Aviah's pondering.

We continue to trust Yahweh no matter how hard life becomes.

But, after years of saying such truths to her sons, she hadn't the strength to utter such a statement if her heart continued to wrestle with Yahweh's goodness.

Help me in my unbelief. A familiar-enough prayer these days.

Aviah refused the dates Naomi offered. To Naomi's surprise, Aviah leaned forward, placing a hand on her arm. "I've also come because of your daughter-in-law."

Naomi scowled, her mouthwatering appetite for the sweets vanishing. "What do you mean?"

Aviah released her hand. "Supposedly, Ruth brought an idol with her, one of Chemosh."

Naomi startled at the accusation. Ruth would do no such thing, preferring instead to cling to Yahweh, but should the truth ever get out about Eshmun and Yassib and the idols they made…

She bristled, like any mother would when defending her own. "I've known Ruth for several years. I couldn't ask for a better daughter-in-law. She is one who loves Yahweh and the law with her whole heart. Surely you don't believe such idle prattle?"

Aviah had the decency to flush bright red. "I've only come to share what I've heard. Someone says that Ruth clings to her Moabite ways and refuses to change."

A tight knot settled in Naomi's stomach as she studied her old friend. "Do you believe everything you hear, Aviah? Haven't you seen my daughter-in-law stay standing by my side when no one else has come forward, other than Boaz?"

Aviah averted her gaze. Finally, she nodded in agreement. "No, I don't believe a word of it, although at first, I wasn't certain. Your Ruth drew water and helped me carry my jug back to my home. She was most eager to help, even if my initial welcome was less than hospitable. I want to apologize to you. I should have visited you much sooner."

Naomi's breath caught at Aviah's contrite tone. She had felt so alone in her old home, and now this blessing of an old friend reaching out to reconnect filled her with gladness. "I'm thankful you came today. And perhaps you can tell the other women how Yahweh blessed me with such a thoughtful daughter. That is how I see her, like my flesh and blood."

As soon as the words left Naomi, a sense of gratitude swept through her, perhaps the first since losing her husband and sons.

She *was* grateful for Ruth.

Ruth had left all that she had known without a word of complaint, and for what? To glean in the fields until her fingers blistered raw? A humbling thought.

Aviah offered a weak smile. "I'll do my best to curb the gossip. When Ruth offered help, I was afraid of what the other women would think of me. I even led her down a side street to avoid stares, and her carrying a heavy jug all the way without complaint. I'm ashamed of my behavior. Will you tell her I am sorry?"

"I think you should tell her yourself." Naomi smiled to soften the sharpness of her curt reply.

Aviah chuckled as she rose from the mat. "Still as frank as ever, Naomi. Would you believe me if I told you I missed our chats over the fire? I have missed you very much. Tell Ruth to come to our home, especially now that everyone is free from fever again. It would honor us to have you as guests."

Naomi's smile widened as she touched her old friend's shoulder. "Nothing would please me more."

CHAPTER FIFTEEN

Ruth kissed Naomi's cheek before leaving their courtyard. In the days following Aviah's visit, Naomi continued to revive in her spirit, little by little. She smiled more readily. She ground the barley Ruth brought home without complaint, proudly pouring each ephah into the storage jar. Naomi had warned the gleanings wouldn't be enough for the entire winter, but Boaz's generosity had extended to his workers, and Ruth could hardly carry her satchel home, brimming with barley to the point of spilling over the sides.

When Aviah visited a second time, she had brought a jar of pungent vinegar, and together, the three women set about cleaning the one storage pot that hid dead mice. And when Naomi left to retrieve food to serve, dipping out of their meager supply, Aviah leaned to whisper to Ruth a heartfelt apology that made her throat tighten with emotion.

The older woman had patted Ruth's cheek, assuring her not to worry about the gossip. More and more women in the village had heard of Ruth's hard work in the fields. Her devotion to Naomi had not gone unnoticed. Indeed, Ruth wondered if she caught a note of admiration in Aviah's whispers.

Nor could she deny her excitement at being invited to Aviah's home for a meal in the coming days. Truly, the gift of friendship took away some of the anxiety of living as a foreigner in a strange land.

Despite her fatigue, she resolved to bring as much barley as she could before the harvest ended. She hoped that when the wheat and olives ripened, she would glean a second and a third time. If only she might thank Boaz, but as the owner of his farm, he hardly stayed long enough in one spot for her to approach him. Maybe it was her shyness that kept her feet planted to the ground whenever she spotted him in the fields.

As she hurried down the hill, a man waited to the left of the road, nearest Zakai's land.

She slowed her steps, her hand grazing her sash where Mahlon's sling nestled beside three smooth stones. She recognized the thin form. Radah, Zakai's imperious son. She hadn't seen him since the disastrous visit to Naomi's half sister, Machla.

He wore a shorter tunic today, his spindly legs pale and hairless.

Stepping onto the road, he blocked her. "I wish to speak with you." With a voice breaking in pitch, he squared his shoulders as if somehow he could stretch to his fullest height.

She tried not to giggle, swallowing her smile.

"You are living in our house, and it displeases my abba, and it displeases my imma to have no rent paid."

Her humor dissipated into the hot morning air. "Naomi says your abba came to an agreement with Elimelech to rent the land. Why would my father-in-law sell his property? He never intended to lose his family's inheritance."

Radah's eyes widened at her boldness—a boldness which, in desperate times, had certainly honed to a lethal point. Naomi would be proud.

"I know nothing about renting the land. My abba swears it is his."

"Was the business deal done at the city gates in front of all to see?"

His scowl deepened, his brows pinching together, but he didn't argue with her. Instead, he appeared almost confused, his cheeks reddened, and his full mouth pulled in a sullen pout.

If no one had witnessed the deal, or heard of it, then Zakai's claims would come to nothing.

Securing the strap of her satchel over her shoulder, she edged away from him. "If you'll excuse me, I have work to do in Lord Boaz's field."

Radah moved a second time, shuffling to the right as if to further block her. "Wait! Don't go just yet—"

Furious now, she barely evaded him, her arm brushing against his. She must not let such a young man bully her, even if he was as tall as she was. A shiver rippled through her, one due to past experience. If Radah wanted to hurt her, he could easily do so when standing close to her.

When she safely ducked past him, she turned, anger chasing away her fear. "Were you the one following me the other day, and rustling around in the dark outside our courtyard, trampling our garden to shreds?" Her voice rang out louder than she intended.

Radah opened his mouth as if to protest but stopped as a long shadow fell across the road. Without a word, he scurried away, jogging in his attempt to escape Ruth's side. She might have chuckled at the cowardly sight if she wasn't so angry.

She whirled to see Boaz standing in the middle of the road. As engrossed as she had been in her conversation with Radah, she missed hearing his quiet approach. He strode toward her, concern warming his expression.

"Forgive me if I interrupted a conversation, but I saw him repeatedly block your path on the road." His gaze remained intent on her, the former intensity fading away as a hint of a smile quirked his lips. "Although I'm uncertain you needed my help, after all. I don't think I've witnessed a young man run away so quickly."

She struggled to control her breathing, her chest rising and falling rapidly. "It was Radah, Zakai's son."

"I did overhear some of your conversation. Has he bothered you before?"

Embarrassed at the strange encounter, she nodded. "I think he's been following me in the morning and evening. We heard someone outside our home late at night too."

Boaz remained quiet as they walked together. Already, a crowd had gathered in the center of the fields where Joab would shout his orders, and of course, plenty were staring at her and Boaz. Despite his silence, the muscle near the hollow in his jaw jumped once or twice.

"Would you allow me to escort you home in the evening?" he asked evenly.

Now, it was her turn to be speechless. "I—"

He hurried to add, as a flush crept up his neck and cheeks. "I can arrange for another servant to accompany us so that everything appears proper. I had hoped to visit Naomi and see if she needs anything. At least allow me to look around the exterior of the courtyard wall and ensure all is well."

So he had heard a fair amount of the conversation! Her pulse thrummed again, though this time it was far more pleasant than in her encounter with Radah. How could she refuse such an offer? "Naomi will be pleased to see you, I'm sure."

"Good." He cleared his throat. "I have very fond memories of that home. When I was just a boy, I would run over to that courtyard and sneak a fig or two from the trees. Elimelech's abba never once scolded me, although he asked for my help when the figs needed to be picked. Instead, he offered to teach both of us how to ride and hit a target with a sling."

Her fingers brushed against her sash where the leather straps of Mahlon's sling peeked above the fabric, the action drawing Boaz's attention to her waist.

His eyebrows arched high as he studied her. "You have a sling?"

A smile crossed her lips. "My husband's. If Elimelech blessed you with instruction, Mahlon did the same for me."

She had heard some of the story regarding her father-in-law and her neighbor growing up together, but she couldn't deny her curiosity about a young Boaz sneaking into the pitiful orchard to steal figs with the sheer daring that only a mischievous child could possess.

An amazed chuckle rumbled deep in his chest. "I should very much like to see you use it. Did you know Elimelech?"

"No, my lord. He had passed long before I married his son."

Boaz's expression softened. "And you miss your husband."

Her voice caught. "Yes, I miss him."

"Ah." His answer was as gentle as the breeze ruffling her brown headscarf, and with it came the invitation to share more. To be understood.

"He was a wonderful husband, so kind and patient with me." She checked herself just in time before she blurted how much Boaz reminded her of Mahlon. The way he looked at her now, as if only she existed.

She took a deep breath and continued. "I had never known about Yahweh when I married Mahlon. I had heard rumors from my parents regarding the strange practices of the Israelites. My abba scoffed, noting the Israelites were haughty with their infinite rules. And he was quick to point out how the Israelites found other gods. But when I met Mahlon and Naomi, it was like I could see for the first time. Truly see. Naomi shared all she knew of Yahweh, from the creation of Adam, to Moses leading the Israelites out of Egyptian bondage. Never once did she tire of my endless questions. They showed me a better life, and I wanted to be closer to their God of Creation, to Yahweh. I wanted to believe He could accept a woman like me, a Moabitess. Because of the love shown to me from my new family, I knew I could trust Yahweh. That He was and is a good and holy God. The only God."

Boaz's sharp intake of breath made her stop.

She peeked at him beneath lowered lashes, with an embarrassed laugh. "Perhaps this sounds absurd to you, especially coming from a Moabitess."

Was she a fool to share so much of herself? Perhaps she had stretched the boundaries of what was appropriate, especially when speaking with a man so used to power and wealth. He had far bigger concerns than to listen to her ramble so.

"No," he said with a hint of awe that warmed her right down to her toes. "I think it sounds beautiful. My imma first encountered Yahweh when she helped two Israelite spies hide from soldiers. Her name was Rahab, and she later married my father, Salmon. In a way, you remind me of her."

She wanted to keep talking with him and ask questions about his mother and his life, but they had reached the edge of the field where she would need to join the other gleaners. Before she could say anything further, Joab rushed to Boaz with a list of needs to be taken care of. Was it her imagination, or was Boaz reluctant to leave her?

He held up a hand, stilling Joab's frenzied recounting of the northern field, which lagged because of the workers, before turning to her. "Thank you for sharing what you did."

Such simple words, yet she could hardly deny the flush of pleasure they brought her. How exactly did she remind him of his imma? The way he spoke of Rahab, with that reverent tone…

She had no right to assume anything with such an innocent comment.

As she joined the other women and a few cautiously greeted her, she noticed that Abigail hung back at the edge of the group. Nor did the young woman seek to join her side as Joab led the workers and the gleaners to another field, one far closer to Boaz's home.

Nothing could prepare Ruth for the sight of that building. It put Zakai's house on the hill to shame. Even Elimelech's home, which was significantly bigger than the house in Kir-hareseth, could easily fit inside the walls of Boaz's massive courtyard.

Beyond the palatial house, she spied the olive grove, ancient with twisted roots. During the olive harvest, servants would beat the trees with a long stick to send the ripe olives cascading to the orchard floor and gather the fruit in baskets. The grove captured her attention, drawing her into the sun-dappled depths where light and shadows danced side by side.

What a peaceful place to wander and think.

Something intentionally bumped against Ruth's shoulder, hard and unyielding. Abigail scowled at her. "The barley won't wait, especially with you gawking at the lord's grove. By the time you move your feet, the fields will be picked bare."

Ruth followed slowly while Abigail strode away. Shocked at the vitriol pouring from Abigail, Ruth kept her distance. She had no desire for a public fight, especially after Radah's ridiculous behavior. Abigail, thankfully, didn't wait for her. Instead, she ran ahead to the gleaners, as if determined to avoid Ruth.

Harim leaned against a tree trunk, rubbing his hobbled leg. "Ignore her, Ruth. She's a jealous one, and no matter how hard she tries to catch Lord Boaz's attention, she fails every single time. He's shown her nothing but kindness because of her drunken abba, but the master is gracious to each of us."

"I'm sorry to hear about her abba. I suspected as much the last time I saw her bruised face," Ruth admitted. "She is hurting inside, and there lies the poison. Wounded people do what they know best, and that is to injure others."

Abigail had refused to share more about her home life, and Ruth would never pry, but that didn't mean she couldn't empathize.

"Her abba is well known in this village for his vile habits." Harim spat out the last word with disdain. "He too worked for my old master, Levi. But Levi let that one go because of the drink."

"Will none of the other women take Abigail in and shelter her?"

Harim moved toward her, his crippled foot dragging on the ground, leaving a trail of a single line in the dirt. "You can't save someone who resists. Believe me, that girl is made of marble."

She nodded. Part of her feared such an astute observation might also lend itself to Naomi. She couldn't save Naomi from bitterness. That burden was Yahweh's alone to carry.

Ruth slowed her pace so she could accompany Harim. He had been reserved the first time she had met him, preferring to eat alone and keep to himself when gleaning. But the more she spoke with him, the more she liked him. She reached inside her satchel and pulled out an extra scarf. "Naomi insists on a gift for you, to keep you from burning beneath the sun."

Harim took the scarf, his hand trembling. He bound it on his balding head, covering his greasy locks of white hair. "Your mother-in-law was one of the loveliest women I had ever had the pleasure of meeting when we were young. Tell her I will treasure this gift always. I look forward to matching wits with her when she comes to barter."

Ruth chuckled, having witnessed Naomi's prowess in the marketplace. As she slowed her pace to match Harim's, another woman joined her side.

Sarah grinned at Ruth while gesturing to Ruth's satchel. "I have yet to see anyone glean as fast as you. How are those fingers of yours?"

She glanced at her scratched knuckles, her skin dried from the hot wind and dirt. "My hands might be like old leather hide by the time harvest ends."

"I'll bring you my imma's salve. Your hands won't be so dry if you rub it in every night."

"Thank you." Ruth smiled as she readjusted the strap of her satchel. Sarah easily matched Ruth's stride, distracting Harim with a discussion on the best way to make desserts from date honey, a thick syrup extracted from dates and mixed with cardamom, salt, and olive oil.

"It's how you fry the seeds that matters," Sarah protested when the older man impatiently shook his head.

"You bake it until it's crispy or use it in a cake," he answered but not without a wink directed at Ruth.

Amused, Ruth listened in as they continued to argue over sweetmeats. Perhaps Naomi was wise to not worry about what others thought—even if her bluntness sometimes chafed. Yahweh continued to provide, even in friendship. A more unlikely pair Ruth would never have found, but Sarah and Harim made the monotony of the field bearable.

With Sarah and Harim bantering back and forth while gleaning, Ruth concentrated on her work, the predictable movements of snatching barley and sliding it into her bag now second nature to her.

Farther and farther she drifted forward, the chatter dimming behind her. Ahead, the men cut the barley with their sickles swinging in large arcs. She stopped and took a moment to slow the rapid beat of her heart and keep away from the blades, when another conversation drifted her way—one that made her hackles rise.

Abigail had cut in front of Ruth, close enough to interfere with the men and their sickles. The young woman stuffed a handful of gleanings intended for Ruth into her satchel. A harvester whirled around to see Abigail gather a second, heaping armful. He scowled as he gestured to the ground. "Those aren't for you. The master will be displeased if you take everything intended for Ruth."

Abigail snorted, her back to Ruth. "That sly Moabitess? Don't think for a moment she hasn't flirted with other men for such favors. Why not leave the barley for an Israelite?"

Bile rose in Ruth's throat as she watched Abigail defiantly gather yet another armful of barley. The harvester grunted as if disgusted, but he resumed reaping the standing crop, while giving Abigail wide berth.

Ruth moved to the left, keeping far behind Abigail. The insinuations made her skin crawl. Had someone else convinced the young woman to believe such awful lies?

As Ruth continued to glean, another harvester, an older man, noticed her efforts and dropped extra barley. He waggled his fingers at Ruth and pointed to the ground so she wouldn't miss the spot. It seemed wherever she trod, left or right, someone responded with kindness. She knew she had Boaz's influence to thank for it. She hadn't seen him since he had met with her on the road early this morning.

As the sun descended, she said goodbye to Sarah and Harim. Before Harim left, Ruth opened her satchel to share additional barley. He shook his head, refusing her gift with an amiable smile. Despite his difficulty balancing on one good leg to pick the gleanings, he appeared content with what he had.

Regardless, he caught her off guard when he patted her on the shoulder and tipped forward with a conspiratorial whisper. "Tell Naomi thank you. She is blessed to have you as a daughter, Ruth the Moabitess. Very blessed."

So he had heard Abigail's bluster. Perhaps Abigail had intended her voice to carry to Ruth and those nearest her.

She left the fields with a smile on her face, regardless of Abigail's former coldness. The young woman studiously avoided Ruth, staying close to the other women clustered together in a large group as their laughter trilled. Ruth felt no anger toward her, only sorrow and compassion. She knew what it was like to feel wracked with insecurity and self-loathing.

If Abigail wanted to take the gleanings intended for Ruth, so be it. She would share. Yahweh would continue to provide, as He had proven so faithfully. As she reached the road, she remembered Boaz's promise to accompany her home. He had spent much of his time at the far end of the field, too far to hear Abigail's slur.

Ruth paused at the edge of the field. Should she wait for the lord, or proceed home without him? The prospect of encountering Radah wasn't nearly so terrifying now that she knew who was following her.

Surely Boaz had better things to do than watch over her like a mother hen. Other pressing matters now drew his attention. With a sigh, she headed toward the road running parallel to the field. She had taken all of ten steps when a familiar thudding of hooves shook the road behind her.

CHAPTER SIXTEEN

Ruth glanced over her shoulder just as Boaz dismounted from his horse.

"You wouldn't leave without me, would you?" He smiled as he gathered the reins in one hand and led his horse toward her.

"I thought you must attend to other matters, my lord," she answered, dismayed when her pulse skipped a beat at his presence. "I don't want to take you away from your estate."

All at once, her mouth dried at the idea of riding with him.

He drew up beside her, the reins clasped loosely in his fist. "Truly, it's no trouble. I've asked Joab to join us. I hope you don't object to the additional company."

She shook her head, suddenly mute. True to Boaz's word, the foreman jogged across the field, the horn bouncing with each long-legged stride.

Boaz scanned the fields with a satisfied air. "It's a lovely evening for a walk. I'd be happy to carry the barley for you."

She exhaled with relief. No ride then, just a walk.

Before she could say no, he reached out with his free hand. She unslung the bag from her shoulder and handed it to him.

"Unless you would prefer to ride on Beracha instead of walk?"

She shook her head. "Beracha?"

His grin widened. "It means blessed. Beracha has been my faithful companion these past four years. She loves to race, and so I indulge her as often as I can. She also has a fondness for my grapes, and that weakness I can't indulge. My men have to watch for her sneaking treats whenever we get too close to the vineyard."

A giggle escaped Ruth at the idea of a horse bold enough to steal grapes. "Not unlike you with the figs on Elimelech's land."

His eyes rounded at her quip, and then he laughed, a rich, throaty sound that made Ruth grin.

"I must admit, I've never witnessed a horse loose in a vineyard. A sight to behold, I'm sure. Your grapes must be as wonderful as your barley."

"Then you should see my vineyard," Boaz answered warmly. She blushed, helpless to prevent the heat spreading to her cheeks.

When Joab approached them, his eyebrows quirked high as he glanced from Ruth to Boaz. "My lord?"

Boaz composed his face, but a hint of the smile lingered. "We'll walk Ruth home to Naomi and offer a quick welcome."

Joab offered a slight bow and slowed his pace. Significantly so, as Boaz led his horse.

Boaz looked down at her as they walked down the road leading to Naomi's land. "Did you have a successful day?"

Ruth struggled to match his stride and was grateful when he slowed as well, providing plenty of opportunity to chat without losing breath. Regardless, it was difficult for her to maintain a steady voice.

She decided not to mention Abigail's behavior. "I did, my lord. Wherever I went, I found plenty of barley. My mother-in-law will be so pleased with your generosity." Then she added under her breath, "As am I."

"Ruth, you needn't use titles with me. I'll answer to Boaz just as well," he said thickly after a moment, but the light shining in his eyes did not diminish. "Family takes care of each other. It is the right thing to do, as you have so beautifully demonstrated with Naomi."

She mulled over that last statement, a curious dampening sensation stealing from the joy of a walk with him. Boaz's thoughtfulness, though full of favor, carried none of the spark that Mahlon's gestures once had. If only Abigail realized Boaz's generosity had nothing to do with Ruth but stemmed from his care toward a relative.

Dare she reintroduce the conversation they had earlier in the morning, discussing Yahweh and loss? She wanted to know more about his wife and son, but discretion cautioned her from prying too quickly. If and when Boaz was ready, he would share.

So, instead, she asked him questions about threshing and the final stages of the harvest. He answered readily, with contagious excitement as he pointed to the location of the threshing floor.

She stood on her tiptoes to see above the rolling land, the farthermost curve of the earth elevating the threshing floor above the rest of the valley.

Boaz rubbed his horse's nose when she bumped against his shoulder. The mare whinnied, as if ready to run again, but Boaz appeared content to stroll with Ruth. He gestured to a swath of land. "Over there, the farmers share an open space, each man taking his turn to thresh."

"And what happens next?" she asked, interested to know more about his life.

"Do you want the short version or the detailed version?" He leaned ever so slightly in her direction with a teasing smile.

"The long version," she answered promptly, delighted when his grin widened, flashing white teeth against tanned skin.

He glanced at her, his gaze approving. "I ensure the large bundles are secured with rope and placed a few feet apart. Then my donkeys kneel while my men fasten the bundles to the packsaddle. When the driver gives the signal, the donkeys rise and march to the threshing floor. It's fifty feet across, shaped like a circle. Oxen without muzzles pull a threshing board over the grain, and the thresher sits or stands upon the instrument, with his goad in his hand to hurry the animals."

Ruth stopped in the middle of the road. Though the threshing circle was too far away for her to see clearly, Boaz had painted a vivid picture with his descriptions.

All that wheat and barley pressed down, neatly crushed beneath the weight.

"I'm not boring you, am I?" He came to a halt beside her, his brows dipping downward, as if he cared what she thought. "Harvesting can be a dull business, although I've always loved this season."

Her voice wavered ever so slightly. "No, I'm thinking about the oxen trampling the grain, and the immense pressure created before the grain is finally set free."

He nodded slowly. "We call it the *dush*. To be tread under foot."

She exchanged a long look with him, one full of understanding.

"Not unlike Naomi feels at the moment, or you, Ruth," he murmured as he gripped the reins.

"Or you, my lord." How easily the formal title slipped from her, cautioning her of the vast chasm between them.

He sighed as he studied his sandals for a moment. "Yes, I have felt that trampling in my life. I lost my wife and son four years ago. There are days when it feels like it happened yesterday, and days when it feels an eternity has passed since I last saw their sweet faces. Perhaps that hurts the most—the fading of a memory, dimming with time, until I can no longer picture their features as I once did."

The moment came to ask the question that had plagued her thoughts since she learned he lost his family. "How did you cope with such a terrible loss?"

He inhaled deeply. "I didn't do so well in those early years."

Would he share more of his past with her? The only sounds came from their sandals crunching on the road and Beracha snuffling from behind Boaz.

He finally added, "At first, I buried myself with the duties of the farm. I even wrote poetry when I had spare time."

"Poetry?" She couldn't help but raise her eyebrows, bemused at the image of such a large man who spent his days outdoors, hunched over a small desk with a papyrus beneath his fingertips.

He huffed a self-deprecating laugh. "Poorly written poetry, stuffed somewhere on a forgotten and dusty shelf in my home. But mostly I prayed. Every single day. Joab can testify to the times I spent on my knees in the olive grove, begging Yahweh for answers to my grief."

"And did you find your answers?"

Boaz's answer was halting. "I didn't hear an audible voice, but I sought after His presence, where I found a measure of peace. And the more time I spent in the olive grove, the more I realized how much I needed to depend on Yahweh. I couldn't rely on my wisdom or strength or good fortune. I had only Him."

She found herself most drawn to the picture of him praying in the olive grove, a bittersweet image. "And Yahweh was enough for you."

He nodded. "Yes, He is enough for me. In a sense, my loss brought me closer to Yahweh and set me truly free."

How she wished Naomi might feel the same way in time. If only her mother-in-law might recover the full joy of Yahweh again. As they approached Naomi's home, Boaz shifted the strap on his shoulder and guided Beracha, while Joab followed from a safe distance.

"I see the fig trees I snuck fruit from as a boy," he said, bringing a lighter mood to the conversation.

Ruth glanced at the trees in desperate need of pruning. "They're shriveled, but you are welcome to them when they ripen, my lord."

Twin dimples carved into his cheeks at her sudden invitation, one she had not properly thought out in advance. But when he smiled, his face transformed into something boyish and charming despite the beard and the silver threads at his temples. Features that made him all too attractive.

She averted her eyes as the heady thoughts threatened her composure. She would not be Abigail or Sarah, all starry-eyed with wonder.

He handed the reins of his horse to Joab, who by now had jogged again to reach Boaz's side. Although Naomi and Ruth had done a fair amount of work to the courtyard and home, it couldn't compare to its former glory. Ruth bit her lip as she led Boaz into the courtyard.

Naomi had her usual chickpeas simmering in a pot over the fire. A nearby plate of fresh round bread made Ruth's mouth water. A quick assessment of the chickpeas in a bowl earned a wince when she realized she hadn't enough food to offer her guests.

When Naomi entered the courtyard with a jug, she nearly dropped it at the sight of the men. "My lord!" She clutched the jar close to her chest, her eyes widening.

He held up a hand. "Just Boaz, Naomi. We've known each other long enough to forgo formality, as I've told Ruth. I was just telling her how I used to climb Elimelech's trees as a boy."

Naomi chuckled as she shot Ruth a curious look. "Yes, I remember Elimelech telling me similar tales. Although his favorite stories include racing with you all the way to the gates of Bethlehem. I never learned who won the bulk of those races."

"The true winner will remain in secrecy. But no one, and I do mean no one, could balance bareback like Elimelech."

Naomi's cheeks were two bright spots, and her eyes sparkled as she continued to trade childhood stories with Boaz. How good it was for Naomi to share memories with someone who knew her husband so well.

"Would you care to eat with us?" Naomi spread out her hand to the food, as if she were serving a delectable banquet of the richest fare.

To Ruth's surprise, Boaz and Joab readily agreed. Of course, Naomi was merely extending hospitality, and their acceptance was also one of hospitality. Secretly, Ruth loved how he protected Naomi's dignity, treating the invitation as a wonderful courtesy.

"I had a guest bring honey and dates," Naomi murmured. "Give me a moment and I'll find them."

Ruth also ducked into the house to bring Boaz and his foreman a water pitcher. Though she knew he was staying to break bread with them, she was not prepared when he followed her.

He kicked off his sandals, nudging them to the side, refusing to mar her floor with dirt.

Somehow, the action felt intimate, seeing his bare feet—as intimate as the offer to ride his horse.

The evening sun shone through the gaps in the ceiling. He said nothing as he studied the ceiling and the floor and the rickety table, which had once been a source of pride.

He palmed the back of his neck as he inspected the pillars. His strong throat bobbed as if he swallowed hard. "Do you sleep upstairs?"

Embarrassed, she stuttered out an answer. "Y-yes, both of us."

He probed the low ceiling, his fingers easily indenting a cracked, brownish patch. "I'm afraid one of you will come crashing down if you put your weight on the wrong spot. This ceiling is about to collapse. And when it does, someone will be seriously hurt."

She couldn't disagree with his assessment. Both she and Naomi had avoided sleeping on the flat rooftop. The stuffy room at the top of the house collected all the heat from the day. If she wasn't so exhausted every evening, she would find it difficult to rest at all.

"Would you allow me to send someone to fix the beams and your roof?"

"You are very thoughtful, but I cannot pay."

"I don't want you to pay," he said quietly as he reached out a second time with a long, muscular arm and easily touched the old mud plaster covering the branches. "Consider it a gift. A gift need only be accepted, not earned."

This time, beneath the pressure of his fingers, a sizable chunk fell loose, tumbling to the floor and shattering to bits.

Someone elbowed her sharply in the ribs. Naomi shook her head with her brows raised, warning Ruth to quell any further protest.

When Boaz finished his inspection of the ceiling, a faint smattering of dust covered his black hair. He ran his fingers through the tousled strands, shaking out the remaining crumbs of dried mud. "I'll send someone tomorrow, if Naomi approves."

Naomi clasped her hands together, beaming with delight. "Thank you, Boaz. Ruth and I would fix the roof if we could, and in fact, Ruth has tried, but the work is hard, and she is exhausted these days."

If only Naomi wouldn't utter such presumptuous things. What must Boaz think of such a shameless request? Naomi, however, asked if he would like to see the garden, which was next to the empty stable tucked in the room behind the main living area. While he slipped on his sandals, Naomi called out, over her shoulder, "Will you find the honey and dates, Ruth?"

With a silent groan, Ruth located the jars of honey and dates kept safe in a medium-sized clay pot used for storage and to protect against rodents. As she entered the courtyard, she heard voices drifting in the breeze, and as she suspected, Naomi had started a conversation Ruth probably wouldn't approve of.

"She can't do much more. When she comes home at night, she can hardly keep her eyes open." Naomi's thin voice carried around the side of the house.

Ruth hardly dared breathe when she heard Boaz's deeper tone.

"I'm worried about her too. We must encourage her to rest," he admitted.

"I try, but she's determined to take care of me."

Then Boaz responded, the words too muffled and low for Ruth to discern. She had assumed he was too busy to observe her working among the gleaners. Perhaps she was wrong.

"Radah waited for her?" Naomi exclaimed with tight fury, scattering Ruth's turbulent thoughts.

Alarmed by the turn of the conversation, Ruth balanced the wooden bowl laden with dates and the twin pots of honey and carried them to the courtyard, where Joab sat cross-legged. When her mother-in-law returned to the fire, Naomi's flushed cheeks and Boaz's searching gaze that landed on Ruth showed something was afoot, but Ruth wasn't so certain she wanted to know what her mother-in-law might plan next.

CHAPTER SEVENTEEN

The Bethlehem marketplace rumbled with noise, especially as harvest came to a close. Naomi wandered toward the tables loaded with fragrant spices and rolls of fabrics. Realizing Boaz's workers would be at the house today, she left early in the morning to barter for what she needed. Pistachios would be a delightful change, but she didn't dare indulge in the treat.

Her food supply, at least, stayed well stocked, thanks to Boaz's visit. He sent baskets of supplies along with the men charged with rebuilding her home. Cuts of roasted mutton tantalized, along with a basket laden with herb-infused bread, dried fruits, and clay jars filled with the most fragrant olive oil she had ever smelled or tasted. He sent something else that made Ruth grin—four oval stones as perfect as could be, weathered by nature, each rock fitting snugly into Mahlon's sling.

It was almost too much of an abundance for two women, and Naomi gladly provided lunch for her recent visitors.

For the past week, a group of four strapping men had all but filled the rooms with their masculine presence and laughter as they knocked down the rotten ceiling and secured it with new beams. Yesterday, they had coated the wood with a mud mixture, smoothing and shaping the plaster until not a speck of sunlight danced on the floor. Their good-natured teasing reminded her too much of Mahlon and Chilion, especially when one man—a youth, really—splashed the others with water while washing his face before eating.

Though she smiled at the antics, sorrow trailed far too close.

She pined for her sons, the way she had ached for water during the long trek to Bethlehem.

Yet the heavy sorrow of the past weeks had subsided as Ruth continued to point out the simple blessings Yahweh provided. Soon they would sleep beneath the stars on a new roof. The enormous clay jars lining the courtyard wall were overflowing with barley. The biggest surprise of all occurred this morning when one of Boaz's men dragged an ornery female goat with an udder nearly bursting with milk and secured it in the stable section of the house. When Naomi tried to milk the goat, the creature bleated its scorn and nearly butted Naomi with its two small but sharp horns, hoping to escape the narrow stall, earning a snicker from her. A stubborn goat, with an attitude not unlike hers.

As she ran her hand over the goat's coarse hair, she had whispered in its ear, "You will learn, impatient one. Soon enough, I'll set you free to wander in the grass. Until then, I'll need to milk you."

Naomi could hardly wait to show Ruth Boaz's latest gift. Surely Ruth would come to realize how much Boaz cared for her. No landowner treated a gleaner so well. Naomi had studied him that night from across the crackling fire while sharing her meager supper. His gaze strayed to Ruth, over and over, like a flower tilting toward the sun. And his smile, though readily given to all, dimpled whenever directed at Ruth.

Why didn't he pursue her daughter-in-law openly? Why was he so careful, as if afraid of frightening Ruth away? It had taken only a handful of meetings with Elimelech, his intent to marry Naomi clear almost from the moment he had watched her draw water from the village well. Elimelech had been a man sure of himself, who knew what he wanted, and didn't think twice. He acted first, then worried later.

Boaz, although similar in age to her husband, acted completely different.

However, she couldn't deny his keen interest in Ruth. How respectful Boaz was, coming to her as the matriarch of the household, to ask her permission to provide an escort for Ruth and to repair her home!

"Ask her yourself if you wish to escort her," Naomi's blunt reply had been enough to make his mouth round with shock. "Ruth is more than capable of deciding on her own. You won't find a more levelheaded woman in all of Israel."

Secretly, she hoped he would seek out Ruth, and if giving him every opportunity to talk to Ruth meant pushing them together, then Naomi was more than happy to oblige.

She edged sideways between two tables, one laden with filmy scarves decorated with dangling beads. If only Ruth could wear something so pretty, in a color complementing her green eyes.

"*Naomi.*" A woman uttered her name as if it were a curse.

Naomi raised her head to see Machla standing on the other side of the table, clutching a scarf dyed in a magnificent amethyst hue. The rare scarf would cost a fortune, thanks to the dye made from snails along the Canaanite coast. The seller waited beside Machla, his eyes bulging as she wrinkled the precious scarf in her tight grip. "Please, don't damage my wares unless you intend to buy them."

Ignoring his plea, Machla dragged the unfortunate scarf to her chest. "I've heard rumors you've been busy, and the ceiling in that old home is finally repaired."

Naomi ignored the snide tone. She casually studied the array of scarves, even though she knew she couldn't afford one. "Yes, the work is finished. My roof is as sturdy as the day Elimelech first built it."

The subtle rebuke did not go unnoticed. Naomi caught Machla's stare out of the corner of her eye. She pretended not to notice, and withdrew another scarf from the pile of fluttering cloth, this one a brilliant crimson mingled with indigo and lined with blue beads. Too garish, and not Ruth's style at all. She realized she ought to put the scarf down and escape before Machla invited further trouble, but pride kept Naomi's feet pinned to the ground.

Machla's lips puckered as if she had tasted sour vinegar. "I understand Boaz helped fix the roof."

Naomi dropped the vibrant scarf immediately onto the table, no longer willing to suggest she would purchase it. "Yes, he sent his workers. Did you realize he is related to my husband? Boaz promised me he would take care of family."

Unlike others I know.

She had hoped Machla might extend some hospitality, or at least a visit, especially since they shared the same father.

Despite the blessings of prosperity and status, the passing years had only hardened Machla, cementing old hatreds and imagined slights.

And to think I demanded the other women call me Mara. Bitter. No wonder they avoided me during those first weeks.

Was Machla proof of the end result if Naomi refused to release her pent-up anger?

Her half sister seemed to feel Naomi's censored thoughts. Machla's gaze slipped to the scarf in her hands. She flung it to the table, among all the other glittering ware, her face creased in harsh lines as if nothing pleased her. "How fortunate to have the favor of one of the most powerful men in all of Bethlehem. But are you sure he has your best interests at heart?"

A faint thread of warning wrapped through Naomi. Arguing in a public market for all to see would only bring harm, but neither could she let Machla get away with such accusations.

"We are very fortunate. Lord Boaz's care has blessed my daughter and me."

Machla snorted. "A man's favor shouldn't be bought with feminine wiles, wouldn't you agree? Perhaps you should educate your Moabitess daughter-in-law on how the Israelites conduct themselves. Or do you remember the law, Naomi? All those years spent in the Moabite territory, surely you've forgotten who Yahweh really is and what He requires of His people."

Specks swam in Naomi's vision as the insult sank in deep. Was Machla the source of the slander about Ruth? Naomi had long assumed it was one person stirring up strife. Machla had every reason to want her gone, especially if Elimelech's land bordered Zakai's land.

"I have not forgotten Yahweh or His commandments. Have you? The law states to show hospitality to foreigners. It demands care for the hurting widow and the hungry orphan. When I lost everything, Ruth followed me, forsaking a well-to-do family and the possibility of marriage to a Moabite man. But she willingly chose Yahweh and never lost hope that He would see us through, even if it meant poverty."

Naomi's throat tightened as she considered the full extent of Ruth's sacrifice and devotion to her and to the God of Israel.

Ruth's tearful plea echoed.

"For wherever you go, I will go, and wherever you live, I will live. Your people will be my people, and your God will be my God. Where you die, I will die, and there I will be buried."

Naomi punctuated her next words with her finger, jabbing into the swirls of fabric on the table. "You will not besmirch Ruth's name anymore. And you will tell your son to keep away from her. No more will Radah stalk Ruth's every footstep, nor will he creep around our house at night to frighten us!"

Machla blanched as the barbs hit their intended mark. Naomi refused to cower as she squared her shoulders, though her heart pounded with an erratic rhythm at Machla's visible hatred. Would this feud over ownership of the land continue indefinitely?

Machla leaned over the table, hissing under her breath. "You both should have stayed in Kir-hareseth, where you belonged."

By now, other men and women overheard the loud conversation, and the seller of the scarves retreated to a safe distance.

She searched her sister's face and saw only a stranger. "I came home, hoping to rejoin with family. Yet you, my half sister, have avoided me, while demanding every coin I own, including the house over my head and my millstone. I have asked nothing from you, not even the rent of my lands owed me. Instead, your husband refuses to pay me. Your plans won't work. What have I done to offend you so? Is it greed for my land? Or are you still spiteful because our abba favored my imma?"

Machla fled then, her mouth a white line as she pushed her way past curious onlookers. The shopkeeper snatched the ruined scarf from the table. Dismayed by the conversation, Naomi escaped the table, stopping only to purchase cumin powder. The earthy spice flooded her nostrils as she paid for a small bag filled with herb. Already she had need of it, considering the throbbing headache blossoming at the back of her skull.

The walk home brought her past Boaz's land and Zakai's. She studied the shorn fields, searching for any sign of Ruth, but the work had moved farther west, closer toward Boaz's magnificent house.

If only her half sister had cared enough to reach out to Naomi, how very different circumstances might be. She had been so disappointed with Machla's lack of response. So disappointed with what felt like Yahweh's indifference.

Yet somehow, Yahweh had led Ruth to Boaz's field. Several farms surrounded Elimelech's land, spreading in every direction. What if Ruth had found another farm that fateful morning? Or what if she had stepped across the road to Zakai? As Ruth was so quick to point out, Yahweh had proven faithful—just not in the way Naomi expected. But He had tended to her needs through Boaz, offering a roof and storage jars full of golden kernels.

Machla's snide remarks pierced Naomi afresh. *"Surely you've forgotten who Yahweh really is."*

For the past several years, she had absorbed Elimelech's position as the teacher and guide of the family, intent on passing her beliefs and traditions to her sons. In this recent testing, she had forgotten Yahweh's goodness and His love.

At last the gated courtyard appeared, and she entered her home. The men had assured her they would leave before noon. She sighed with pleasure at the sight of the new roof, the mudbrick already dry in patches, thanks to the sweltering sun. How wonderful to sleep tonight with a cool breeze caressing her face. Elimelech would be so pleased to see his beloved home restored to its former state. He would be proud of her, and Ruth too.

She was about to duck into the house when a small white figure with a set of horns peeked around the corner and bleated out a welcome, or a warning.

The goat somehow had worked its way loose from the pen. It cautiously watched Naomi, the amber eyes blinking with distrust.

As Naomi approached it, her hands outstretched, the goat darted left toward the courtyard wall. And there, to her horror, the lid of the storage pot lay broken on the ground, exposing the large jar to the elements. She rushed to the side and peered into the pithoi. A cry escaped her as she stuck her hand into the jar and touched the air. Someone had stolen their barley.

CHAPTER EIGHTEEN

Ruth mended a rip in her satchel as she watched the sun ascend into a rosy sky. But she couldn't enjoy the brilliant sunrise, not after discovering that someone had pilfered a significant portion of their supplies. Who would do such a thing? She couldn't imagine the men Boaz had sent to fix the roof capable of such a betrayal.

While Naomi shopped in Bethlehem, someone else must have sneaked into the courtyard and let the goat loose with the intent of stealing or causing mischief. If that goat hadn't been so stubborn and wily, they might be short both barley and milk.

Ruth shivered in the cool air as she poked her bronze needle free of the leather, her work finished once the knot was tied. She silently rose from her mat, while Naomi slept close by.

They had talked long into the night, too rattled to sleep. Without the storehouse of barley, surviving the coming months would prove too difficult to bear.

Nor had Machla's accusations regarding Ruth's alleged faults helped matters, instead stirring old fears to the surface. Hadn't she done everything she could to win over her imma's friends and neighbors? Despite Naomi's reassurance, Ruth feared she would never be enough.

She couldn't fully ease Naomi's grief. She couldn't even provide to the extent she wanted to.

But Naomi's latest suggestion made Ruth feel even more inadequate.

Her mother-in-law had insisted. "Why not approach Boaz and ask him to be your kinsman-redeemer? He would provide for you."

Ruth had held up a palm, warning the conversation could go on no longer.

For over nine years, she had waited for a baby. Against her understanding and every desire, Yahweh had closed her womb, designating her barren. No man wanted an infertile wife. She would never feel the soft swell of a belly or the tiny kick of life hidden inside her. Shouldn't she just be grateful for what she had?

After depositing the needle into a box kept in the upper room, Ruth found one of her worn tunics. She dressed slowly, dreading what to do next. Dare she ask Boaz for more help, especially after he had given her and Naomi so much?

Her thoughts troubled her as she walked the familiar path leading to Boaz's farm. To her relief, Radah remained out of sight. Had he stolen the grain? He didn't need it, not when his abba owned significant land. Perhaps Naomi was right. Zakai would do whatever it took to frighten two widows away and claim the land for his own purpose.

When she reached the halfway point to Boaz's land, another figure ran down the road, waving at her. She recognized Sarah. When the young woman reached Ruth's side, she bent over, panting. "I saw you in the distance and hoped it was you."

Almost shy, Sarah pulled out a round clay jar sealed with wax and handed it to Ruth. "For your hands, as promised. I know you need the barley, yet you've shared with me and Harim every chance you get."

A thoughtful gift, as if Sarah knew about the last encounter with Abigail and the other women who worked for Boaz and wanted to make amends. While the men had been quick to listen to Boaz and treat her with respect, the women had been far harder to read.

"I also wondered…" Sarah took a deep breath, but her eyes sparkled with mischief. "If you would meet a young man? Completely respectable, I assure you. You've likely seen him alongside my Gilead. His name is Aharon—Joab's son—and he's a hard worker, just like you."

Ruth pocketed the jar carefully into the bottom of her satchel just as the first horn blew, signaling the harvesting had begun. And thankfully, sparing an immediate answer. What to say? While she had no desire to offend her new friend, she wasn't particularly thrilled with the prospect.

Together, Ruth and Sarah hurried past the fields, past Boaz's property and olive groves. When she drew closer to the men harvesting, her eyes must have widened at the sight of lush green leaves entwined on posts dug into the ground. Boaz's vineyard.

"Did you know you can pick the grapes when they ripen?" Sarah asked as she pushed back her headscarf. "Boaz allows gleaning for all of his crops and orchards. When the men beat the olive trees, scattering olives to the ground, they cannot beat the tree a second time. Yahweh has blessed him above all others. After the famine had decimated villages and cities, somehow Boaz kept working his land, tending his crops, and giving to everyone in need. He saved many lives during those lean years. Why he does it, I do not know."

"Grace." Ruth turned to the young woman beside her. "Unmerited favor but full of mercy."

Sarah nodded, her expression pensive. "We call it *hesed*. Extravagant grace. It hasn't always been so in Bethlehem and the surrounding villages. For many years, every man did what was right in his own eyes, regardless of who he hurt. Dark days, from what I've heard and seen."

Ruth pondered Sarah's halting confession. Boaz was a treasure, indeed. How many righteous and good men had she encountered? A handful. But oh, the things they accomplished. She might not feed a village, but she would do what she could to show those around her hesed. As she picked up the freshly cut barley, her bag slowly filled, and her resolve strengthened.

By the time noon arrived and the sun shone nearly white in a cloudless sky, her fingers ached and her back ached, but she moved swiftly, even if her mouth dried and her ears rang. She didn't stop to eat and rest with the others, her desire to refill what was lost consuming her focus. Instead, she nibbled on a chunk of stale bread she had packed, continuing to glean long after the others had left the field.

"Ruth," a familiar voice commanded her attention.

She glanced up to see Boaz's concerned expression. His eyes darkened as he studied her. He held out a waterskin for her to take. "Have you had anything to eat or drink?"

As she straightened, she swayed in the heat as she reached for the waterskin. His fingers brushed against hers, and to her surprise, that little muscle in his jaw bunched, yet again.

"I'll be fine," she croaked, her throat far more parched than she realized. The drink of water slid down, barely quenching her thirst. Instead, it roared to life as she drank more.

He nodded at the stone fence encircling the vineyard. "There's some shade in the vineyard, if you care to rest. My invitation to see it still stands."

She hesitated a moment too long. Was it her imagination, or was that disappointment she saw flash across his face?

In the meantime, Sarah called her name and waved before pointing to a mat where bowls of roasted grains and jars of honeyed water lay in an inviting circle. Sarah's intended, Gilead, stood beside her with another man Ruth recognized. Aharon, Joab's son. The men watched her with unconcealed curiosity.

Boaz turned to see the commotion, his eyelids hooded, when he saw the men next to Sarah. "Or perhaps you have other plans. I see Gilead has brought Joab's son, perhaps someone to introduce to you?"

She had no desire to chat with Gilead's companion, even if he appeared attractive enough. Instead, a curious longing, one she had tried hard to suppress, rose stubbornly to the forefront of her thoughts. The more time she spent with Boaz, the more she wanted to linger and visit with him.

"I should like to see your vineyard," she admitted, and was rewarded with a quirk to his lips.

Ignoring the others, although she waved at Sarah just long enough to see Abigail scowl from the edge of the crowd. Never had Ruth been on the receiving end of such a spiteful look. Yet as she walked alongside Boaz, she could have sworn she saw Abigail wipe tears from her eyes with the frayed edge of a headscarf.

Dismay flooded Ruth as she approached the stone hedge surrounding row upon row of twisting vines, planted in uniform rows. Budding grapes, too small to harvest, hung in small clusters.

"What is the matter, Ruth? You needn't come if you don't wish." He sounded pensive.

She pushed aside all thoughts of Abigail's unveiled hatred and Machla's vicious slander circling around the village to focus on Boaz. "It is an honor to see your vineyard, but I suspect there may be others who would disagree...." Her voice trailed as she struggled with how to explain her insecurities.

He waited for her at the gate, swinging the door open for her. "Yes?"

"It's just that I am a Moabitess, my lord. Our people have never been at peace with each other. Even now, I feel the displeasure of others over the extra grain and provisions you've blessed me with."

"It's Boaz," he corrected her as he continued to hold the gate open long enough for her to enter. "I suspect it hasn't been easy for you, sojourning in a strange land. I had hoped

Naomi and you would feel at home, regardless of what others say or do."

Naomi had said the same thing, albeit in a far more stringent manner.

Ruth ducked her head, suddenly overcome with emotion. Had her abba carved too many wounds into her heart, rendering her broken?

Boaz leaned in. "My imma, Rahab, was a righteous woman, regardless of her past in Jericho. When my abba, Salmon, asked her to hang the red cord from her window, she listened and found deliverance for herself and her family. As the years passed, the other Israelites saw her value and her dedication to follow what was right, even if she had once been branded as an innkeeper at the city gate."

Ruth didn't need to have him explain what an innkeeper did. The innkeepers, the brightly painted women who waited by the city gates for willing customers, plied their age-old trade in Kir-hareseth as well.

But his admission filled her with wonder.

Boaz's imma, though once a fallen woman, had found a new life and a new identity with the Israelites?

He fingered the nearest vine, the smooth, green curl wrapping around his finger. His expression was thoughtful as he tugged his finger free. "Did you realize I graft vines together, and the new vine soon melds with the old vine until you can hardly tell the difference?"

She shook her head, mesmerized.

He plucked a green leaf and placed it in her hand, gently cupping her fingers over it before letting go. "I believe Yahweh did the same with my imma, grafting her into the tribes of Israel. He changes us, Ruth. The more we seek Him, the more He makes us like Him. He grafts each of us into the vine. It doesn't matter what past a person comes from, not when we seek Yahweh with a heart of repentance. I know my imma grieved over her past. Yet Yahweh healed what others broke inside of her. He made her new again."

She glanced at the fragile leaf. "I wish Naomi could experience such healing."

He traced a coiled vine with his finger. "It takes time." When he looked at her, his brown eyes, the color of cinnamon bark, warmed with compassion. "And you, Ruth, have you experienced healing? You will forgive me if I say this—but I see some of myself in you, chasing my grief away with endless chores."

Instead of alarming her, his bold observation cracked open something locked tight inside her, something she hadn't dared speak of even to Naomi. How could Ruth share her loss when Naomi had shut down so completely?

"It's easier to do than to think or feel."

"But you must allow yourself to grieve, to feel the loss, the dush, before you are truly set free."

She recalled his conversation as they walked down the road, past the hidden threshing floor, where wheat and barley endured unimaginable pressure. Was this how Yahweh refined His followers? Removing the chaff to leave the kernel of grain behind?

Tears filled her eyes as she drew a deep, shuddering breath. If she let those tears fall, they might never stop. They escaped, regardless, no matter how hard she tried to hold them back.

A hand touched her shoulder, clasping briefly, the weight solid and comforting. Someone called Boaz's name, yet he remained by her side while she dashed away her tears. His expression remained tender as he watched her.

No wonder he had extended so much compassion to her, considering the story of his mother. What a rare gift to the hear the story firsthand from him. She sensed a deep loneliness within him, equal or greater than her own. She had Naomi. And he, his servants.

Yet one truth remained. A man could be beloved by those around him and still be very much alone.

As evening fell, Ruth carried her barley home. Her arms felt surprisingly less tired than before. The muscles in her body had slowly hardened from labor, becoming distinct. Life outside the city had proven more delightful than she realized. She liked the feel of the crumbling earth beneath her fingertips and the fresh breeze whispering against her damp skin. Later, in the afternoon, she had joined the women working together to tie the cut barley sheaves into large bundles and load onto carts.

Nor could she deny the impact of Boaz's respectful treatment of her. No longer did the men gawk at her or the women whisper as much. The conversation she shared with Boaz in the vineyard played over and over in her mind. He had shared something deeply personal, and it left her wanting to discover more, to peel back the layers of such a fascinating man. A foolish thought, perhaps. But one she couldn't shake.

So immersed in her thoughts was she that she nearly missed a voice calling to her.

"Ruth! Over here!"

To the left of the field, Gilead and Aharon waited, along with Sarah. She suppressed a twinge of irritation, forcing her face to smooth into a pleasant expression.

"Come." The younger woman pulled on Ruth's sleeve, her tone pleading. "I want you to meet someone."

Ruth wanted nothing more than to dig in her heels like the belligerent caravan donkey she had ridden, but Sarah tipped close, her breath tickling Ruth's ear. "This is Joab's son, Aharon. He stands to replace Joab one day as foreman." A girlish giggle escaped her as she eyed Ruth for some hint of approval.

Ruth's flat answer, "I see," did nothing to discourage her friend. Dragged by the arm, Ruth allowed herself to be led to the two men. Up close, Gilead, with his tawny, wild hair, resembled a young lion. Full beard and a toothy grin, and a personality to match. It was easy to understand why Sarah, who was so bubbly, might be attracted to such a vivacious man.

"So this is Ruth." Gilead clapped Aharon on the back, practically forcing him to lurch forward.

In contrast, Aharon hardly spoke a word as he unslung his bow. He regarded her with tight lips, his black hair and wiry stature similar to Joab. She hadn't been impressed with him the first time she saw him with that sullen pull of the mouth. Instead, she recoiled from his stonelike expression until she realized, after Gilead dominated the conversation, that Aharon might be shy.

"What do you think of Bethlehem so far?" Gilead asked her.

She chose her answer carefully, knowing full well every word could be picked apart later. Why fuel more gossip? "It's lovely. Similar, in some ways, to Kir-hareseth, with the same fields and crops."

"And different in other ways." Gilead nodded, directing a shocking wink in her direction. "Will you ever return to Moab?"

Even Aharon's quiet interest seemed piqued as his gray eyes studied her, but she had no desire to share titillating stories of her past. "This is home for me, and I intend to live out the rest of my days on this land," she answered firmly. Every word was true. She had grown to love the countryside, even the bleating sheep that had overrun Elimelech's pastures.

"I doubt the crops of Moab could compete with our harvest this year. I've never seen such a yield. The master says Yahweh has brought double blessings, and who can disagree?" Gilead said, but Ruth didn't answer his challenge. Out of the corner of her eye, a familiar green robe flashed. Abigail marched to the road, her chin lifted while ignoring Ruth and everyone else.

"She thinks entirely too highly of herself," Sarah said under her breath once Abigail had passed.

"Look at her, a gleaner, no less," Gilead sneered, not bothering to lower his voice.

Ruth darted a look at her friend, who covered her mouth in shock. Sarah's eyes watered after a moment. "Oh, Ruth, I am so sorry. I'm certain Gilead didn't mean to insult you. Or me, for the matter." She punched her intended in the arm.

"Ow!" he exclaimed, but his expression turned rueful. "Sarah tells me I'd be better off choosing silence most days. I meant no offense."

Ruth offered a small smile as reassurance. She had accepted her lot, finding life much easier for having done so. "None taken. It is the truth, after all."

Sarah frowned, her hand dropping to her side. "It's just that Abigail carries herself with such airs, and no one really likes her."

"How can you say that?" Aharon demanded suddenly, his eyes narrowing—the first statement he had spoken during the entire conversation. "Don't you know what kind of home she comes from?" He looked over his shoulder, almost as if latched on to Abigail's retreating form. Ruth saw his fist clench by his side.

"She's a terrible flirt, Aharon. All the men have been on the receiving end of her fluttering eyelashes," Sarah protested.

"Almost all the men," Gilead said with a smirk as he waggled his eyebrows, but Aharon merely glowered when he finally tore his attention from the road to his friend.

"She is not as bad as you say," he said defensively.

Poor Aharon, forced to watch Abigail flirt with everyone but him. To think, Abigail pined for what she couldn't have, and never realizing fully what was right in front of her.

Ruth couldn't help but pity both of them, but it was time for her to leave. Whatever ridiculous plan Gilead and Sarah had concocted in advance, it clearly wasn't working. She knew only too well that uncomfortable feeling of pent-up longing. There was no reason to waste her evening, or Aharon's, any further.

She muttered a polite excuse to leave, ignoring the crestfallen disappointment displayed on Sarah's face. Nor did Ruth glance at Aharon again. Instead, relief at having escaped a bungled, even if well-intentioned, matchmaking session flooded through her as she retraced her now-familiar path home.

Relief, yes. But also a little sadness, if she was honest with herself. Like Aharon, she felt her gaze tugged—pulled, not toward her friends but the verdant vineyard with the tender fresh shoots and dangling grapes promising refreshment. There, in the cool greenery, where the sun had scattered dappled shadows across Boaz's strong features, she had felt his hands clasp hers, his fingers warm while pressing a leaf into her palm. Telling her she too could be grafted into this marvelous country, along with the people she had grown to love.

Her pulse thrummed with the recollection. She closed her eyes momentarily, breaking the sight of the lush foliage, and forced herself instead to study the empty road ahead.

***

That night, by the fire, Ruth ate beside her mother-in-law. The goat, now named Jael, bleated mournfully from the stable, as if afraid to be alone. Stars flared one by one as the fire crackled in front of them, scattering a shower of sparks to drift in the night air.

She found herself unprepared for Naomi's urgent questions. "You didn't tell Boaz about the thefts?"

Ruth sighed, thinking of the vineyard again. "No, Imma, we spoke of other things."

Naomi perked up almost immediately, her bowl of roasted grains forgotten. "Oh? What things, exactly?"

"He told me of his imma, Rahab, who lived in Jericho and later married Salmon."

Ruth avoided looking at Naomi, but she could sense her mother-in-law's excitement as she scooted closer to Ruth. "Jericho, you say? From a wealthy family?"

"No, she was an innkeeper rescued by Yahweh. I understand she became a well-respected woman in the tribe."

A gasp came from Naomi as she cradled her bowl in her lap. "Don't you see, Ruth? This is Boaz's way of trying to put you at ease."

"Oh, Imma, *no*. He asked me if I had fully grieved Mahlon, and truthfully"—Ruth set her unfinished bowl on the mat—"I haven't."

"You can't wait forever to move on with your life. You're still young. Lovely too."

"He sees me as a daughter, and I am convinced his attention, which has always been most respectful, is only that. There must be at least fifteen to twenty years' difference between us."

"But do you care for him?" Naomi's insistent question pierced through Ruth, right to her innermost being.

Did she care for him? Dare she admit she searched for him every single time she gleaned in his fields? Or that her ears pricked whenever someone mentioned his name? She missed his conversation long after he left to attend to other business. Boaz spoke to her as an equal, sharing his innermost thoughts. Mahlon, though a flirt and a tease, didn't speak of Yahweh. Mahlon's interests had resided elsewhere—a future pottery business, a new home in a better section of Kir-hareseth, or a boisterous game of *senet* with his prized Egyptian set of ivory pieces. Boaz might have been much the same as a younger man, but life experience had refined an abiding love for Yahweh. A searching to understand deeper matters.

Naomi pressed a hand against her chest. "No man remains unmarried forever—not if he can help it. Nor woman either. There are other young maidens and widows who would snatch him, if given the half the chance."

Ruth knew what else Naomi would say. Be bold as a lion and speak up for herself. But for all the hesed Boaz had shown, not once had she any sign to think he wanted to marry her.

"The hour is late, and I am tired." Ruth's refusal to answer the question was met with silence. Naomi exhaled slowly as she retrieved the empty bowls, her frustration evident.

Ruth climbed the stairs to the new rooftop and sank down on her mat. All around was a moonlit vista of fields stripped of harvest. She bowed her head and beseeched Yahweh for answers. Surely there was a reason He had brought her to Bethlehem. She thought it was to take care of Naomi until the very end.

"What would You have me do?" she asked, her head still lowered.

But the only voice that whispered back was one of fear.

As the stars twinkled overhead and the moon rose higher in the sky, Ruth lay on her back with her arms behind her head and stared at the black sky. Naomi had turned in for the night on the mat next to Ruth's.

She had just closed her eyes when Naomi's next question startled her. "Why did you come with me to Bethlehem?"

Ruth rolled her head to the side to meet her mother-in-law's troubled gaze. "You rescued me. You and Mahlon. I had never known what safety felt like in a home until I moved into yours. You taught me about Yahweh by the way you cared for me and for each other. I knew you differed from everyone else, and I wanted to be just like you."

"Bless you, daughter," Naomi murmured. "I hated what your abba did to you. No man should hurt a child like that. I know you left a terrible home, but I've feared you might come to resent me in time and wish for Kir-hareseth again."

Ruth sighed. "I can't put a price on knowing Yahweh, especially after the pain and betrayal caused by my family. How could I go back to my abba? Or my brother, even if he offered a wealthy marriage? I would have been bound to a world no longer mine, regardless of the comforts provided. A gilded cage, where I would be forced to serve false gods. I am forever grateful to you for teaching me of the one true God. How could I abandon you? No matter what circumstances I encounter, I belong to Him. I won't leave you. Whatever comes, we'll face it together with Him."

Naomi seemed to chew on Ruth's confession. The older woman's face relaxed, losing the harsh lines about her mouth. "Thank you, Ruth. I cannot lie and say I haven't wrestled with Yahweh this past month. I also feared I might have discouraged your faith."

Ruth thought of Boaz's challenge along the road, and later in the vineyard. How pain and suffering had the power, when used by Yahweh, to shape a man's or a woman's character, and later, bring a fruitful harvest. "I just wish none of this loss hurt so much. For both of us."

Naomi pulled her blanket up to her neck. "I'm so sorry, my dear. I wish it were different too." She reached out a hand and clasped Ruth's, with fingers cold and trembling. "But I'm so glad you are here with me. I couldn't have survived without you, and for that, I'm very grateful. I promise I won't force you to do anything you don't want to do. I won't be like your abba. I only want what is best for you."

Ruth gripped her mother-in-law's hand and squeezed tightly. "I love you, Imma."

Naomi's voice broke. "I love you, Ruth."

CHAPTER NINETEEN

Two days later, a knock at the door interrupted Naomi while she swept the floor. With a new roof, the floor remained cleaner than before, but wielding a broom brought a sense of normalcy. While cleaning, she worried over Ruth's exhaustion the past two days. Fretted about the theft and Radah's strange behavior. The knock brought a welcome distraction. When Naomi opened the door, Aviah stood at the threshold with a basket looped over one arm. With a weak smile, her friend thrust the basket to Naomi. "I come bearing gifts."

Naomi bade her friend to enter, relieved to break the monotony and loneliness of her long day.

Aviah bent to untie her sandals. "I have only a moment to visit before I watch my daughter's twins."

"Bless you for bringing treats," Naomi said. "Come in and share a cup of honeyed water with me. Your honey, I might add."

Aviah remained silent as she placed the basket of supplies on the table. As Naomi brought the pitcher and a cup to the table, Aviah slowly eased onto the bench, as if debating whether to leave or stay.

Naomi plunked down the pitcher and cup, determined to discover the reason behind her friend's long face.

"Did you find who stole the grain?" Aviah asked as she took the cup.

"No. Though I suspect Zakai might have something to do with it. His son followed Ruth several times. What if it was Radah or Zakai sneaking about to frighten us at night and later entering to take the barley?"

"They have no need of barley," Aviah said as she raised the cup for a sip.

"No, they don't need barley. But Zakai wants us gone. He feels the property belongs to him."

Aviah wrinkled her nose after she drank, but Naomi realized it wasn't the water disgusting her. "Machla told the women at the well that Ruth comes from a wealthy family, one that served Chemosh. Since the former rumors didn't work, she is now hinting Ruth might have been a priestess before she married Mahlon."

Naomi hissed under her breath as she rubbed her temples. Hadn't she told Machla that Ruth came from a prestigious family? Machla had twisted the information to something grotesque.

"I'm sorry, Naomi. I told the others the rumors are not true," Aviah said, with a tiny wrinkle between her black brows.

"At least we finally know who to hold responsible for such vile talk," Naomi admitted grudgingly.

"Zakai wants Ruth removed from Bethlehem, and he won't stop until he's convinced others. He swears he will have your land by the end of barley season. He wants to plant a vineyard in your fields. Why he needs such a thing is beyond me."

"Do you think anyone will listen to his nonsense?"

Aviah waited a moment, her answer slow but thoughtful. She set the cup down with a decided clink. "No, I don't. Ruth's devotion to you and her hard work and noble character while in the fields has preceded her. There are many who would vouch for her character. I think this angers Zakai. He's no longer respected in our village, and it bothers him."

Naomi pushed away from the table. Why had she foolishly clashed with Machla in the marketplace? Why hadn't she swallowed her pride and walked away from the useless fight no one had any chance of winning? No doubt Machla had slunk away with shame, especially when others heard Naomi's bold accusations concerning Radah. Now her half sister wanted revenge.

She couldn't control her shiver. "It will also make him reckless. Let us hope he reveals himself for who he truly is."

"You'll need proof to take to the elders, before you accuse him of anything," Aviah warned. "Zakai now admits, at least, that he rented your land. Of course, he claims he paid you. He says he will remove his sheep soon, to leave you full use of the fields."

A minor victory.

Her breath came out more shakily than she'd care to admit. "What can I do with the fields at this point? I would rather rent them for the grass and receive money. Now that the harvest season is over, I can't hire anyone to plant a new crop."

"If I had enough *minas,* I would invest in your property," Aviah admitted carefully. "But I know my son-in-law can't take any additional financial risk. I asked him on your behalf. You need a man with plenty of coin to purchase your land for you. But Machla is determined no one will ever rent from you again. The lies aren't only about Ruth. Machla's said terrible things about you as well. She says you are a shrew to work with, bitter and heartless. I believe she referred to your name as Mara."

Naomi's headache throbbed again as she considered the mess she had made of things when picking a fight with her half sister. When would she learn to trust in Yahweh's will instead of taking things into her own hands?

CHAPTER TWENTY

The gate at the house remained open. Ruth smiled when she heard feminine chatter, easily picturing Aviah and Naomi sharing bread coated with honey while sitting by the fire. Aviah's visits, more and more of late, brought a spark of joy.

As she reached the gate, a young man darted around the stone wall of her courtyard, as if caught eavesdropping. She recognized Radah's lean form. He halted when he saw her. Staring back into those beady eyes with a glare she hoped could chisel rock, she gritted her teeth as she marched forward. She doubted she could pivot on her heel and run fast enough to evade him, even though he made her skin crawl. It was far better to advance and show no fear.

He kicked a stone, sending it skittering across the road.

"Why are you here?" She bypassed any pleasantries.

"I'm not hounding you, as my aunt says." He shoved a hand through his hair, forcing the ends to stand straight. "All right, I have indeed followed you these past days."

"You frightened Naomi. Was that you at our house late at night?"

"No," he said, with a hint of incredulity. "I would never do something like that."

If she could slip inside the open gate, she could slam the door shut and bar him from entering. She edged toward the gate, keeping a firm hand on her satchel.

"Ruth, please believe me. I followed you to make certain you were safe." He fiddled with his sleeves. "I was curious. My imma and abba said so many awful things about the Moabites, and I had never met a Moabite before. I wondered if what they said was true."

"You should have spent your hours working with your abba. Didn't you tell me your abba refuses to tolerate laziness?"

Radah flushed as he mumbled, "My abba says *many* things."

"So I've heard." Ruth's dry response made Radah further shuffle on his sandaled feet.

"I've worked hard enough for him, but it doesn't matter. Nothing I do will ever please him. Precious little makes him happy these days. He wants more and more land, and he won't stop until he gets it. Every morning, he sits on his rooftop and stares at Boaz's holdings. He wants to be the most respected man in Bethlehem, but to my abba, that also means the richest."

She recoiled at the idea of so much hatred and covetousness, all tangled together. A horrible web, difficult to escape.

"Stealing from our jars won't make us run. Nor will your imma's lies. I have no idol of Chemosh. Nor was I a priestess."

"All right, fair enough," he said, "And I didn't steal your barley, but I know who did."

She had one hand on the roughened door by now, but his declaration made her freeze.

"Oh?"

"It was that young woman with the hair the color of gold. She gleans in Boaz's field beside you. I saw her sneaking out of your courtyard. I wouldn't be surprised if it was her stealing your gleaning. She carried a basket."

Ruth had a sick feeling about who that woman might be.

Her stomach curdled further as she thought of how she had tried to be kind to Abigail, the effort clearly wasted. By now, Naomi's voice mingled with Aviah's as the older women entered the courtyard.

Seeing an opportunity to be done with the conversation, Ruth nodded once. "Goodbye, Radah," she said as she slipped into the gate.

"Radah? Is that really you?" Naomi cried as she marched toward the gate, dust kicking up beneath her sandals.

He held up both hands, as if to ward from blows. "I'm only here to explain. And to warn you."

Ruth almost felt sorry for him.

"Warn me about what?" Naomi demanded as she blocked him from entering the courtyard. Aviah hovered in the background, hidden next to the wall.

"I know who stole your barley." His tongue darted over his red lips, suddenly nervous as his gaze darted left and right. "You won't tell anyone about this visit?"

Aviah snorted, stepping into view with her hands on her plump hips and the silver earrings dancing from her ears. "We will make no such promise, young man."

Radah recoiled when he spotted Naomi's older friend. His skin blanched, and he backed onto the road. "I really must oversee my abba's threshing." Before Ruth or Naomi could say anything further, he cut across the road and into Zakai's barren fields.

"Did you hear Radah accuse one of Boaz's workers of stealing our grain?" Ruth asked the women.

"No." Naomi frowned as she drew a bolt on the gate. "Is this the woman troubling you in the fields?"

Ruth nodded. "Abigail is her name. Her behavior worsens each day I glean. She was jealous of the extra grain Lord Boaz left for our family."

Aviah's startled gasp checked Ruth from admitting more.

Naomi rubbed her chin, as if deep in thought. "But Ruth, I went to the market during the afternoon that day around the same time when you and the other women normally glean. Could she have taken our barley?"

"I don't know. I haven't always seen her in the field. Sometimes she's arrived late, without explanation." Ruth tried to stifle her shock and failed. She had suspected Abigail's jealousy, of course. But to hear Radah's accusation so plainly, so bluntly, caught her off guard. She felt nauseated by the idea of the young woman creeping into her home to heartlessly commit such a heinous act. Did Radah speak the truth? If so, what would happen to Abigail?

"The law demands action for theft, a repayment to set things right again, and a sacrifice to the priest," Aviah added, her eyes narrowing as if reading Ruth's thoughts. "Someone is lying."

CHAPTER TWENTY-ONE

The barley harvest drew to a close, the fields mostly stripped bare and the sheaves of barley bound and placed in carts to be loaded into Boaz's storehouse. All morning and afternoon, Ruth heard about the weeklong celebrations, the betrothals, including the many plans for the next year. She listened to the conversations, glad to be included as she gathered the last of the barley strewn across the remaining fields.

Harim shared with her that in years past, Boaz opened his home to offer a splendid feast to the community. She had heard the same story from Sarah, but Harim, who was in a chatty mood this day, noted Boaz no longer did so.

The older man loudly whispered, "Due to so much theft, the master sleeps on the threshing floor until morning. While his men relax and celebrate their wages, Boaz will guard the harvest."

She flinched, remembering Naomi's state of panic when pointing to their storage jar. How violated they had felt, discovering nearly half the pot gone. She hated the idea of Boaz subjected to a similar threat—one far more dangerous, considering the sheer amount of wealth heaped in piles along the threshing floor.

"Why not move the threshing floor to his private property, where high walls can protect against intruders?"

Harim swung out his hand to illustrate his point. "You need open spaces and a constant wind for the winnowing to blow away the useless chaff. After the threshing, the men toss up the barley with their forks so that the wind does most of the work, and the kernels fall to the ground, as perfect as can be. Don't look so worried. The master isn't a fool. He sleeps with a stout sword by his side. No one has dared bother him."

Boaz slept alone, with no one else to watch over him? She shouldn't be surprised. After all, as Naomi had previously explained, his name meant "protector."

As evening approached, Ruth grabbed another handful of a gleaning, when someone bumped into her from behind. Her satchel tipped forward, spilling precious barley to the ground. Ruth raised her head to meet Abigail's hard gaze, her eyes bright and glassy like chips of obsidian.

"Watch where you are going." Abigail's voice rang loud and clear for everyone to hear, but for Ruth's ears alone, the young woman whispered, "No one wants you here, Moabitess." Before Ruth could say anything, Abigail trod on the fallen barley with her filthy sandals, grinding it into the dry soil. Ruth's throat burned as she watched Abigail saunter away, as if nothing had happened. Ruth rescued what she could, scooping handfuls into her satchel. Someone knelt beside her.

Sarah nodded at the satchel, her fingers already digging into the kernels to bring up fistfuls. "If you open the bag, I'll help put in the barley. Four hands will make quick work."

"Thank you," Ruth murmured as she opened the satchel as wide as possible while Sarah cupped heaping handfuls, tossing the barley into the bag

"Horrible woman," Sarah said, her voice shrill enough for everyone to hear. "Abigail was cruel to bump into you. I saw it happen, as did nearly everyone else. Someone needs to put her in her place."

Jealousy proved a terrible master. How chilling to think of the scarcity in Abigail's heart, driving her to such brokenness. Ruth continued gleaning into the late morning, but she couldn't shake the image of the younger woman's bruised face or the tears she had wiped from her eyes when no one else saw.

Dare Ruth beseech Yahweh again on Abigail's behalf? Would her prayers bear any fruit at all? She was tiring of showing compassion for someone who, as Harim noted, remained as hardened as stone.

By the time the horn sounded and the men and women left for the field for lunch, Ruth held back from eating just yet, gleaning every portion she could find. The extra she found, she liked to give to Harim, who could no longer balance on his good leg.

She drifted to the northern edge of the field, searching the ground and picking what she could. Most of the workers sat in circles, eating roasted grains and loaves with vinegar. Her mouth watered, but she kept retrieving every fallen sheaf. She had a little longer to work—at least before Boaz came and insisted she rest.

A smile crossed her lips as she straightened, her thoughts envisioning the enclosed vineyard and the curling vines wrapped about sturdy posts.

"What are you smiling at?" a cross voice demanded from farther ahead.

Dreading yet another encounter, Ruth dragged her gaze from the field to see Abigail at the top of a small hill as she glared at Ruth. The younger woman stood far enough away to raise her voice.

But whatever dread she had at dealing with Abigail soon fled in horror. Ice filled Ruth's veins, chasing away any ire.

A low hiss came from the left of the mound, unearthly and full of hunger. A creature the same shade as the barley and wheat slunk forward, its paws padding silently on the dirt. It flattened its ears when spotting prey.

Abigail squeaked, her voice strangled as she turned to view the direction of the sound.

A lioness, weak with hunger, judging from the row of ribs poking beneath its skin, crouched low, with tail up and hindquarters ready to pounce. A young lioness but no less dangerous. The mangy coat and the fact that the beast had crept up on harvesters during the day suggested an illness.

It growled again, as if in warning.

"Ruth, w-what do I do?" Abigail dropped her basket to the ground, spilling a whole day's worth of barley at her feet. She appeared petrified on the hill, incapable of fleeing.

Surely the other harvesters would hear the sound by now, but none of them would reach Abigail in time to help. With shaking fingers, Ruth unslung her satchel, letting it drop to the ground, regardless if it split next to her feet. She dug into her sash and pulled out Mahlon's sling then one weighted, smooth rock tucked next to her waist.

Steady my hand, she prayed as she slipped the rock into the sling. Oh, this was madness. She couldn't take a lioness down… she couldn't…

Her husband's encouragement whispered to her. *"It doesn't matter how tiny you are."*

Breathing deeply to steady her nerves, she met Abigail's terrified gaze. "Keep your eyes on me. Don't look away."

The sling whirled in her grip, the speed picking up, bringing a rush of air against her face, and a low, familiar whine. She felt the sling move, the vibrations rippling down her arm, choosing instead to focus on the lioness, not the strings pinched in her grip. Mahlon had taught her to feel the angle of the wind blowing in through the plains. A southwestern wind, she judged as it brushed against her tunic and legs.

The lioness sensed Ruth, its black nose twitching. Shifting on its paws, it opened its maw, the growl morphing into a blood-curdling roar, full of fangs and rage. It coiled into itself, back legs pumping as if to spring at any moment.

If she released too soon and at the wrong angle, the rock would veer off course, skittering across the fields, or worse, injuring Abigail.

Oh, Yahweh. The lioness leaped into the air, claws unleashed.

She released the bottom string, and the rock flew.

It struck the lioness in the flank, causing it to flip on the ground, earning an enraged howl. With a blur of movement, it rose to its feet, shaking its head. Still very much alive.

Dimly, she was aware of a man's hoarse shout from behind, calling her name. But she had already reached into her sash, her grip stronger now as a thrill shot through her veins, steadying her. The second rock she slid into the pouch and without hesitation, spun the strings and released again.

This rock sailed harmlessly past the lioness's head, landing somewhere in the soil with a useless bounce. Too fast. Too careless, sheer desperation hindering her aim.

Had she injured the lioness the first time? She had only one rock left. She sidestepped to the left, careful not to get entangled in the bag at her feet, and moved farther away from Abigail, drawing the brilliant amber eyes to follow her instead. It obeyed, tracking her as the new prey. A thin red trickle dripped down its side.

Her fingers slid into the sash for the last rock, but she touched only fabric. In her haste, the last rock had slid free. Before she could do anything else, something whizzed past her, sinking into the lioness with a thud. An arrow quivered from the neck as the beast toppled in a cloud of dust.

Abigail's scream pierced the air just as Ruth's legs collapsed from beneath her. She sagged to the earth, suddenly faint as the realization sank in that she or Abigail might have died. Men rushed into the field, a cacophony of voices surrounding the fallen lioness. Aharon ran past Ruth and up to

Abigail, engulfing her in a one-armed embrace while the other hand gripped a bow.

But before Ruth could move, brawny arms scooped her up and she found herself pressed against a massive chest with a heart beating so hard, it felt as though it might break free.

She glanced up to see Boaz's face, his features drained of color.

"Ruth, Ruth, speak to me—are you injured?"

Her throat and lungs closed as he abandoned the scene behind them, his long legs striding as fast as he could. Past the faces of curious and frightened workers, their mouths rounding with shock. Past the bound sheaves of barley and the carts used to carry the harvest to storage.

"Is Abigail safe?" Her voice sounded so breathless as he carried her. He moved swiftly, as if fear dictated his every step.

His dark brows lowered ominously and his arms tightened around her. "Yes, thanks to Yahweh. And you. I've never seen such a sight in all my life. I thought you were gone, and her too. We heard the lion growl, and thankfully some of my men keep bows handy at all times. Ruth, you are truly not hurt?"

She tried to shake her head, difficult when so close to him. "I'm only dizzy and a little embarrassed for fainting. I don't want to weary you."

He attempted to chuckle, the sound strained. "You weigh no more than a bit of chaff, so light you might blow away in the breeze."

Someone ran beside them, huffing for air. Sarah's pale face appeared at Boaz's side. "My lord, is she harmed?"

"No," Ruth answered, though her forehead oozed warmth and the sky spun above her. "All I need is some water and a moment to catch my breath. I confess it was more excitement than I'm used to."

"And get a bite to eat. I doubt you've had much since breakfast, if that," Boaz added as an afterthought. The frown reappeared. "Will you come with us, Sarah? I'm taking her to my home. She can rest there in the shade, and you can stay with her for as long as she needs."

Ruth gaped as she saw the massive estate up close, surrounded by the wall layered with rock. It rivaled any of the wealthy homes in Kir-hareseth, including her abba's, which had impressed her as a child. But unlike Yassib's home, full of idols and an uneasy presence, she felt strangely welcomed as Boaz headed through the opened gate and into the courtyard. Stables and a garden, spilling with flowers and vegetables, lay to the side of the house. A ritual cleansing pool waited from the opposite end, framed by a row of doum palms.

Sarah darted ahead to the house and opened the massive cedar doors as Boaz carried Ruth inside. It was much cooler in the main chamber, free from the oppressive sun outside, thanks to the thick rock walls plastered white and a high ceiling, allowing the heat to rise. Tapestries hung from the walls, and a floor paved with flat stones kept the temperature lower. They stood in a greeting hall, and to the left, she saw another room with a table and chairs and a bench with lined with plump cushions.

He gently lowered her on her feet, his hands spanning her waist. His gaze, intense and almost fierce, studied her.

"When I said I wanted to see you use the shepherd's sling, that wasn't quite what I had in mind," he said.

Her legs felt like limp mallow leaves, every limb shaking from the encounter with both the lioness and him.

"I have only Yahweh to thank for guiding my aim," she answered, still in awe of what had happened.

"You said Mahlon taught you to use the sling?"

"For over nine years. He was an excellent teacher." And he had been. With no children to occupy her days, she had gladly spent her evenings walking outside the city gates with her husband, out in nature, among the powdery cliffs and bluffs of Kir-hareseth. The precious memory, however, was soon eclipsed by the man in front of her.

"For that, I am extremely grateful," Boaz's voice dropped to a whisper. She noticed his heart still beat furiously beneath his tunic.

Sarah coughed loudly in the silence that followed, and Boaz immediately released Ruth, his expression clouding as if he had revealed too much.

"I'll see to Abigail," he murmured before pushing on the door and stepping out into the bright light. "Please, in the meantime, consider yourselves my guests."

CHAPTER TWENTY-TWO

R uth sipped honeyed water, the liquid sliding down her parched throat. Sarah sat beside her, her face slack with something akin to awe as she studied the room. Sunlight filtered through a series of latticed windows, casting elegant scrolls on the paved floor. A row of shelves, hardly dusty, contained carved boxes and tied sheets of papyrus. Did Boaz's poetry hide in such a box, tucked away from prying eyes?

If only she could give him a gift as thoughtful as the stones he had sent her. If she purchased a scroll for him, would he write again?

The cushions, stuffed with feathers, felt oh so soft behind Ruth's back. The table before them was laden with plates of roasted mutton, sticky pastries filled with crushed pistachios, and a bowl of thinly sliced melons. All brought by an older servant woman, intent on plying them with an endless stream of dishes.

"You are still pale," Sarah said from across the finely carved table, her disapproving tone similar to Naomi's.

Ruth sighed, her fingers curled around the cup. "It will pass as soon as I finish my drink. I've got to gather up the barley I spilled."

"I don't think you'll need to worry about lost barley. I have a feeling you'll be sent home with plenty to spare." Sarah nudged the plate of melon slices closer to Ruth. "We have a feast to enjoy. Best not let such food go to waste," the younger woman said as she snatched a green slice.

Ruth found she had no appetite, her stomach protesting, gurgling when she thought of the danger avoided. She held up a hand, refusing the plate.

"You saved my life—"

For a moment, Abigail appeared as though she might bolt to safety. Instead of a mouth curled with disdain, Ruth saw only a trembling bottom lip. Abigail's golden hair was in disarray, and her dusty cheeks bore evidence of tear stains.

Compassion filled Ruth as she rose from the table and approached Abigail. "Won't you join us? There are plenty of raisin cakes waiting. Sarah and I can't eat it all."

Abigail clasped her hands in front of her, her gaze disbelieving, sliding to Sarah, the table, then Ruth. A very different Abigail, no longer sneering or pretending. No more bravado to cover a host of insecurities.

Ruth offered what she hoped was a welcoming smile. After all, she couldn't be more frightening than a lioness, despite the way Abigail cowered before her. "I think you'll find the cushions very comfortable. We will make room, won't we, Sarah?"

Sarah arched an eyebrow, but she scooted over all the same on the bench and patted a seat next to her.

"Why would you do such a thing for me? Why invite me to eat with you when I was so cruel?" Abigail asked in a choked voice, her hand fluttering to her bruised cheek. "I don't understand."

Ruth looped her arm through the younger girl's and guided her to the table. "I know something about being given kindness I didn't deserve."

She thought of Mahlon, rescuing her, the daughter of a corrupt idol maker, when no one else cared. And of Naomi, patiently teaching Yahweh's truths over a similar dinner table—though far less plentiful, but filled with laughter and love.

To Ruth's surprise, Abigail wept, her noisy sobs shaking her slight frame. She threw her arms around Ruth's neck, tears dampening the collar of Ruth's tunic.

Ruth enfolded the younger woman in a hug, her eyes welling.

When Abigail pulled back, her nose red and sniffling, she laughed weakly. "I told Aharon to wait outside for me, at least until I talked with you in private. There are so many things I must say. But first, I wanted to apologize to you."

"I had only hoped for friendship," Ruth admitted. She hated to bring up the subject, but she needed the truth. "I was more than willing to share gleanings. Although, I must ask— did you take the barley from my home? Radah, Zakai's son, swore he saw you outside our house."

"No, I never entered your home," Abigail answered slowly. "But he offered me money to harass you until you left the fields for good."

Speechless, Ruth could think of no reply.

Abigail's shoulders slumped forward. "Fool that I was, I took the shekel. I have no excuse. I can't blame my abba, since he didn't even know about the deal." She raised her head, her features bleak. "I'll understand if you decide to hate me. I will replace the barley I took from you in the fields. Only Radah can tell you the truth about what he stole."

Would he reveal everything? Radah had made Ruth uneasy from the moment she had first met him. Her skin crawled with the idea of him lurking about the courtyard late at night. A hush filled the room as Abigail's admission sank into Ruth, alarming enough to send fear spiraling through her yet again. She reached for the back of the chair to steady herself. On one hand, Abigail had done something despicable, worthy to be addressed before the elders of the city, but she also stood before two witnesses, admitting everything freely, asking for the chance to atone.

"I forgive you," Ruth said, and she meant it. "I know your law—our law—allows us to make restitution with Yahweh when we sin. Make it right with Him first, and the rest we will discuss later, over a shared meal."

Abigail sniffled again as she dashed away fresh tears.

"And if you need a place to rest, to be safe, Naomi and I will find something for you, even if it is with two lonely widows."

The younger woman's smile wobbled. "Aharon will ask permission from his imma. Hopefully, I'll stay with them from now on—if Joab approves. I was so blind with jealousy over you and all this—" She pointed to the richly appointed furniture and the tapestries on the walls. "I didn't realize how much Aharon cared. It was his arrow that felled the lioness." She paused, her voice cracking again. "But it was you who saved me."

***

Ruth did not wait long for Boaz's return. In fact, she suspected he waited outside the doors of his house to allow Abigail a moment of privacy.

When he entered the hall, he paused at the sight of her. "Ruth, all is well? If you are ready, I will see you home."

To her surprise, Sarah mumbled an excuse for needing to see Gilead and ducked out of the room before Ruth or Boaz could protest, the door slamming in her hurry. Which left Ruth alone with Boaz, other than a kindly old servant, who had insisted on offering a second bowl of dates to the table already loaded with plates. So perhaps they weren't alone, as it seemed.

She attempted to keep her tone light, to chase away the intensity of his gaze. "Thanks to you, I've eaten more than I ought. Any more date pastries or sweetmeats, and you'll have to wheel me out in a cart."

He smiled, though it didn't quite touch his eyes. In fact, if she believed it could be true, she might think that fear lurked there as well.

"I saw a most contrite Abigail outside now, and I must say the change is striking. I know you saved her life, but something else happened." He folded his arms across his chest. "I've never understood her animosity toward you. It makes no sense.

You've been sweetness to her, letting her steal the barley I intended for you. Not once have you complained."

"She is terribly immature, but I understand her abba is a cruel man, and I've encountered similar men. Please, don't turn her out yet."

"Was your abba such a man, Ruth?" He stepped closer to her, his voice so low no one else could hear. He reached out a hand and then lowered it to his side.

"Yes," Ruth whispered, her mouth dry. "He was. But I had a rescuer. Yahweh. If not for Mahlon's and Naomi's great kindness, I might have ended up like Abigail."

Didn't Boaz see how Abigail viewed him? Like a mighty warrior of old? One who had the power to pluck a woman from her miserable existence and bring her to a place of safety? Was he blind to how attractive he was, that gentle spirit providing for so many? Compassion filled Ruth as she met his scrutiny without flinching. If only Abigail had learned to trust Yahweh and His timing and provision, so much suffering might have been avoided.

"Abigail might have had aspirations regarding a particular landowner with a magnificent vineyard."

He blushed bright red. "I have never, ever conducted myself in such a manner that would give her or any other maiden ideas regarding marriage or—" He sounded strangled, letting his last thoughts dangle in the open air. "I'm half tempted to ask her to never visit my fields again based upon her behavior."

"I know, my lord. You've been one of the most honorable men I've met. Unfortunately, to a woman who has known only cruelty, such kindness can be misconstrued. You can't blame her for dreaming of something better." Ruth curbed herself before she pointed out how much time he had spent with her.

The heated look he shot her nearly seared. "Why, Ruth? Why would you wish me to give Abigail a second chance to glean in my fields?"

She tipped toward him, her whisper only for him to hear. "Grace, Boaz. Undeserved grace, as I have been given. I choose to forgive her."

He exhaled before plunging a hand through his hair. "Such mercy."

Her heart beat again, unsteady. "As have you shown."

But his next words took her off guard, settling deep into the dry cracks of her soul, soothing like a melting balm. "It's easy to be kind to someone like you, Ruth. Not so with Abigail. That takes courage, and I do believe you might be one of the most courageous women I have ever met."

CHAPTER TWENTY-THREE

Naomi had only one thing to say after Ruth's finished tale told over yet another fire.

"So you stared down the lioness and won."

Her dry tone earned a snicker from Ruth, but truthfully, Naomi quaked within, her fear of losing another person she loved boiling to the surface. She poked at the glowing logs and feathery ash with a stick, shooting embers every which way in the breeze.

"Debatable. I scared it, mostly. Someone else shot it with an arrow. But I've had requests from women to learn the art of the sling." Ruth sounded almost jovial, her posture relaxed as she held out her palms to the warmth of the dancing flames.

How could her daughter-in-law joke about such a near miss?

Naomi jumped up from the courtyard hearth, pressing a fist against her mouth. Darkness flooded inside her, just as awful as when Lotan threatened her and Ruth with slavery.

"Imma—wait."

A muffled cry escaped Naomi, one she tried to push down inside. What if Ruth too died? Naomi couldn't imagine… Agony so engulfing as if to swallow a woman whole.

An arm slipped about her shoulder, and she heard her daughter-in-law's soft voice pleading, "I'm here, Imma. I'm safe and sound. You are safe and sound."

"I can't lose you too, Ruth. For a moment, I saw myself alone at this fire. Friends are precious and come by to visit, but family stays with you, and to lose family is to lose myself."

"You won't say farewell to me any sooner than Yahweh determines. You once told me He created us, so it reasons He is sovereign over our last breath."

Naomi shuddered, but she clasped Ruth's hand.

"And even if it is just you or I, alone in this land, loving Him would still be worth it. You would not lose yourself, because He made you to rest in Him. Don't look at what you've lost, but be thankful for what you had. Life is still precious. See how far we've come, across a dangerous caravan trail, past the lifeless sea of salt, right to this valley. We will get to the other side of this pain and see the sun rise again," Ruth added as she raised her head to scrutinize the deepening sky heralding nightfall.

How strange and wonderful and convicting for Naomi to hear her own words brought back to her, when the student became the teacher. Ruth clung to hope, no matter the circumstance. Naomi allowed a smile as she lifted her attention to the heavens, stretching as far as she could see.

Yes, their world had changed completely. Yet the crystal stars above remained the same. The hunter. The virgin. Even the moon clinging to the expanse like a drop of liquid silver.

All with a marvelous design, set into the sky by Yahweh's might and power. He remained the same, day after day.

There remained things she didn't understand in this weary life. Such as Boaz, who circled around them, providing care, yet always holding back. What would it take for him to embrace Ruth? Or for Ruth to seek more? And then there was the troubling situation with Radah and Zakai, the son just like his abba, a greater threat, perhaps, because of weakness lurking inside a craven heart. Naomi did not know how to resolve these issues using her wisdom, but she knew whom to trust.

As her heartbeat slowed, no longer thundering in her ears, she squeezed Ruth's hand as they headed back to the warmth of the fire.

No, she didn't fully understand why Yahweh had allowed such a gutting loss to begin with. Why He refused to remove every burden that came her way. Yet somehow, He gave her exactly what she needed for the day. Blessings, tucked into seemingly small things but no less remarkable—as Ruth had pointed out. Hidden gifts in a garden, and in the gleanings found in a cousin's field, and in the offerings of rekindled friendships. Gifts intended to stir her heart to a place of gratitude and wonder instead of debilitating fear.

That, perhaps, was enough.

CHAPTER TWENTY-FOUR

"Where did the goat go?"

Ruth heard Naomi's frantic cry from the courtyard. She had just returned from a walk, enjoying the wide-open scenery stretching as far as she could see, pondering the past events of the week, including Naomi's renewed warmth and her desire to speak about Yahweh. In addition, Abigail's remarkable change had sent Bethlehem into another frenzied round of gossiping, although this tale carried a far happier ending, as Abigail sought to undo the damage she had caused.

And then Boaz…Boaz and his face white with worry, carrying Ruth to his house.

That thought she dare not let unfurl fully and examine where it might lead. Yet it plagued her all the same.

So when Naomi's frantic call bounced off the walls, it brought a welcome distraction to the matters weighing on Ruth's heart.

She rushed outside to the stable area where Jael usually was penned for the evening, peering into the stable room where Naomi stood among the straw. The pungent scent of animal and a dirt floor hit Ruth's nose. Despite plentiful straw and a small trough of water, there was no sight of the goat anywhere.

"This is my fault." Naomi ran the back of her hand against the beads of sweat forming along her hairline. "I didn't close the stable door."

"I didn't close the gate either, Imma. It was open when I came home," Ruth answered, mentally kicking herself for such a careless mistake. Had they lost their only milk supply? Jael had proven to be an invaluable member of the family.

"No, not the gate." Naomi's eyes widened as she pushed past Ruth into the courtyard, where the door to the courtyard swung ajar.

"I'm sorry, Imma, I didn't think to close it."

"It's just as much my fault, if not more. Don't blame yourself."

Ruth hurried after Naomi. Past the courtyard, the long road leading to Bethlehem appeared deserted. Ruth checked the exterior of the courtyard. A pair of small brown quail scurried as fast as they could into the swaying grass, but there was no sign of the white goat. Naomi's chest heaved as she jogged around the house, her breath coming in noisy gasps. "We'll look tomorrow. It's the Sabbath, and I don't know what else to do."

Normally, the start of the Sabbath brought a moment of peace for Ruth. The bread had been baked the night before, and the house freshly cleaned. It was a time of rest and reflection, not chasing after a rebellious goat.

But she couldn't let such a precious gift escape. They *needed* that goat.

"I'll search for it. It couldn't have gone far, could it? What if I find it in Boaz's field next to ours? I'd hate for him to discover Jael grazing on his property. What would he say?"

"As long as you don't go too far," Naomi reluctantly agreed. She arched her neck, studying the deepening sky. "Don't stay out late. Once it's dark, you'll never know what trouble you'll stumble into. I won't risk another lion, no matter if you do carry a sling."

Ruth hid her smile, tucking the sling and three weathered rocks into her waistband all the same.

The terrain outside the house was familiar to her, the sloping fields like the lines of the back of her hand. She headed south, walking as rapidly as she could. When she heard a bleat in the far distance, her ears pricked. To her left, Boaz's vast estate beckoned, the latticed uppermost windows open to the breeze. To her right, the hills, where a network of caves and hollows hid all sorts of animals.

She had already wandered so far, searching for Jael. She reasoned she could walk to the caves and back before nightfall. Regardless, guilt pricked her. The Sabbath was meant for rest, not work. Did rescuing an impish goat count as such?

Jael bleated again, breaking any indecision. She ran until her lungs felt as though they might burst, following a narrow gulley that cut through the land like a jagged scar, etching a deep groove toward Boaz's home. She peered over the steep edge, the riverbed long since dry. Tuft of weeds stuck out from the soil. Would Jael head into a gulley? She didn't think so.

But the caves in the hills, fathomless holes hiding danger, brought a tingle to her spine. What if Jael ducked into a cave? Perhaps she should wait until morning. Some shepherds kept their flock in the network of caves. Did Boaz have a similar spot for his sheep?

Another bleat, this time much louder. Almost plaintive, like a child's.

Scrambling over the rocks, Ruth darted up the hillside while clutching her tunic in a fist to keep from tripping over the scattered boulders. Her sandals failed to find purchase against the loose soil, forcing her to let go of her tunic and use her arms for balance.

There Jael stood at one rock outpost, jutting from the cliff side.

"I see you, little one." She exhaled with relief. A stitch in her side slowed her, giving her ample opportunity to study the sharp incline. Dried grass grew in clumps, just like in the gulley. What if she grabbed a fistful and pulled herself?

If possible, the goat narrowed its eyes, chewing on a piece of cud. Carefully, Ruth climbed, using the grass as leverage while speaking low to Jael. The goat stamped its hoof on the rock, scattering pebbles. Ruth wasn't prepared for the mighty jump of the stocky creature. She reached out both arms, hoping to dive and catch it if need be. She touched only air, as Jael darted away every time she got close enough to grab a handful of hair.

When it lowered its head, as if to butt her, she lunged to the left. But its small, sharp horn caught on her gown, the sound of ripping fabric loud enough to make her hiss.

"You stubborn, stubborn thing!" she cried out, placing her hands on her hips. "I won't let you best me."

The embarrassment of losing the precious gift Boaz had offered Naomi forced her onward. Blissfully unaware of the stress it caused, the goat bounced easily higher and higher, its hooves finding purchase on the craggy rocks protruding from the hillside. If it wandered into a cave, she might never find it.

She batted that awful thought away and focused on matching the goat's speed. The ties of her sandals slipped free, and the wooden soles refused to give her the same flexibility as the goat.

She darted again, hoping to grab the goat by the neck, when her foot landed wrong.

With a gasp of pain, she fell to the ground, clutching her ankle. By now, the sandal had worked free. She wiggled her toes, each one thankfully moving, but she had bruised an ankle with that clumsy landing.

The goat bleated its triumph as it stood above her, finding refuge on a higher rock.

"Ruth! Ruth!" a man shouted in the distance.

She heard the familiar pounding of hooves against the valley floor. Boaz raced like a wild man. Never had she seen his horse reach such speed, dust billowing in its wake. She tried to stand up, her balance off, and stumbled against the rock. If he wasn't careful, his horse would trip and Boaz would tumble to the ground. Was he chasing after her? He must have seen her from his estate.

He dismounted with a jump, running toward her.

"Ruth, what are you doing out here, all alone?" Anger sharpened his otherwise gentle tone. "Surely, after all that happened this week with the lioness, wandering through the hillside is reckless."

She looked upward to the hill just as the ridiculous goat bleated again. "The gift you so generously gave me ran away, and I wanted to bring her home before she came to harm."

After retying her sandal as swiftly as she could, she stood to reassure him.

Boaz eyed the ledge where the goat stomped a tiny hoof in defiance. A smattering of rocks tumbled down the hillside. She glared at the stubborn creature, who resisted all efforts to be rescued.

"Your tunic—it's ripped." He sounded horrified.

She waved a hand in the air, dismissing his concern. "Jael butted me, snagging the linen. I'm more concerned about bringing her from the ledge, safely home."

He frowned—no, scowled—at the offending ledge as if it was a foe to be conquered. "Wait here. I'll get her for you."

Before she could protest, he clambered up the rock, nimble as Jael despite his size, his sandaled feet finding the narrow cracks and ledges of the rock. Jael darted again and eluded his long arm swinging out for her.

"Shall I approach from the other side?" Ruth called out.

He shook his head as he climbed. One more swipe at Jael and yet another miss.

"I have many goats, but there is only one Ruth."

She didn't know what to make of that comment, nor could she reply when he continued to leap from one rock to the next, his feet as sure as a gazelle's, all the while crooning to Jael to stay put, which shockingly she did with a relieved-sounding *baa* from the highest point.

A triumphant grunt escaped Boaz as he snatched the rest of the rope dangling from Jael's neck, leading the goat down the steep hillside, choosing the safest path.

His actions felt overly protective. A shadow crossed his face as he walked beside her, with Jael trotting beside them. When they passed the old riverbed, he staggered, if but for a moment, his fists clenching on the rope, the knuckles stretched white. There she saw it—the remains of the gully, now dry, yet carved deep into the earth. She had run past it earlier, so intent on searching for the goat, not even dreaming the gully was the site of so much pain for Boaz. Was this where he lost his wife and son?

He caught her staring at the gully.

"My wife walked a similar path with our boy." His voice sounded hoarse. "The rains came so swiftly that day. None of us are certain what happened. Perhaps my son found something of interest, or did he retrieve a lost lamb? Did she try to save him? We hadn't had rain in years, so the old riverbeds felt safe. But not that day. She loved being outdoors—said the wilderness felt less claustrophobic than weaving inside the house, and her wanderings gave her freedom to dream and think. I was too busy with the fields to be with her. As if the only thing that mattered were my lands and my crops. When Gila needed me the most, I failed her and our only child."

Joab had warned her Boaz would never forgive himself for losing his wife and son.

Ruth held her breath as she listened to his impassioned speech. "It's not your fault, Boaz." Somehow, her words felt so inadequate considering his loss. She touched his arm. "I am truly sorry for all you endured."

He blinked rapidly, as if forcing tears away. "I hate that old river. When I saw you from my rooftop, heading in this direction, I feared the worst. Another lion, perhaps. Or a snake. I couldn't bear to see such loss again."

"But you cannot always fear the worst," she protested. "We must not stop living because of the past. I refuse to live my life in such a manner, worrying over every risk."

He bowed his head, his jaw flexing and his voice tight. "Forgive me. It is not my place to tell you how to spend your time."

She had no wish to hurt him or to see this gulf widen between them. "Remember how you challenged me in your vineyard and asked if I had been set free from grief? Have you been truly released?"

"I no longer weep as I once did," he admitted slowly.

"But will you remain in your house, a beloved lord, but always alone because of the fear of losing others? Is this your freedom?"

Hovering over her, he just stared. Then he whistled for his horse. After gathering the reins and the rope, he silently led her and the horse and Jael to Naomi's house. The distance was short, yet it felt unbearably long. Boaz's broad shoulders rolled forward, as if carrying a troubling weight. His heartfelt confession when stumbling across the gulley mirrored her own unspoken thoughts. Grief had changed them both.

She wanted to reach out and embrace him, to somehow comfort him. For all these years, he continued to mourn for his lost family. Would he remain alone and childless for the rest of his life? She couldn't deny this growing desire to be something more to him, something beyond just impoverished kin in need of charity. Then again, why would any man want a woman with a barren womb? She pressed a hand against her belly, more heartbroken than she could have ever imagined.

When he reached their courtyard, he opened the gate for her, allowing her to move first. The color in his cheeks heightened and his mouth parted slightly, but still he hadn't answered her challenge. He stood unsmiling, with a closed expression, making her wonder what he was pondering.

What a fool she was to assume his previous confession at the gulley had been intended to draw her closer. How could she have so easily forgotten his protest regarding Abigail's attention? All these young women casting themselves at him, with no semblance of dignity.

She felt winded when they reached the door of the house. Did he view her just as desperate and just as foolish?

When the door opened, Naomi set the jar of oil on the table and rushed to greet her daughter-in-law. But the massive figure of Boaz filled the entrance, his fist clutching a rope leading to a contrite goat in tow.

"We found Jael in the hills," he said, pulling back enough to allow a tiny figure to duck inside the room. Edging sideways to fit through the narrow doorway, Ruth brushed past Boaz's frame, her head lowered and the scarf loose about her tumbling curls, hiding her from view. Naomi, however, missed none of the emotions playing across her neighbor's face.

Boaz had only one person in his vision. Ruth. He barely hid his longing beneath stilted manners. After an exchange of bland and forgettable pleasantries, he cleared his throat and finally handed Jael's rope to Naomi.

Her intuition honed to sense any aberrations, she wondered if she could encourage him to stay. Whatever troubled Ruth and Boaz surely could be discussed over a meal. "Will you celebrate the Sabbath with us? I was about to set the table."

He shifted his weight at her invitation, rubbing the bridge of his nose with a finger, as if uncomfortable in his own skin. "Not today, cousin. I'm too tired this evening. Tomorrow I'll be threshing all day, and in the evening, I'll have a meal for my workers. The week has more than enough planned. But you are welcome to come and celebrate with us tomorrow."

Ruth, however, seemed quieter than normal, her head averted as she took over Naomi's task, refilling the oil lamp. Why wouldn't her daughter-in-law at least acknowledge Boaz and say farewell? Besides, how long did it take to refill one tiny clay lamp?

After a few more banal comments regarding the threshing and last tasks of the harvest, he gave a swift goodbye and practically fled. Ruth kept her gaze trained on the oil lamp, her fingers wiping the spilled edges of the oil. Then she sank down at the table and cradled her head in her arms.

"Ruth?"

"No, Imma. I need to be alone, just for a moment," came the throaty answer from behind the arms.

Shaking her head, Naomi led the goat to the stable and secured her inside, barring the door. Something had happened between those two, but what exactly? In the quiet of the stable, amid the pungent smell of straw and animal, she prayed for wisdom.

The next day, at noon, Naomi prepared a second simple meal, even though she longed to see what delicacies Boaz might have offered at his estate. But Ruth would have none of it, preferring instead to mope about the house, sweeping the floor over and over, or washing the walls.

Naomi brought a plate of bread, and her daughter-in-law carried a pitcher of honeyed water to the table. The bowls filled with roasted grain brought a pang to Naomi. If only Boaz had joined them the night before. How she missed a masculine presence at her table.

His absence only strengthened her resolve to speak to Ruth and lay out the plan she felt Yahweh had urged in the quiet hush of the stable.

It was a bold plan, requiring such courage, but she knew Ruth could do it.

After invoking a blessing, Naomi spoke without preamble. "You must go to Boaz tonight. After the celebrations, when he has eaten his fill and his heart is merry and all is well with the world."

Ruth choked on her drink, sputtering and gasping for air. She wiped her mouth, her eyes rounded, bright as jewels, as she stared at Naomi.

Naomi prayed silently before she opened her mouth a second time. In fact, she had prayed for weeks, searching for a sign. Surely Boaz bringing Jael was promise enough of Yahweh's will. "I promised I wouldn't force you, Ruth, and I meant it. But I can't stand by and say nothing either. My sweet daughter, haven't you seen how he looks at you? He could scarcely tear himself from your side last evening. He cares. More than you realize."

Instead of the usual protests, Ruth set her cup on the table, her fingers quivering. Emboldened by the silence, Naomi took Ruth's hand in her own. "Yahweh has given you a rare gift. Boaz is an honorable man, and he views you in the same light."

Ruth sagged against the bench, though she didn't pull from Naomi's grip.

Naomi's heart swelled with tenderness at her daughter-in-law's woeful expression. She patted Ruth's cheek just as she used to cup Mahlon's cheek when comforting him.

"My daughter, shouldn't I seek a resting place for you, that it might be well with you? Now, isn't Boaz, with whose servant girls you have been working, a relative of ours? In fact, tonight he is winnowing barley on the threshing floor. Wash yourself, put on perfume, and wear your best clothes. Go down to the threshing floor, but don't let him know you are there until he has finished eating and drinking. When he lies down, note the place where he lies. Then go in and uncover his feet, and lie down, and he will explain to you what you should do."

Ruth closed her eyes, her breathing shallow.

A terrifying prospect to seek a man and to be so vulnerable. Yet Naomi hoped Ruth would see her worth and seize the moment.

Naomi leaned forward, clasping her daughter-in-law's shoulder. "I am proud of you and the woman you are. No man could ask for a better wife."

"I will do everything you say," Ruth answered after a weighted pause. "But I can't deny I am frightened."

Relief sweetened Naomi's smile. "Of course you are. But what if Yahweh is calling you to trust Him? What if this is the miracle we've been praying for? What bigger sign do you need, to trust Him to lead and protect both you and me?"

Ruth chuckled. Her tremulous smile swiftly dissipated. "You make it sound so simple, but what if Boaz rejects me? I'm barren, and I'm older too."

Naomi shook her head, adamant, as fresh insight flooded her. "No, Ruth. He won't reject you. I suspect he is just as afraid as you are and in need of encouragement. He doesn't want a concubine. He wants a wife. Perhaps he is afraid of hurting your reputation. Any other landowner would have taken what he wanted. Boaz is a powerful man, but he is also noble. What if he has been waiting for your decision all along?"

Ruth startled, her eyes darkening.

Naomi continued after a deep breath. "And, my dear, did it ever occur to you that the fault of your womb lay with my son? Both of my boys were feverish as children. I have often wondered if that might be the reason why neither you nor Orpah carried babes. Perhaps with this marriage, Yahweh will bless you in a manner you couldn't even imagine."

Ruth pushed away from the table, a hand pressed against her abdomen. "I challenged Boaz the other night, asking how long he would remain alone because of fear. And now, it appears I must humbly take my own advice."

Naomi smiled.

Ruth sighed as she stood. "Pray for me, Imma, for I need your courage. Would you believe the lioness was easier to face?"

"Yahweh will provide exactly what you need. We simply must trust Him." Naomi rose from the table, excitement thrumming through her veins. "And I know just the tunic you'll wear tonight."

CHAPTER TWENTY-FIVE

R uth waited on the rooftop. She had spent the evening preparing and praying, her whispered pleas to Yahweh uttered during her bath. Her hair had been washed and anointed with perfumed oil, thanks to Aviah. Not the fruity persimmon but a spicy musk evocative of the sunbaked fields she had tended. The unfamiliar scent felt foreign and yet somehow right. A fresh start.

She had no desire to be ensnarled in the past any longer. Fingering the glossy curls hanging down onto her shoulders, the strands somewhat damp, she marveled over Naomi's encouragement and at the memory of Boaz searching for her during the Sabbath.

What would he think about the wedding dress she'd borrowed from Naomi? Would he think she was pretty? He had only seen her covered in dust, wearing rags.

Naomi had gasped when she finished tying the embroidered sash around Ruth's narrow waist. "You are like a rose, Ruth."

Naomi's warm approval brought renewed reassurance to Ruth's injured soul.

Next came the silver earrings, which danced every time she moved her head. So long, they nearly grazed her shoulders. A testament to a different time, one of happiness and prosperity and blessing.

Could Yahweh repeat such marvels a second time? Especially after so much loss?

She sheltered her eyes with her hand while studying the empty fields. Men and women drifted home to Bethlehem, the road cluttered with revelers shouting and laughing. How different from Kir-hareseth. In the city, she had longed to hide during the celebrations. But here—she desired more than anything to join in with the Israelites. To be one of them.

She could wait no longer, hiding on the rooftop. Nightfall approached. Had Boaz enjoyed his wealth, satisfied with the cheers of his workers and the song of a musician, while eating the choicest cuts of meat and the softest breads? Regardless of the festivity, he would remain all alone on the threshing floor throughout the night. Her pulse quickened at what she might find.

The threshing floor lay in a wide circle, as wide as Boaz's courtyard and just as flat. A low stone rim provided a small barrier but not enough to impede the warm wind sweeping across the plains. A breeze nudging Ruth forward. Mounds of barley waited, and next to the piles rested wooden winnowing forks with stout prongs. Beyond the rim, a horse whinnied softly.

She placed a steadying hand at the entrance of the threshing rim, her heart nearly failing.

Moonlight highlighted a man asleep on the packed ground, surrounded by sifting piles of discarded chaff, lifting with the breeze to float away. With cautious steps, Ruth crept forward, flinching when her sandals crunched on the straw strewn everywhere across the smooth, chalky earth. With a shuddering breath, she struggled to slow her racing pulse.

Help me, Yahweh. I'm afraid.

Yet when she drew close to Boaz, her fear subsided. This was the man who ordered his workers away from her. He had shown her favor, even to the extent of providing extra grain in such a way that her reputation or dignity wouldn't be besmirched. He had watched over her from afar, never once making her feel uncomfortable. In fact, he had remained so cautious and respectful that she would never have assumed he cared, if Naomi hadn't concocted this plan to draw him out from his cocoon of safety.

He had become—dare she say it—a dear friend. There were few men she respected, but he had risen to the top, and not because of his wealth but for his honorable character.

And she longed for so much more. Her pulse continued to race until she felt dizzy enough to faint.

She would test the depth of his character this night, for no one else was near to hear either of them on the threshing floor. No one to see him pull her close, if he so chose.

With a muscular arm flung behind his head, Boaz slept deeply, his chest rising and falling to a slow rhythm. Asleep, he appeared far younger. She bent to study him in the moonlight. Below a crooked but charming nose, his beard covered a firm jaw. What long lashes he had, a dusky shadow against his cheekbones.

Slowly and silently, she lowered herself to the threshing floor. He stirred beneath the woolen mantle thrown over his sandaled feet. A sword lay within easy reach, the moonlight glinting along the sharp blade.

Before her resolve failed, she pulled away the wool garment to cover herself, the brush against his skin disconcertingly warm to her chilled fingers. With a mumbled cry, he jerked upright. The cloak tugged away from her, leaving her exposed to the cool night. Unable to move, she felt as though she was made of granite. She could only stare at him, helpless. Had she made a mistake in coming after all?

As she shifted closer to him, he gave a startled gasp, followed by a furious, "Who is there?"

"My lord," she whispered, "it is I, Ruth, your servant."

"Ruth?" he echoed, as if he didn't quite believe his eyes, or his ears. "Why are you here?"

Gulping, she placed a hand on his arm and felt his skin jump. "Spread your wings over me, for you are a redeemer."

There, Yahweh help her, she had said it. She had offered him marriage, all in a hurried breath before she lost all courage. She had offered everything of herself. Every limb trembled as she waited for his response. Clouds rushed to cover the moon, and darkness hid his features, yet she heard an audible swallow.

"My daughter…," he began, his voice rough.

Her heart sank as shame heated her cheeks. He didn't want her. Did he think her a fool, or worse, a harlot? A sob threatened to break free.

"My daughter," he said again, this time gentle. "Ruth, look at me."

She raised her head.

"May you be blessed by the Lord, my daughter. You have made this last kindness greater than the first in that you've not gone after young men, whether poor or rich. Don't be afraid."

The wind stirred a curl loose from the pin in her hair as the moon broke free from the clouds. He leaned forward, his eyes searching hers, and again, she smelled the scent of wheat and earth, cinnamon and leather. Her every sense seemed attuned to what he might say or do next.

"I will do for you all that you ask, for all my fellow townsmen know you are a worthy woman. And it is true that I am a redeemer. Yet there is a redeemer nearer than I. Remain tonight, and in the morning if he will redeem you, very well, let him do it. But if he is not willing to redeem you, then as the Lord lives, *I will redeem you.*"

A thrill shot through her at his slow emphasis on the last words. And fear too, as his statement slowly registered. She sensed a yearning within him but also an unspoken caution restraining him. She had humbled herself, only to find that another man might be closer in line than Boaz? Naomi had never mentioned such a possibility!

A strangled sound came from Ruth's throat, betraying her distress. "Who is the other man?"

"His name is Levi."

Levi. The man who refused to take care of Harim and cast out Abigail's abba? A man driven by greed and a friend of Zakai's? She felt as if the blood had drained from her face.

"I've heard nothing good about him. Some of your workers have left his farm to harvest with you." She told him the rest about Radah and Zakai and the greed lurking beneath polished manners and false piety.

His shoulders heaved with a ragged sigh. "I know, Ruth. I didn't want to frighten you, but yes, he's driven by coin. However, that may be to our advantage. A Levirate marriage means a man will marry his brother's widow, raising the eldest son to inherit the fallen brother's property."

Beside herself, she drew into a ball. An arm slid around her shoulders, pulling her close to a solid chest. He grasped her chin with his other hand, gently but urgently raising her head to meet his gaze. "Ruth, if Yahweh so blessed us with children, it would honor me to raise our first son in Mahlon's name."

Although she had hoped for his answer, she still gasped at his willingness. Boaz would ensure that the land was not included with his wealth—a tremendous sacrifice. "You would redeem everything and ensure Elimelech's line continues?"

"Yes," he said thickly, "and you would be worth it, my beautiful Ruth. You've blessed me more than perhaps you realize. Why wouldn't I honor Yahweh's commandments and Elimelech? From the moment I first met you, I couldn't make myself walk away, even though I warned myself a hundred times. And if I was free to do so, I would kiss you right here, right now, and I would tell you how much I lo—"

He halted suddenly, sending a shiver rippling through her, but the arm wrapped around her, warm and secure, a shelter against the night, made no move to tip her chin closer toward his.

She rested her head against his shoulder, her joy dimming.

Why, Yahweh? She had prayed, and this action had felt right. Had she misinterpreted the will of the Most High?

"Don't cry. All will be well. I give you my word—I will take care of everything." Boaz reached out and tucked the stray lock of hair behind her ear, the action tender and full of promise when his thumb caressed her cheek. "Lie down until morning. I don't want you to walk alone late at night." He said it as an invitation rather than a command. "Please. Stay with me."

Heart pounding, she dashed the tears from her eyes and gathered the edge of his cloak a second time and tucked herself into it. He was so close she felt the warmth radiating from his long form. How small she was compared to him. They lay in silence, the sound of crickets chirping and the rustle of the wind sweeping across the flattened ground. She could easily reach out a hand and brush against his legs. A sigh escaped her as she shifted to a more comfortable position on the ground. In response, his hand flexed, almost as if he wanted to touch her but dared not.

She held her breath, realizing that something precious had blossomed between them, and the wrong move or word could easily destroy this new tenderness. He must have sensed it too.

His voice deepened, low like a rumble of thunder before a storm. "Sleep, Ruth. I will watch over you. I won't see any harm come to you."

Someone traced Ruth's cheekbone with fingers featherlight. She opened her eyes to see Boaz leaning over her.

"Good morning," he said with a hint of huskiness.

Behind him, the sky warmed with tones of pink, the sun still hidden beneath the horizon. Around her, evidence of Boaz's labor, the golden piles of barley, hid them from view. All at once, the memory of last night came rushing to the forefront. Awareness of his closeness shot through her, and she realized something firm pillowed the back of her head and neck—his arm, which surely must be all prickles by now.

As she sat up, her hair tumbled to her shoulders. His cloak draped about her brought a renewed sense of intimacy. When had he tucked it around her form, keeping her warm from the chill of the night?

"G-good morning," she stammered.

If he had any regrets about her late-night visit, he didn't show it. His gaze wandered to her unbound tresses, his expression one of pure delight.

"You are not a dream," he murmured as he reached out to touch a lock of her hair, letting it slide through his fingers. "I was afraid I would wake up and find you nothing more than a pleasant illusion, and if so, I would wrestle with a cruel reality come dawn. But you are really here. Sitting on my threshing floor. You truly wish to marry me."

Suddenly, she felt very shy, sitting so close to him, her arm brushing against his. "I truly wish it."

He lifted her chin with a finger and breathed deeply, as if inhaling her perfume. "I am not too old for you? There are many other good men, much younger, much more handsome." How vulnerable he sounded as he studied her lips.

"No," she interrupted, "you are the only man I want, and…I think you are very handsome. I thought so from the first day I saw you."

His warm hands dropped to her shoulders, and he pulled her in, resting his forehead against hers. "Ruth—"

She waited, her heart pounding all the more.

"Don't tempt me beyond what I can handle."

Unable to help herself, she smiled.

"All night, I argued with Yahweh while plotting how I could secure our marriage. There is nothing more I would wish than to spend the rest of my days with you by my side. How right you were to challenge me near the gully. I was too afraid to lose again, but it was more than that. I dared not hope you would see me, gray-haired as I am, in such a manner. And then you came to me last night, as lovely and as courageous as can be. I want you to know that no matter what happens, I have always admired you. And yes, dreamed of you."

She reached to touch the silver threads at his temples, her fingers smoothing the hair.

With a small groan, he added, "But I must do the right thing and go to the city gate with the other leaders and first ask this other man, who is your closest redeemer, if he wishes to take first place according to the custom of our law. Land must be transferred, and family lines protected before several witnesses. I have to trust that Yahweh will lead us both. Do you understand?"

"I do," she whispered as she withdrew her hand. And she did. Boaz was a man of honor, and he would not forsake the law, yet when he pulled away from her, she thought she saw him blink away a sheen in his eyes.

"Yet how can I walk away from the treasure before me?" he breathed, as if torn by the prospect. He shook his head as if to clear away rebellious thoughts. "No, we will trust Yahweh. We must."

And she too would do what was honorable and marry to protect Naomi, but would she be obligated to marry a stranger? The idea wedged itself into her thoughts, sharp and uncomfortable, like a jagged piece of obsidian. She truly didn't want anyone else other than Boaz. As if afraid to stay so close to her another moment longer, he struggled to rise to his feet, offering her his hand and pulling her up to stand by him.

Boaz glanced over his shoulder. "Dawn is here, and my men will come with their carts. I don't want anyone seeing you here with me."

She nodded, realizing once again he was intent on protecting her and her reputation. A lesser man would have caved to his desire, and she had sensed Boaz's desire from the moment she had asked him for marriage.

"Will you give me your shawl?" he asked. When she picked it up from the ground, he took it and spread out the fabric, the wind ruffling his hair. Then he reached for a wooden ladle and scooped precious handfuls of barley, carefully filling her scarf before tying the ends to form a satchel. "I can't have you returning to your mother-in-law empty-handed."

"Thank you," she said as he carefully handed her the satchel.

"And I will return to you with an answer." He reached for her, his fingers wrapping around hers. For a long moment he held her hand, his thumb brushing back and forth against her knuckles. He squeezed and let go. She immediately missed the warmth of his touch. Would this be the last time she would see him? His gaze, troubled, met hers with unspoken concerns as he reached for his sword and his horse.

She left the threshing floor, the weight of the barley as comforting and solid as always. A promise of provision. Of the depth of Boaz's regard.

Oh, that Yahweh would provide one last time.

"Please," she prayed out loud as she reached the road where she could see Naomi's home and courtyard. "Please, make a way."

The sound of hooves pounding the ground reached her ears and, helpless to resist, she watched Boaz race toward to Bethlehem.

CHAPTER TWENTY-SIX

When Ruth pushed open the door to the house, she found Naomi waiting at the table with an oil lamp burning. The scent of oil mingling with smoke, a pleasant smell of home, greeted Ruth. Had Naomi slept through the night, or had she waited through the early hours of the morning for her? The wide room with the freshly plastered beams felt warm and safe after the cool morning air. The musty smell no longer lingered since Boaz's repairs. Everywhere Ruth gazed within the room, including the stable behind the wall, she saw yet another indication of his lavish care.

Her mother-in-law jumped up from the bench with the energy of a younger woman. She enveloped Ruth in a warm embrace.

Ruth waited as Naomi leaned back to study her. "You spent the night with him? All is well?"

She unslung the heavy weight of her scarf and handed it to Naomi. Her mother-in-law's eyebrows shot upward as she hefted the scarf and carried it to the table.

"Oh, you must have good news! He sent you home with this tremendous gift? Sweet girl, didn't I tell you Yahweh would provide? Didn't I tell you Boaz wanted you?"

Ruth wearily sank onto the bench, and Naomi chatted happily as she untied the ends of the indigo scarf, allowing the barley to pool. She ran her hands through the plump kernels then paused when she raised her head to meet Ruth's gaze.

"You are silent this morning. This does not bode well. You should blush like the bride you will soon be."

Ruth toyed with the scroll-like embroidery edging the sleeve of her tunic. It would be best to present everything to Naomi and get her advice. Her mother-in-law had never steered her wrong in the past.

"I did as you asked and lay down at his feet. It was just the two of us there. He asked who I was, and I told him."

Naomi's gaze sharpened as she sat next to Ruth. Her voice hardened. "Tell me he was an honorable man. I can't bear the thought of you used or hurt."

Ruth shook her head, the heavy earrings tinkling. "I had nothing to fear from him, Imma. He called me his daughter and said he would redeem me. He said my request for marriage honored him. You were right—he was too concerned about frightening me with any advances. He kept mentioning younger, more handsome men, but I assured him I wanted no other."

Naomi grinned widely, the lines crinkling from her eyes. In her enthusiasm, she slapped the table with her palm. "I knew it! You had only to be brave and show him how you felt." She nearly crowed her victory as she covered her mouth with her hand. "Thank You, Yahweh! Thank You! I knew you had the courage, Ruth."

Ruth couldn't share her mother-in-law's excitement. Her emotions had gone from dizzying heights, hearing his tender answer, then plummeting to despair when he told her of Levi and the law.

Naomi's jubilation faded. "Why do you look at me with such a sorrowful face? I don't understand."

"Boaz said there is another kinsman-redeemer, a man closer to us. Before I left the threshing floor, Boaz raced to the village to speak with the leaders at the gate. He said if the other man will redeem me, then…good."

"Good?" Naomi's jaw dropped. "How is this good, exactly?" An expression of pure dismay replaced her former mirth. "I didn't know we had another redeemer."

"I understand Boaz will speak to the leaders about the matter today," Ruth said as she pulled the weighted earrings from her aching earlobes. She carefully placed the silver jewelry on the table, anxiety coiling tighter and tighter within her gut. It had been hard enough asking Boaz to marry her. She couldn't imagine approaching a complete stranger with such a request—especially the man who stood in the way.

"Imma, it is Levi who is the redeemer."

Naomi's jaw dropped. "*No*, Yahweh."

Alarm spurted within Ruth's bloodstream as she watched her mother-in-law pace back and forth on the floor. "I've heard about his greed. Do you know him?" Ruth demanded.

"He is a landowner, far enough outside Bethlehem that you and I have not met him. He never had an interest in Elimelech or me. I scarcely know the man, though I've heard tales about his avarice. I didn't even consider the possibility of kinsman status since Boaz feels more like family. I thought Levi was married, but who knows in the years that have passed? Is he a widower?"

"I don't know. Harim told me he injured his leg while repairing Levi's storage barn. I understand Levi is good friends with Zakai."

A pale sheen glistened on Naomi's brow. "We must go to Aviah immediately. Her house is near the gate. Perhaps she might know of something about this matter. No one else has the same pulse on the village news. But if Levi is greedy as people say, then what would stop him from wanting our land? Or you, my daughter?"

I will return to you with an answer. Boaz's fervent promise, laden with unspoken things, brought renewed hope.

"Boaz raced to the gate early this morning," Ruth admitted, keenly aware of her mother-in-law's weighted stare.

Naomi's gaze flickered with momentary approval. "Then he realizes how serious the situation is, and I would assume he will do all in his power to ensure you stay out of that man's hands."

Aviah led Naomi to the rooftop overlooking the city gate. "Do you want to watch from this point? I doubt anyone will notice us so high, especially when meetings are so noisy." The rooftop offered a pleasant spot to view the road leading to Bethlehem's gate. Aviah had decorated the space with braided mats and large cushions stuffed with feathers, creating a cozy space.

But Naomi couldn't relax among the silken pillows. She peered over the plastered wall, her hands resting against the thick bulwark, warmed in the morning heat. A group of men had already pressed near the benches. Some of them she could hardly view without tumbling over the side of the wall.

Aviah must have had the same thought, as she tugged a fistful of Naomi's tunic, pulling her back to safety.

She closed her eyes against the sight of so many men gathered below. Men who would discuss her daughter-in-law's fate. Would Boaz prevail? Doubt wrestled within her, stabbing holes into her rekindled faith. A hideous voice whispered to her that Yahweh had allowed her husband and sons to die. He had allowed her to feel the blight of poverty. Yet Yahweh had also redeemed Moses and her people from Egypt's oppression, providing an escape route from a deadly enemy. Surely He could handle the troubles of an unknown widow.

Her fingers curled. *Yahweh, help me in my unbelief.*

He had also given her a faithful daughter-in-law, Ruth, who had won this community with her love and dedication. He had restored her friends to her and brought Boaz. She had a home and a garden. Life remained, fragile but alive.

He would provide again. She knew He would answer her cry for help. Perhaps not in the manner she chose, but He would ultimately prove trustworthy.

Do Your will, for I will submit.

She opened her eyes to see Zakai saunter through the gates with a man at his side. Zakai's garish saffron tunic gleamed beneath the sun, and the other man, Levi, wore a tunic and overcoat the color of sand. He had a long, reddish beard and thinning brown hair barely stretched across a sunburned dome.

A man who, though he was the closest of kin, had never once checked on her, or offered any help, despite the law.

"Miser," she mouthed to herself. No, she wouldn't see Ruth married to such a man.

A familiar presence warmed Naomi's left. Ruth. She too leaned over the side, the wedding gown a brilliant splash of color against the plastered wall and the wind toying with her long curls beneath the fringed headscarf. Her gaze homed in on one man—Boaz. He moved directly into Naomi's line of view. Towering over the other men.

Ruth backed away from the bulwark, her face strained. "Imma, how can I bear to watch?"

Bless her daughter-in-law. Who could blame Ruth for loving Boaz?

She covered Ruth's hand with her own. "You've sought after Yahweh in every area. He knows the secret longing of your heart. Trust Him."

CHAPTER TWENTY-SEVEN

Ruth counted ten elders who greeted Boaz as if old friends. He wore the same gray tunic as he had on the threshing floor, and his tousled hair, further ruffled by the wind, made him even more endearing. If he was nervous, she couldn't tell.

To her shock, he gestured to Zakai, pulling Naomi's brother-in-law to the side, while the other men spoke with a balding man with a red beard. Zakai jerked out of Boaz's grip. His cocky smile flattened as he straightened his coat, smoothing imaginary wrinkles. But when Boaz leaned in to say something else, Zakai flinched.

To be a fly and buzz near Zakai's sleek, oiled hair and witness that conversation!

At last, Zakai held up his palms as if in surrender, and as more men hunkered in a circle, taking available spots on the ground or the stone benches to observe the morning's meeting, she sensed whatever power Zakai thought he might have had somehow ebbed away.

Backtracking his steps, Zakai joined another man, Radah, lurking at the edge of the assembly. Abba and son nearly touched heads, conferring, as Radah dragged a palm across his face.

"Come over here, my friend, and sit down." Boaz's resonant voice recaptured Ruth's attention. Levi sank down on the nearest bench. Boaz directed the elders to take the best seats reserved on the other stone benches.

She marveled at the influence he held, that men would cease their chatter to listen to him. Even the restless shepherds and farmers crammed near the elders stopped talking, leaning on their staffs as if to hear every word.

Boaz joined the men as they parted on the stone bench, leaving him plenty of room. But he sat next to Levi, clapping him on the shoulder as if they were the closest of friends. "Naomi, who has returned from the land of Moab, is selling the piece of land that belonged to our brother Elimelech. I thought I should inform you that you may buy it back in the presence of those seated here and in the presence of the elders. If you want to redeem it, do so today."

Ruth gasped at Boaz's casual shrug of his shoulder as if the matter were nothing.

"Steady, Ruth," Naomi's whisper flooded into Ruth's ear. "Boaz knows what he is doing. If he gives away too much of the situation and how it matters to him, Levi will snatch it all."

Was this shrewd maneuvering? Not a soul knew how precariously her fate hung in the balance.

Levi spat on the ground, his lanky form lounging on the bench. "Naomi, the widow? Does the house even stand on that land? No wonder she needs to sell it if she was stupid enough to leave Bethlehem in the first place."

"Vile miser," Naomi muttered under her breath. Ruth rested her palms on the bulwark and leaned over, equally repulsed. She would rather live in poverty than bind herself to such a spiteful creature.

A nervous chuckle rippled through some of the men.

Boaz leaned against the bench. "Perhaps you are right. It's been over ten years, the property suffering under neglect. But if you will redeem it, tell me, because there is no one but you to do it, and I am next in line after you." He spread out his hands as if helpless, but Levi's answering smirk did not bode well. Ruth clenched her fists, dread overriding any former confidence.

The balding man laughed under his breath. "I will redeem it. I hardly think you need more property."

Someone else spoke. "But it's fallow. No one has planted a crop in years, and Zakai has let his sheep run wild over the fields, chewing the grass right to the ground. Rumor has it he refuses to pay to rent. A separate matter we should discuss. Perhaps Elimelech abandoned his farm because the soil was useless. Barren, if you ask me."

Murmurs rippled through the assembly. For once, Levi appeared uncomfortable, wiggling on the hard bench, his smirk disappearing. "Has the soil more clay than dirt? How much coin are we discussing?"

Boaz appeared sympathetic as he flung out an arm, encircling Levi. "One other thing I forgot to mention. On the day you buy the land from Naomi and also from Ruth the Moabitess, you must also acquire the widow of the deceased in order to raise up the name of the deceased on his inheritance."

Levi rolled his shoulder to break free from the claustrophobic grip, his jaw slack. "What?"

Boaz struggled to hide a yawn. "Ruth the Moabitess. Yes, you'll have to marry her, of course."

Ruth wanted to slap her palms against the bulwark in frustration. How calm Boaz appeared! How did he do it? Nonchalant, as if he were discussing roasted almonds sold at the market.

And although Boaz hinted nothing wrong with a Moabitess, Levi wouldn't know this, since he likely spent his days listening to Zakai's wild tales.

She angled a look at Zakai, who paced back and forth while staring at his friend.

"Oh, you dirty liar," she breathed. "You can hardly cut into the conversation now and say what a prize I am."

Naomi snickered beside Ruth. "I can't believe it either. Zakai dug his own pit. In hoping to scare us away, he frightened only Levi."

"I can't redeem it myself, or I would jeopardize my inheritance. Take my right of redemption." Levi shook his head, half rising from the bench as if he might escape. "No, I cannot redeem it."

With a good-natured grin, Boaz pulled Levi down onto the bench. "Make it legal before the assembly."

Grunting, Levi stooped to untie his leather sandal. He removed it and slapped it into Boaz's outstretched hand. "Buy it for yourself, and Yahweh help you with such a foolish decision. Who would saddle himself with such a woman?"

Boaz held up the sandal for all to see, the elders and the growing crowd of mostly men, but also women arriving from the well, their water jugs forgotten.

His voice shook with excitement. "You are witnesses today that I am buying from Naomi all that belonged to Elimelech,

Chilion, and Mahlon. Moreover, I have acquired Ruth the Moabitess, Mahlon's widow, as my wife, to raise up the name of the deceased through his inheritance, so that his name will not disappear from among his brothers or from the gate of his home. You are witnesses today."

Ruth clasped her hands to her face, tears streaming through her fingers. Dare she look at all the people below, so many who might judge her?

To her shock, the resulting voices spoke as one, reverberating against the walls. "We are witnesses." The elders and all the people sitting at the gate leaped to their feet to surround Boaz, voices breaking into shards of hooting, shouting, and clapping.

She lowered her hands. Joy waited below—something she never dared hope for again. Boaz's grin widened with pleasure as the lead elder, a man with white hair and crooked back, raised his frail hands to still the noise.

"May the Lord make the woman entering your home like Rachel and Leah, who together built up the house of Israel. May you be prosperous in Ephrathah and famous in Bethlehem. And may your house become like the house of Perez, whom Tamar bore to Judah, because of the offspring the Lord will give you by this young woman."

"Thank you," Boaz replied. "I am indeed a blessed man, to take such a wonderful bride into my home."

"It's about time, Boaz!" someone shouted from the crowd, and Boaz threw back his head and laughed.

Naomi and Aviah's simultaneous hugs squished Ruth between two older immas, both women giggling and crying like young girls.

Boaz's voice rang loudly over the shouted well-wishes, "But now, my friends, one last matter of a serious note."

People plugged the gate, crammed as tightly as possible, allowing no entry or escape from Bethlehem. In the distance, Ruth saw Zakai grab his son by the shoulder, jerking him farther away, only to stumble against an irritated shepherd.

"You know what the law says about theft. We have a heinous example, involving stealing from a person in need. I must bring forth Zakai and his son, Radah."

CHAPTER TWENTY-EIGHT

Feet as light as wings, Ruth raced down Aviah's mud-brick steps. She ran out of the open courtyard and into the street, past the row of houses beside the encompassing wall and the rustling palms. If she hurried, she might catch Boaz. The outraged Israelites were slow to disperse once Boaz made the case for restitution, declaring Zakai and his son must pay double for what was taken, including rent for grazing and theft of grain, and finally offer a sacrifice to Yahweh for forgiveness. As for Radah's stalking of her, the Bethlehem men shouted with a combined fury that brought prickles to Ruth's skin.

Zakai had raised his chin, imperious at the calls for justice, but Radah had predictably bolted, only to find himself pinned down by two burly shepherds who were far too used to rebellious sheep resisting a thorough wool shearing. The elders would take care of the matter, and Boaz, after seeing the law served, edged his way through the crowd, graciously accepting congratulations. Perfect for slowing him down.

He saw her at the gate. Breaking free from the surrounding men, he rushed to her with that long-legged stride, engulfing her in a hug that lifted her sheer off the ground. Twirling her in a circle, he whooped like a boy, regardless of who saw.

When he set her down again, his cheeks were bright and his eyes sparkling. "Is there someplace private where I might speak with you?"

She led him to Aviah's courtyard. Once the door of the gate shut, he didn't wait, capturing her face between his two palms.

"My Ruth," he said, his voice thick.

"Your Ruth," she echoed as she gazed up at him. She stood so close to him she could feel every breath he took. He kissed her finally, and it was nothing like Mahlon's kisses. This was slow and tender, his lips lingering over hers, chasing away the dark days and nights long with sorrow.

"How is it that Yahweh brought you to me, to my field?" he murmured into her ear as his arms banded around her a second time. "How can it be that I am blessed beyond belief?"

She couldn't hide her smile as she rested her head against his chest. Grace. The only answer was the grace and the goodness of Yahweh. He alone had brought them to a place of safety and delight once again.

He murmured against the top of her head. "I wanted so badly to tell you I loved you. So many times. Ruth, I love you with every fiber of my being. I thought I might lose you, especially if Levi knew what a treasure he stood to lose."

She pulled back enough to see his serious expression, unable to resist teasing just a little. "You had me fooled. For one awful moment, I feared you didn't care at all when you mentioned Naomi's field."

He reached up and brushed her hair aside, his palm warm and solid against the back of her head. "Never. But can you blame me? Levi is ruled by greed. I had to be calm and collected. I knew if he took one look at you—"

"He'd be expecting a bride with twisted horns and no teeth, I'm sure. Who knows what Machla and Radah have said at this point?"

"We exposed their lies for the entire village to see. After I left you at the threshing floor, I knocked on every door I could think of, pulling the elders and anyone who would listen. I sent a message to Zakai and Levi to come. Levi assumed he would wrangle a deal, purchasing land—although I didn't tell him whose land."

"And Zakai?"

"He thought he would convince enough people to see you removed, but when faced with the public opinion of others, he couldn't continue to whisper falsehoods in the dark. I warned him not to interfere, and that I had witnesses observing his son near your land."

A tremor skipped down her spine, and his hands spanned her back, possessive and firm. "You don't have to be afraid of the slander, Ruth. People are not blind."

"They don't see me as a foul Moabitess widow with tattered clothing?" she asked, partly jesting but also partly in awe over the warm reception she had just witnessed. She truly was one with her new people and the reality of it hadn't quite sunk in yet.

"No, those words do not do you justice. I shall have to think of a poem to capture these moments. How gracefully you moved when you gleaned in my fields. And now, the way your green eyes spark with fire, filled with love for me."

Then he bent his head and captured her lips again.

She wasn't certain she could contain much more joy, but the sight of two older women, eyes wide as plates, mouths gaping open while they tried to peek over the rooftop, made her giggle and break the kiss.

Boaz glanced up, his smile mischievous, etching twin lines on either side of his cheeks. "Do you think they know the news?"

"We know!" Aviah called out, cupping her hand over her mouth. "Don't mind us. Please, continue with your poetry." The older woman snorted when a grinning but red-faced Naomi elbowed her in the ribs before they ducked from view.

Ruth smothered a laugh. "I should like to hear this poetry," she admitted.

"Hmm," he answered, quirking an eyebrow, as he drew her close again, "it makes you think about our children, doesn't it? What skill will they have? The sling or the stylus?"

"Perhaps both. As long as they serve Yahweh, I couldn't ask for anything more."

His gaze warmed. "I couldn't ask for anything more either. Your faith shines like a lamp for all to see. I found myself surrounded by men congratulating me on my good fortune to find such a bride. Ruth, your service to Naomi and your character have inspired many. To think you came to me last night and chose me—" His voice cracked with wonder.

"Because I love you, Boaz. You are the noblest man I have ever met, kind and wise and generous. There are many decent men in Israel but few who seek Yahweh like you. How could I desire anyone else?"

The look he shot her had the power to melt her into a puddle. "My beautiful, beautiful Ruth." He raised her hand to his lips. "We have much to be thankful for."

She blinked, wetness on her cheeks—this time from tears of gladness. Tears she would never hide or repress again.

"What's this? You are crying." Boaz wiped her cheekbone with the edge of his thumb.

"You're right. I am thankful. But I think I've learned that thankfulness is a choice not dictated by my circumstance but rather my attitude of worship. How can I not worship the Creator who redeemed me? He drew us from a place of darkness into His light. It's a miracle, just like the stories Naomi shared with me regarding Yahweh's goodness."

His mouth parted in wonder as he regarded her. "Ruth, one day our children will need to hear this. You must share your story."

She sighed with contentment as he led her up the steps to the rooftop where Naomi and Aviah waited. As she and Boaz ducked beneath the awning, she watched her future husband be embraced first by a beaming Naomi and later, Aviah. Laughter, including Ruth's, echoed across the rooftop. The time for celebration had finally come.

Although her life had endured a bitter season, watered with sorrow and suffering, Yahweh had proven faithful, pruning her faith and bringing a harvest beyond her imagination, a harvest of grace.

EPILOGUE

One year later

"My sweet baby boy," Naomi crooned to the bundle nestled in her arms. Large eyes, more like Ruth's than Boaz's, blinked at her. Then her grandson yawned and thrust a dimpled fist into his mouth. She sat cross-legged on a rug, surrounded by cushions. Before her, plates of dates, figs, and pastries of crushed pistachios and honey tempted her guests, who sighed and crooned alongside her, each one begging for a turn to hold her grandson.

Aviah reclined on her cushions, her smile approving. "Obed is a fine name for a strapping boy. He will have Boaz's height. Imagine him climbing those trees in the olive grove. You'll have your hands full watching this one. He'll be like a lion, I suspect. A perfect leader for the tribe of Judah."

"You have a son again," another woman added. "How wonderful Ruth shares him so readily with you."

Naomi breathed in Obed's milk-sweet scent and planted a kiss against his petal-soft skin. He snuggled closer, his long lashes fluttering against flushed cheeks. How long since she had held a baby? Her arms had ached for another child.

He would bear Elimelech's name, inherit her husband's lands, and continue the family legacy. But Boaz would raise him. She could not ask for a better man to guide her grandson.

"How blessed you are," Aviah continued, her tone reverent—absent of jealousy or judgment. "Blessed be the Lord, who has not left you this day without a kinsman-redeemer. May your grandson's name become famous in Israel. He will renew your life and sustain you in your old age. For your daughter-in-law, who loves you and is better to you than seven sons, has given him birth."

A blessing from a dear friend. A few of the other women murmured agreement as they sat on finely woven mats in the courtyard. Around Naomi, trees rustled above her head, providing a canopy of shade. The wind brought a cooling breeze as it stirred above Boaz's pool. The house, grand but never imposing, had become a second home to her. Not once had Boaz made her feel unwelcome, treating her with the utmost reverence he'd shown his imma, Rahab, long since passed.

"I will never stop thanking Yahweh for all He has restored to me," Naomi answered as she traced Obed's rounded cheek with her finger.

She would spend every single moment teaching her grandson of the goodness and holiness of Yahweh, of His faithfulness and love. How He had changed her bitter mourning into rejoicing and singing. One day, Obed would share her story with his son, and the next. Who knew how Yahweh might use the simple testimony of two widows relying solely on Him?

Loss would eventually come to everyone—one day, even Obed. She would tell him to cling to the Almighty Creator, the One who laid the foundations of the earth and the sky.

The doors to the courtyard stood propped open, and in the field, Naomi glimpsed Ruth and Boaz, walking hand in hand through the bronzed fields undulating as far as she could see. Her heart swelled at the sight, overflowing with gratitude.

Yes, Naomi would plant seeds of truth in this precious little heart, and Yahweh would do the rest.

Dear Reader,

The book of Ruth is pure literary delight, complete with subtle echoes and a unique rhythm almost poetic as the women in Bethlehem listen to Naomi's grieving and later celebrate with her, when all ends well. Yet it is also a historical account describing the ancestry of King David and, later, Jesus.

Set during the time of the judges, Ruth's story offers a refreshing respite from the tragic stories of immorality and selfishness found in Samson and the Israelites turning to idols. Instead, Ruth offers a glimpse into God's tender heart, and the offering of future redemption. We can view Boaz as a type of "redeemer," foreshadowing Jesus's ultimate redeeming act of dying on the cross. Just as Ruth is granted entry into the Israelite family, we too are grafted into God's heavenly family when we believe in Him, repent of sin, and accept His atoning gift.

Ruth's selfless act both encourages and challenges us to see our neighbors and family in a new light. How can we better serve those around us? Will we make space for the widow, or the single mother, or the unmarried woman, or the foreigner within our churches? Are we willing to seek mentorship from godly men and women and to mentor others closer to Jesus?

Although many are drawn to the romantic tones in the book of Ruth, the story focuses mostly on God's provision during suffering. Like Job, Naomi grieves but still comes to a place of adoration of Yahweh's ultimate goodness. Naomi teaches Ruth about Yahweh. Ruth acts out her faith in practical ways. Both women support and love each other during a painful season. Their mutual faith spurs each other to greater works and deeper trust.

I hope readers will indulge my desire to give Ruth a sling and Boaz the love of poetry. I'd like to think David, with his shepherd's sling and his writing skills, had a secret family example to inspire him. Wild lions are no longer found in Israel. However, during the time of the Judges, all the way to the medieval Crusades, they remained a threat.

If you wonder at the raw themes of grief in this novel, not even I was prepared when I began writing Ruth's scenes. One of my dearest friends, a fellow pastor's wife, lost her husband suddenly, his passing absolutely devastating and shocking. Yet my friend's tender reliance on God's faithfulness convicted and inspired me. Her steadfast hope reminded me of Ruth. God's Word is eternal, rich with instruction. It's more than just a fascinating tale. He worked in Ruth's life, and He's willing to move in yours and mine, providing healing when we so desperately need it.

Finally, trusting in God's ultimate sovereignty and providence, even when our lives fall apart, can bring us tremendous comfort and courage during trials. He works all things for His glory and for our good. Trials refine character and faith, remaking us in His image. Ruth truly is a woman who might have heard at the gates of heaven, "Well done, thou good and faithful servant."

269

Blessings,

Jenelle Hovde

BIBLE STUDY QUESTIONS

1. Do we see chance or God's hand at work when Ruth finds a field to glean? What were some of the risks for unattached young women in ancient Israel? Can you recall a time when God supernaturally provided for you?

2. Boaz demonstrates tremendous compassion. How does he treat Ruth? How might his past relationships have influenced his behavior? How should we treat someone of a different religion, race, or cultural background? What would the Israelites have thought of this young woman? How does Boaz foreshadow Christ to come?

3. How does the ordinariness of Ruth's story encourage you? Sometimes God works in astounding ways, such as Jonah in the fish, or Noah and the ark. Big, bold actions that are earth shattering. Sometimes He works in quiet ways through humble people, yet the results are still remarkable. Ruth is in the lineage of King David and, ultimately, Jesus, our Messiah!

4. How can you live a practical and winsome faith this week? Is there someone you can mentor or encourage? Is there a woman who needs your fellowship, sisterhood, or even adopted motherhood? Your actions may be more profound than you realize.

A SCHOLAR'S VIEW OF MOAB

Ruth, a Moabite woman, was the grandmother of David and a direct ancestor of Jesus of Nazareth. Let's learn a bit more about what her life in Moab might have been like from a historical perspective.

In biblical times a widow, like Ruth or Naomi, walked a difficult path. Her ideal future was remarriage—*if* that was possible. If not, the woman had to return to her father's house or even possibly live with her mother-in-law. Some rules by which she would have had to live:

- Widows wore a special garment, so they were easily identified (Genesis 38:14). Unscrupulous lenders could keep the widow's garment as security for a loan. Eventually, the Mosaic law forbade the practice.

- Should a widow remarry and have a son by her new husband, the child would be considered the dead man's son.

- The law considered a widow's oath to be binding, but a new husband could cancel his wife's vow.

- The law provided that a widow could glean grain, olives, and grapes for food (Deuteronomy 24:19–21). However, in actual practice, a widow would have had a difficult time obtaining such foodstuffs.

Another option for a widow was to live with her son. However, if she had no son or her son was dead, she would fall into double jeopardy. Three miracles in the Bible are about the restoration of a widow's son which also returned the woman's ability to survive (1 Kings 17, 2 Kings 4, Luke 7). The unexpected twist in Naomi's story is that her redemption comes through her daughter-in-law rather than her son.

The Jews knew the Moabites were ancient cousins. They could entertain a relationship that was not possible with other nations or tribes. Lot's relationship to Abraham imparted a familial connection with Moab originating from Lot's incestuous relationship with his daughters. When Lot became drunk, his daughters seduced him. From their offspring came the Moabites. The Septuagint indicated that the name Moab meant "he is my father." Consequently, Ruth and Naomi would have known of the incestuous origins of the country.

Of course, the Old Testament doesn't paint many pictures of what today's world calls romance. We don't find stories of men bringing candy and flowers to woo their girlfriends. Instead, marriages were largely transactional. Love as we conceive it, if it happened, was a bonus.

Later the prophets used the husband-and-wife relationship as a metaphor for God's relationship with Israel. And the Song of Solomon did exalt romantic love. Obviously, the lack of explicit description of Ruth's affair of the heart leaves much to our imagination.

To understand Ruth better, let's talk a bit about religion in Moab.

King Mesha of the Moabites worshiped a deity called Kemosh. In the name of this god, King Mesha went to war, offered sacrifices, and secured many victories. Like the practices that had drifted across the Middle East, the Moabite religion probably had overtones of a fertility cult. Ruth would have grown up in a society that expected everyone to worship Kemosh. Because these societies were polytheistic, they would have allowed for numerous other deities to exist.

When Ruth entered Israel, she would have found a much different situation. The Hebrews believed that YHWH allowed no other idolatrous gods to be recognized or worshiped. When she proclaimed, "Your God will be my God," Ruth made a decisive and final decision never to turn back.

We know something about the Kemosh cult from the Mesha Inscription found in 1966–1969. Other relevant materials were found in fragments containing Moabite inscriptions. Seven seals were found in Assyrian and Egyptian texts. Excavated sites at Dhiban and Tell Hesban continue to reveal such evidence.

For thirty-eight years, the Hebrews had wandered in the wilderness before they arrived on the edge of the Promised Land just beyond the plains of Moab. They were eager to fight any tribe that opposed them. To advance, the Israelites had to fight King Sihon of the Amorites and King Og of Bashan, who was defeated in Moab. On the plains of Moab, Moses reinstated the Law and then transferred leadership to Joshua. When the Hebrews reached the Moab border, they climbed into the highlands. Rather than attacking Moab, they turned back into the wilderness. The Israelites knew that the Moabites had played a significant role in their history.

One of the fascinating stories from this period was that of Balak, the King of Moab, ordering the prophet Balaam to curse the Hebrews as they advanced toward his country. But instead of cursing the Hebrews, Balaam could only recite the Israelites' history of endurance and victory. The message was clear. "The Lord their God is with them." Balak had no alternative but to go home.

Today a twisting mountainous road reaches east stretching toward Aman. The lonely route probably existed in Ruth's day as a trail. The eastern route takes one into the sterile desert that stretches 1,500 miles across the Arabian Peninsula. Ruth had come from a people whom the Israelites knew well.

On the other side of the wilderness, Moab's terrain had mostly gentle rolling hills broken up here and there by steep ravines. The rich grasslands provided pasture for sheep and livestock. The climate was ideal for growing barley, wheat, and similar crops. The ancient transportation route of the King's Highway cut through Moab running from Syria down to the port city of Aqaba. Directly east of the Dead Sea, Moab stood between Edom and Ammon. The valleys of Ammon and Zered as well as the gorge of the Ammon River lined the boundaries of the country. Moab likely covered about 1,400 square miles. The land north of the Ammon River had been assigned to the tribe of Reuben. However, the men of Reuben could not hold on to their land and eventually this portion was absorbed into Moab.

As the future unfolded, other problems arose relating to Moab. For eighteen years King Eglon oppressed Israel until Ehud brought deliverance. In the ninth century BC, a war broke out between Israel and Moab. On the other hand, David sent his father and mother to the King of Moab for their safety while Saul continued to chase him. His son Solomon took wives from Moab. By his actions, the idolatrous religion of Kemosh, the god of Moab, was visited on the land.

Ruth and Naomi's story is set against this backdrop with its many complexities and convoluted history. For Ruth to walk away from this setting took great courage and devotion. She was truly an extraordinary woman.

Read on for a sneak peek of another exciting story in the Extraordinary Women of the Bible series!

AT HIS FEET: MARY MAGDALENE'S STORY

BY ROSEANNA M. WHITE

FRIDAY

They had crowned the King with thorns.

Magdalene felt the pierce of each small sword in her heart as she watched the blood well up on the Master's brow and stream down his face. That precious, familiar face. How many times had she watched emotions move over each feature? She had seen Him laugh. She had seen Him frown. She had seen Him, time after time, smile with love at those who flocked to Him like sheep to their Shepherd, seeking one word from His lips, one touch from His hand.

She had seen Him weep at the death of a beloved friend. She had seen Him wipe away the tears and rejoice when that friend emerged from his tomb.

Impossible. That was what the religious leaders had claimed when He brought life back to the limbs of one dead four days already. That was what they said about so much that He did. *Impossible.*

Someone shoved her from behind, someone else elbowed her in the ribs. All around her, people shouted the ugliest words she had ever heard. "Crucify Him! *Crucify Him!*"

Magdalene pulled Imma Mary tighter to her side, willing her own limbs to grow so that she could better protect her from the savage reality unfurling before them. Only because Imma's head was bowed could Magdalene look over the top of it, meeting the eyes of the other Mary, mother of two of the Twelve.

They needed to break free of this horrible crowd before the screaming men trampled them. Yet *leaving* wasn't an option. They couldn't just abandon the Master now. How could they? For three years, He had ministered to their every need, their every hurt. He had filled their ears with truth that sank all the way to their souls.

He had redefined everything. He had brought light to a world dark with sin and hatred and death.

She felt it now, elbowing them as solidly as the crowd. *Evil.* Surging, boiling, frothing evil. Dark clouds of it gnashing its teeth in anticipation. Her skin prickled, her stomach churned. She had known that very evil, once. She had lived with it, had welcomed it inside her. She had nearly let it consume her.

But He had changed all that. He had cast out the demons, had banished the darkness.

What did it mean, that the darkness was back? What did it mean, that Jesus had let Himself be arrested, that He staggered even now under the weight of a Roman cross?

He could have stopped it. He could have banished this darkness as He had banished it from her soul—with a word, a touch. When He commanded it to, the darkness had no choice but to flee.

The jeering crowd surged again, their knot of women nearly falling beneath the angry feet of the Lord's accusers. They gripped one another fiercely, and Magdalene knew that they each had the same determination in their spirits that she did.

They would stay together. They would see where they took Him. They would be there, every moment, so that if He had the strength to look up and see them, He would know that He was not alone.

Jesus. Jesus! Her soul wept for Him, even though her eyes remained strangely dry. This horror was too great even for tears—tears would only blind her. Tears would put them in danger.

Imma Mary had a hand splayed over her heart as she watched His progress along the long, dirt-packed road. "He warned me," she whispered. "Simeon, in the Temple. When Joseph and I presented Him to God. He warned me that my precious boy would divide Israel. He warned me that my heart would be pierced."

Magdalene had already heard the story, countless times. Each time, she had marveled at the words of prophecy that both Simeon and Anna had spoken over the newborn babe. They had known, when He was but a helpless infant in His mother's arms. They had known and had come to greet their Lord, before He ever spoke His first word.

They had known they were in the presence of God made man, wrapped in fragile human flesh.

Fragile—so fragile. She knew it when she saw other babies and marveled that He had been one too. Yet since she'd known Him, He had been anything but fragile.

He was the healer of wounds, spiritual and mental and physical.

He was the doer of miracles.

He was the Master of the sea and the wind.

He calmed storms.

He walked on water.

He held the laws of the world, the Laws of God, in His capable hands.

But now those hands clutched one of the rough-hewn arms of the cross they had laid upon His shoulder. Splinters pierced His palms—she could see them digging in as He trudged nearer. Obviously whoever had made that horrible torture device didn't care if it hurt its victims before it killed them. Why should he?

Yet she couldn't banish the ridiculous, unimportant thought: Jesus would have made it with more care. He would have planed each surface smooth with all the patience His earthly father, Joseph, had taught Him. Because each item they fashioned in the woodshop deserved such attention. Each was a creation that remembered the true Creation of God.

When Jesus first told that story around a campfire one night in the countryside while He whittled a stick into a toy for one of the children, Magdalene had tucked a smile away into the corners of her mouth and looked to His mother. Imma Mary had been smiling too, at memory of the husband she still mourned. At the time, Magdalene had wondered who had really taught that lesson to whom. She had wondered if, as He put small human hands to small human creations, He was remembering what it had felt like to truly create everything from nothing.

Was that thunder rumbling over the hills? The crowd?

The powers of darkness?

"This way!" she yelled to her companions when a passage opened up through the swarm of people.

Not just people. People and demons. Her soul recognized some of their hissing voices.

She and Imma's sister led the others through the opening in the wall of people, emerging a moment later onto the edge of the road.

He would pass by here. He had no choice. Magdalene's whole self yearned for Him, even as she wished Him anywhere but here. Anytime but now. In any other position.

Why? Why had He let this happen? What did it *mean*? He was the Son of God! Conceived without the seed of a man, placed in the virgin womb of this woman beside her. He was the one man in all of history who had lived a life totally pure before God. He held all power, all authority—she had seen it.

She had felt it. It had saved her from sure destruction.

Yet as she watched, He stumbled—He, whose feet had always been sure upon His path as He brought healing and the good news of salvation to all of Judea and beyond. He fell—He, who had raised up so many who by rights should never be able to lift their own heads. His knees struck the ground—He, who had commanded the storm, withered the fig tree, told them all that they could cast the mountains into the sea.

Would He even be able to stand again? His muscles shuddered, quivered, twitched in exhaustion. As He bowed to the earth, Magdalene got her first glimpse of His back—a sight gruesome enough that she had to avert her eyes, and which elicited a groan from Imma.

She had known they were taking Him to be scourged. Knowing it hadn't prepared her for the reality of the stripes across His back. Each place the lash hit Him, His flesh had been ripped, peeled away.

He had healed so many others, countless multitudes. He had healed them of illness and disease, of injury and defect. He had cast out legions of demons.

Were they the very ones now whispering their mockery into the ears of this mob, who was so eager to spew them back out at Him?

The Roman soldiers yelled at Him to get up, and He tried to obey. He heaved upward, managed to lift Himself and the cross a foot, but then both crashed back down. What would they do? Apply more lashes with the whips in their hands?

No—one of the soldiers scanned the crowd on the side of the road opposite Magdalene and her companions, pointed at the tallest, broadest man he saw, and shouted something she couldn't make out.

It didn't remain a mystery for long. The man, his face a seething storm that mixed rebellion with obedience, shoved his way out of the crowd. A flicker of compassion calmed the storm.

Magdalene looked back down at Jesus for a moment, but then her gaze snapped back to His compulsory helper. He looked to be about the same age her own abba would have been. And there was something familiar about him.

The height. The chiseled jaw. The strong form.

It couldn't be…could it? She had never actually met this man, but the resemblance to one she knew far too well was strong. It must be his father, Simon. So far as she knew, Simon hadn't made the pilgrimage to Jerusalem for Passover for years though. He had been sending his sons about his business around the empire in his stead.

The knots in her stomach cinched tighter. If he was anything like his son, Simon was as likely to kick the Lord in the ribs as to lift the cross from His shoulders. She felt the fresh bruises on her arms, swore she could smell again the wine-laden breath in her face. Heard his slurred accusations stinging her ears. *"This is all your fault! You brought me here, you made me so low! Would that I had never looked on your cursed face!"*

His father didn't lash out, though, whether from his own sense of decency or because of the soldiers barking out orders. He simply knelt down beside the Lord, put his own shoulder beside His, and levered the cross-beam over onto it. He stood again as if it weighed nothing, as if he hadn't at least five decades of age on his muscles.

Now when one of the soldiers pulled Jesus to His feet, He managed to hold Himself upright, though still He swayed. How much blood had He lost? How many bruises mottled the skin she couldn't see?

At the soldier's next bark, Jesus started forward again. His gaze lifted from the road, perhaps when He heard the keening of His aunt and the other Mary, and landed on them. Each of them, lingering for a moment on His mother before moving to Magdalene.

"Where is it you want to be, Mary?"

He had asked her that question several times over the years—each one, a pivotal moment in her life. Each one solidifying her decision to follow Him. He didn't ask it now, not aloud, but she could see it in His eyes.

Where is it you want to be, Mary? Will you flee too?

She held His mother tighter and lifted her wobbling chin. She would remain exactly where she had sworn to Him years ago she would be. She would follow Him even now. She would not let a moment of His life slip by without her.

His gaze moved back again, to His aunt and the other Mary. Was He wondering where their sons had gone? Why they were not here with them?

No. He knew. "Daughters of Jerusalem," He croaked, voice rough, gaze gentle and loving as it moved from one of them to the other, "don't weep for Me. Weep for yourselves. Weep for your children. For the day is coming when they will say, 'Blessed are the barren, the wombs that never bore.' Days are coming when people will beg for the earth to cover them."

And they would face it without Him? Then Magdalene would indeed wish for the hills to fall on her and cover her. She had faced life without Him before—empty years of supposed pleasure that only brought pain, of ambition that led her to scorn. Years of waste and ruin.

She wouldn't go back there again. She would *not*.

A Note from
THE EDITORS

We hope you enjoyed another exciting volume in the Extraordinary Women of the Bible series, published by Guideposts. For over seventy-five years Guideposts, a nonprofit organization, has been driven by a vision of a world filled with hope. We aspire to be the voice of a trusted friend, a friend who makes you feel more hopeful and connected.

By making a purchase from Guideposts, you join our community in touching millions of lives, inspiring them to believe that all things are possible through faith, hope, and prayer. Your continued support allows us to provide uplifting resources to those in need. Whether through our online communities, websites, apps, or publications, we strive to inspire our audiences, bring them together, comfort, uplift, entertain, and guide them. To learn more, please go to guideposts.org.

We would love to hear from you. Write us at Guideposts, P.O. Box 5815, Harlan, Iowa 51593 or call us at (800) 932-2145. Did you love *A Harvest of Grace: Ruth and Naomi's Story*? Leave a review for this product on guideposts.org/shop. Your feedback helps others in our community find relevant products.

Find inspiration, find faith, find Guideposts.

Shop our best sellers and favorites at
guideposts.org/shop

Or scan the QR code to go directly
to our Shop

Printed in the United States
by Baker & Taylor Publisher Services